PRAISE FOR *A WHISPER TO A SCREAM*

"The eternal struggle of the harried American woman is analyzed here, with surprising adeptness and compassion... fearless truthfulness..."

—*Publishers Weekly*

"Some books you read, put down, and forget all about, but I promise you this won't be one of them."

—*Kindle Fire Department*

"I could easily imagine I was reading non-fiction, so well drawn were the characters in the book. With fluid prose and realistic dialogue, the novel is as much a psychological study as a novel about contemporary marriage—the daily demands of raising a family, career versus children, infertility, infidelity, extended family, and hobbies outside of work and home."

—*The Book Dilettante*

"This is the type of book where you get so engrossed with the characters' lives that you feel you become part of 'the friendship.'"

—*CMash Loves to Read*

"Whatever your takeaway, I think you'll find immersing yourself in the lives of Annie and Sarah is an experience worth having—five stars."

—*BigAl's Books &Pals*

"(The) writing is smooth and entertaining, leading the reader right to the heart of the story. Her words tell us of the true strength of the human spirit."

—*Breakout Books*

"No one got one single thing out of me for two-and-a-half days because I could not get my nose out of the books."

—*Empty Nest*

"It was less like reading a book and more like talking to two old college friends."

—*Tiffany's Bookshelf*

A *Whisper* — TO A — SCREAM

THE BIBLIOPHILES: BOOK ONE

All the best,
Karen Wojcik Berner

KAREN WOJCIK BERNER

ISBN-10: 145659365X
ISBN-13: 978-1456593650
Cover and Formatting: Streetlight Graphics

"Blood of Eden"
Written by Peter Gabriel
Published by Real World Music Ltd.
International copyright secured
Courtesy of www.petergabriel.com

*For my mom, Barbara Wojcik, who passed
her love of reading onto me.
I am eternally grateful.*

PART ONE

CHAPTER ONE

A<small>T THIRTY-FIVE YEARS OLD, S</small>ARAH Anderson discovered something quite shocking. She had Attention Deficit Disorder—she didn't get any. Men saw right through her, noticing the children she toted about, one hanging on her leg and one in her arms, but quickly dispelling her, as if the kids were somehow suspended in mid-air, like receivers on Monday Night Football. She wasn't sure if she had made this correlation herself or had seen it as a joke on the comedy channel. What did her sleep-deprived brain know anyway? How comforting to know her life could be summed up by a punch line.

As she neared the end of the grocery store aisle, she pulled her cart to a screeching halt, barely missing the man wearing a business suit and cyborg earpiece who just cut in front of her. He continued his conversation, rolling over her foot as he passed.

"I'm in an all-day meeting on Monday. How's Tuesday look?"

"Asshole," she whispered, hoping her son would not hear. "C'mon, Alex. Let's get this over with."

The toddler was playing his favorite shopping game, throwing things from the cart at passersby. Alex had a small box of rice in his hands. Sarah mistakenly thought shaking it might amuse him, but instead the little guy was ready to chuck it at the pink-babushkaed head of an octogenarian when Sarah turned around from choosing a linguine. Spotting the just-released rice, she leapt across the aisle, caught it on the fly, and tossed it in the basket. Alex cried at being thwarted. Sarah smiled, only to be admonished by the scarved lady for not knowing how to keep her child quiet in the store.

"These kids nowadays. They run the show, not the parents." The little woman, oblivious to her near-miss, pushed her cart past Sarah's, who stared in shock as the pink head became lost in the crowd of shoppers. Alex cried louder. Sarah gave him some fish crackers and continued on.

At last, they were finished and headed for the check out lanes. "Hey! Record time. You were a pretty good boy in the grocery store. Mommy really appreciates that." Sarah kissed her son on the check. Alex responded by smiling and slapping her in the face.

———— ☙ ————

At home, Sarah put the baby down for his nap. She had time (approximately ten minutes) before she had to get about doing all of the things she couldn't do while he was up, such as cleaning out the refrigerator, emptying the dishwasher, and going to the washroom.

A large part of her day was spent cleaning up after Hurricane Alex, who left a path of destruction in his wake. Like most small toddlers, he had mastered "take out," but had yet to grasp "put in." Duplos were poured out of their container. His bookshelf was empty, and a pile of children's literature lay underneath. Every piece of Tupperware she owned was thrown on the kitchen floor. In the powder room, the toilet paper had been unraveled and left in a heap. Blocks were sprinkled throughout the living room.

Then there was Nicky's stuff. Piles of school papers, library books, and half-done puzzles, all heaped on the dining room table. Green army men sat poised and ready to attack on the kitchen counter. Too bad she couldn't have them report for cleaning duty.

The family room had walls so scuffed up they were begging for a new paint job. Was that a booger? Yes, Alex had used the wall for a tissue again. Video games and their boxes were thrown around the television. Completing the tenement look was a large piece of plywood in front of the fireplace that concealed a half-broken glass door, which had combusted and shattered one night while Sarah and Tom were trying to have an evening for two after the kids went to bed.

Sarah slumped onto the sofa, baffled that she could even live in a place that looked like this. In college, her friends had called her room "the museum." It was pristine. Everything had its proper place. When she would answer the hall phone, Lisa would sneak in and make one tiny change, just enough to drive her crazy. One time, she turned one of her books upside down. Another afternoon, she switched the order of her cassettes, which, of course, were alphabetized. Sarah craved one full day where everything would stay in its place. Smiling at that thought, she sipped some Earl Grey.

The front door slammed open. "I'm starving!" Nicky threw his jacket, hat, mittens, and scarf on the foyer floor.

"Hey, what are you doing here?"

"Half-day. Remember?"

"Oh, that's right," Damn, she thought she had two more hours of quiet. "Welcome home, sweetie." She gave him a kiss. "Did you have a good day?"

"Yeah." He started emptying his backpack—lunch box, home folder, Market Day order form, Scholastic Book order sheet, reminder of Multicultural Fair on Monday night—all dumped on the dining room table. "We had PE and got to climb the rock wall today. We can go horizontally, but when I get into *second* grade, we can start climbing up. When I get into *fifth* grade, we can go past the ledge." Nicholas was the perfect blend of his parents, with his father's looks and build right down to the same blue eyes and dark hair and his mother's wit and touch of melancholy. He was a dear, sweet child who proved to be a formidable opponent for Sarah in the battle of wills to assert his independence that had become a daily event. "And then Robbie threw up all over his desk. Lots of kids are sick in my class. It's going around, you know. Mommy, can I have something to eat?"

They heard a loud howl, followed by the slam of a crib against the wall.

"You woke Alex up." Sarah started toward the stairs hoping to persuade her baby to go back to sleep. She had a sneaking suspicion Alex was on the verge of eliminating his nap. This was unfortunate, for Sarah had every indication that Alex would be her napping child, basing this assumption on his older brother's sleeping habits, which, basically, did not exist. Nicky gave up napping cold turkey two weeks before his second birthday and had not slept anywhere near the average amount of hours required for a child his age since. The later you tucked him in, the earlier he rose.

"But m-o-m, I'm hungry!" Nicky screamed after her.

"I have to get Alex."

"I'm starving to death." He dropped to the floor in a fit that was worthy of an Oscar.

She ducked into the pantry and threw a packet of Fruit Snacks at him. "Here, these should hold you over until I get back downstairs. I'll be right back, and then I'll get you both a snack."

The cries became louder and more irritated with each stair. It was Friday and that meant only one thing. Alex had had enough of Sarah for the week. She picked him up, still crying, despite her pleasant banter and attempts to soothe him. "Nicky's home!" This proved to finally bring a smile to his face. Another person to play with besides Mom. Sarah put Alex down on his blankey in the family room. Nicky bent down and tickled his stomach. Alex giggled, repeating what sounded like "eye" since he couldn't talk yet.

"Here Nicky." Sarah gave him a few of store-bought chocolate chip cookies from the barn-shaped cookie jar. "Mooooooooo." Sarah had bought it as a deterrent, but it was all for naught. She still ate them. Every cookie she ate made her feel guilty on two counts. One, that she was chubby and needed no more sweets ingested. Two, that she had not baked in at least a year. Wasn't that what stay-at-home mothers were supposed to do? Her mom seemed to have the time. Why didn't she?

"Alex, would you like a bottle?"

"Phone!" Nicky announced.

"Hello." Sarah answered it.

"Itsa me."

"Hey you. I was just thinking about you."

"My ears were burning. What about?"

"Remember when I used to come home from school and you would be baking cookies?"

"You talked and talked about what you did that day or later on about who was dating whom. I never thought you would shut up."

"Very funny. Do you remember when…Alex, it's all right. Just some spit up. I'll clean it…Sorry, Mom. What was I saying? Oh, I don't remember now. I lost my train of thought."

"What are you up to this weekend?"

"Well, we've got Tom's Uncle Rich's seventieth birthday party tomorrow. I'm going to wrap Christmas presents sometime. Why?"

"Would you like to bake cookies together on Sunday? Dad and Tom could hang out with the kids while you and I work in the kitchen." Her mother was always reading her mind like that, calling at just the right times, her human safety net.

"That sounds great. I haven't made anything yet."

"Okay. I'll get the ingredients when I go grocery shopping. I'll make a pot of chili for a quick dinner."

"Great. We'll be over after church. We can put Alex down at your place for his nap. I've gotta go. Have to get a present for Uncle Rich after I drop off Nicky at piano. Love you. Bye."

"Bye, honey. Love you, too."

Some people might think it childish, but Sarah and her mother talked on the phone every day. Come to think of it, she was Sarah's best friend, especially during these last few years after having the boys.

"Okay, boys. Nicky get your coat on. Did you go potty? C'mon Alex, let's get your snowsuit on. We need to go."

The phone rang at six-fifteen, right as Sarah was mashing potatoes for dinner.

"Hello?"

"Hi, honey." It was Tom.

"What's up? Where are you?"

"I'm still at work. I got stuck in a four o'clock meeting that ran a little late."

"Sounds like it. When will you be home?"

"I have a few things to tie up, then I'll get on the road. Hopefully, I'll get there before the kids go to bed."

"It's Friday night." Fridays were reserved for movie night with the kids, cuddling together on the sofa, eating popcorn.

"It's stuff I need to wrap up for an eight o'clock meeting on Monday. I'm sorry. I have no choice."

"Okay," came out of her mouth before she could stop it.

When they were newlyweds, Sarah had admired Tom's focus. He set goals and achieved them. Period. While still a computer programmer, he researched other related positions and found that people who had a combination of technical and communication skills were highly desirable. So he attended classes, became certified in project management, and commenced playing the corporate game. Being a project manager would garner the salary that he and Sarah agreed would be enough for them to live on when she became pregnant. One month after Tom secured that position at Icon Software Systems Inc., Sarah went off the pill. Two months after that, Nicky was conceived. Tom's plan proceeded forward.

Sarah was more of a "turn the grant proposal in at the last second" person. She made the submission deadlines, but without a cushion. There was no time for error. Sarah tried to be like Tom, but found it impossible. Every cell in her body prevented it. She enjoyed the adrenaline rush of working under pressure. She could think more clearly having no time to second guess.

Of course, all this went out the window when Sarah became pregnant, and hormones stripped her of the ability to focus on only one thing for more than five minutes, which was the standard amount of deliberation time any woman received once the dear ones arrived. Pregnancy helps females acclimate themselves to cyclic spurts of genius, followed by hours of incomprehension. It is depressing, if dwelt upon, but thanks to the five-minute rule, the thought is gone and out of the woman's head, leaving just the feeling of hope that someday her exiled brain will return before she forgets how to use it. One of the bus moms said it's when your oldest turns nineteen.

"Who was that?" Nicky grabbed one of the dinner rolls that Sarah had just pulled out of the oven.

She hit him with an oven mitt. "Hey, wait for dinner. I'm putting it on the table in about two seconds. It was your father. He's going to be late tonight. He said we should go ahead and eat. Will you get Alex over here so I can put him into his chair? I have to finish these potatoes."

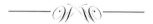

Tom Anderson was heading up a major undertaking. Icon Systems was set to release version 5.0 of its software by first of January. If his team could make this impossible deadline, especially during the holidays, Sarah had joked he would be canonized Saint Thomas of Technology. The new version was in final-release testing right now, and problems were erupting all around him. The Monday morning meeting was to update his vice president on the project's status.

At nine o'clock, he called Sarah again. "Hi, this is taking longer than I expected."

"I gathered."

"I'm going to leave in about an hour."

"Okay."

"Bye."

The lack of words coming from the other end of the phone told him that Sarah wasn't too happy with tonight's outcome. Tom had made up his mind not to work on Friday nights since Sarah started complaining about it so much, mentioning something about it taking away from their family time, but he had to get this release out on time. If this version was successful, Icon Systems might go public, and all of that penny stock might actually be worth something.

Since Sarah stayed home full-time, they had to do some creative financing. She committed to the idea that one parent should be home with the kids; it didn't matter which one. Tom had voiced that same opinion, but knew deep down inside that it would never be him. He liked working too much. His deliverance from child rearing came in the form of his career path. The computer industry had much more financial potential than writing grant proposals. It was a common-sense business decision. After awhile, Sarah agreed.

He had been getting home more and more after the boys were in bed. The upgrade issues seemed never-ending. On Wednesday, the management team had a "boost your spirits" dinner for everyone working on version 5.0. He had to be there. How would that have looked if he didn't show?

Sarah got undressed at eleven o'clock, not willing to wait downstairs in the family room any longer for Tom. She had already fallen asleep once. Who knew what time he would actually come home? Despite grand efforts to avoid it, Sarah caught sight of herself in the bathroom mirror. She stood there, breasts askew, the left one sagging slightly lower than the right. No one had told her about this lovely after-affect of nursing two children. She was beginning to understand why so many women got implants. It is hard to feel sexy when the ends of your boobs blend in with the top of your stomach, creating one large enclosure of cellulite. Fat mountain. How many men would want to ascend that? No wonder Tom did not care what time he came home from work.

CHAPTER TWO

"ARE YOU OKAY?"
"What's wrong with me? Women have babies all the time. Some even have goddamn three or four at the same time, and I can't even have one?" Annie sat hunched over on the toilet seat, another negative pregnancy test falling through her fingers.

"Honey, don't do this to yourself."

"What am I supposed to do?" She was never three days late. Her cycle ran like clockwork. She was sure this time they were pregnant.

John thought about putting his arms around her, but knew now was not the time. He leaned against the bathroom wall, deflated. Just in time for Christmas. Maybe if he was lucky, Uncle Joe would tell him to relax again. "Don't worry, it'll happen. Take a cruise or something." As if he did not know how to make love to his wife.

Annie was dreading the holiday onslaught too, especially the Jacobs Family Christmas Spectacular, when every relative John had in Illinois converged upon her mother-in-law's house for supposed holiday merriment. But the true horror would begin at exactly two o'clock, when Santa arrived. Each child was required to perform something for him—play an instrument, sing a song, recite a Yuletide poem—then he or she would receive a small gift. It was a sweet tradition. Annie thought it was amazing June thought of it, frankly. John had played Santa for the last few years running.

"He is the obvious choice," June gushed last year and in a whisper added, "We wouldn't want any of the kids to recognize their fathers, would we? Then what would happen?"

There Annie would sit, in the back of the room, the only one with no camera, no video recorder, sipping Bailey's on the rocks, praying the whole thing would be over soon.

"So, when will you and John have someone up there? Any plans?" Aunt Molly had sauntered up next to Annie last year. "Of course, I guess you have plenty of time for that, don't you? Oh, wait a minute. Maybe not. How old are you? How old can you still get, well, you know? I can't remember now, it's been so long."

"Excuse me." Annie escaped into the bathroom. She returned just in time to see John's sister, Julie, grab the microphone away from little Sophie who was trying to finish singing "one-horse open sleigh." Julie took the present right out of Santa's hands, threw it at her niece, and yelled into the microphone. "Ralph, could you come up here? You, too, Austin and Boston. That's right, come on up here. Good. Okay, we have an announcement. Ralph, dear, would you do the honors?"

Ralph gladly took the microphone, even if it was only hooked up to a small karaoke machine. "I am very happy to announce that we are going to have another child. Julie is pregnant."

Applause broke out. "Awwww" and "Wonderful news" bounced around the room. June sprinted toward them. Annie had never seen her move that fast, except for the time Uncle Joe knocked over the taco dip two Christmases ago, when June beamed herself to the spot, paper towels and mop in hand, in a matter of seconds.

"Oh, my children!" June was blubbering and hugging them all. "Isn't this a great surprise? When? When?"

"Sometime in late October." Ralph proudly put his arm

around Julie, claiming his pregnant wife as if he were some sort of caveman recently discovered by scientists in Antarctica frozen in a block of ice.

"Oh, wonderful. A toast. We must have a toast. Everyone, raise your glasses. Do you all have something to drink? Joe, would you pour Molly a drink? There you go, dear. Okay, raise your glasses, please. To Ralph, Julie, and baby-to-be number three. May your lives be filled with happiness, as much happiness as you give back to me every day through my darling grandchildren. To Ralph and Julie."

"To Ralph and Julie." All assembled drank to the happy parents.

Air began to slowly leak out of Annie. Her body was closing in on itself. She had to get out of there. The tears were coming now. *Must find John.* Annie could not see him anywhere. She tried to hide behind her glass. Head down, Annie bulldozed her way through the crowd. She was making progress until, SMACK, she ran right into someone. Annie had no choice but to look up. It was Julie.

"Annie, what are you doing?"

"Oh, Julie. I'm sorry. Are you okay?"

Ralph turned from his conversation with Uncle Max. "Julie, what happened? Darling, are you okay?" He rubbed Julie's stomach, glaring at Annie.

Julie stood there, arms crossed, expecting an answer, and there Annie was, bent over, eyes streaming.

"I'm sorry. Something in my eye. Couldn't see you. Great news about the baby." Annie ran upstairs to June's room to retrieve her coat that was heaped on the bed with everyone else's. She shut the door quickly, backed up, and slid down into a sobbing mess on the floor.

"Annie?" John came out of June's bathroom, washing off the last bit of Santa's rosy cheeks.

She looked up. "Did you hear?"

John nodded. "I left as soon as Ralph said the word 'another.' Couldn't let the kids see Santa go pale. Unbelievable. He is such an ass, and God goes and gives him another child."

For two years now, they tried to get pregnant. Tried ovulation detectors. Made sure to have sex on those Rhythm Method forbidden days. Nothing.

Annie got up from the toilet. John went over to her. There they were again, mourning a child that was never created, never destined for them.

After who knows how long, they disengaged. "Oh, I've got to stop this. There's always next month, right?" Annie patted John's chest with both of her hands. "We've got lots to do today. Seeing as I've been denying Christmas is actually coming, we still have lots of shopping to do. Any ideas for your family?"

John let go of Annie. "Haven't a clue. Are you sure you are okay?"

His wife nodded. "It will be good to get out." She bent over her sink and rinsed her face with cool water. " So what should we buy for your sisters?"

"You're female. What do you think they would like?"

"Who knows?" Annie said through the towel as she dried her face.

John had the unfortunate situation of growing up the youngest child in a household of women—two sisters and a mother. His father had died when John was two, and his sisters gladly filled the vacancy. It was as though he had three mothers. Salvation came through the McCann brothers who lived behind them. As soon as he could escape from playing house or dolls, John ran through an opening in the bushes and reclaimed his boyhood, playing football, capture the flag, and Civil War until he was too tired to go home.

John still harbored a vehement hatred of pink, having been

assaulted by it a multitude of times daily by merely cohabiting with his sisters. That was one of the things that had initially attracted him to Annie. She thought it vile as well and usually dressed in monochromatic black or neutrals. Today, she was chocolate brown. It gave her a sleek, casually sophisticated look. After fussing with a scarf for what she deemed too long (approximately two minutes), she threw it across their dressing area in disgust.

"I wish I was French."

"Pardonez-moi? Pourquoi?"

"French women know how to wear scarves. They just wave their hands in front of their necks and—voila!—a perfectly tied scarf appears. How is that possible?"

"I bet the secret lies in Perrier. And you thought it was just overpriced carbonated water that someone squeezed a lime into."

Shopping at the mall on any Saturday would be an ordeal. Shopping at the mall on the Saturday before Christmas would be suicide. Maybe it was all of that canned air, but after a few hours, Annie usually became dizzy and lost focus, so instead they opted for the streets of downtown Naperville, which were packed, but still nowhere near as traumatic. At least they could breathe fresh air while fighting all of the other crazed shoppers going in and out of the various stores.

The mission began after finding a coveted parking space right on Main Street. Many presents to buy. One day to do it in.

"Where do you want to go first?" John crossed the street and looked onto Jefferson.

"Let's see. There's a bookstore down that way. Oh, wait a minute. We are shopping for *your* family."

"Ha. Ha. Oh, I don't know."

She had been trying to conceptualize the right gifts for John's mother, sisters, nieces, nephews, and brothers-in-law, but came up with nothing. All Annie knew was that they would be on the right track for June, Julie, and Joy if they purchased the exact opposite of what she liked.

"What if we just get everyone sweaters?" John said.

"Ding. Ding. Ding. We have a winner! Let's go." They headed across the street.

Carolers dressed in Victorian garb were singing "God Rest Ye Merry Gentlemen" on the corner. For a split second, Annie thought she might hum along, until she felt something ram her in the back of the legs, knocking her off balance. It was a six-year-old pushing his baby sister in her stroller while the parents struggled to keep up, lugging shopping bags.

"Sorry," the little boy muttered, picking up the baby's pacifier that flew out of the stroller upon contact with Annie's legs.

"That's okay, sweetie." Annie smiled at him.

The parents mouthed "Sorry" and "Please excuse us" as they retrieved their children. The bags under the mother's eyes looked as large as the ones she was carrying.

"Matthew, you need to watch where you are going, especially when you are pushing Grace." Handing a huge diaper bag to the father, the mother took over stroller-driving duties, balancing the remaining packages in one hand and grabbing the handle with the other. Matthew moved next to his father, and the little family continued on in a cloud of chaos.

Wherever Annie and John went in Naperville, they ran into children—tons of them. The community was voted the "Number One Place to Raise Children" by some magazine that Annie couldn't remember the name of. At the time, it was great news. Where better to live when she and John were finally ready to start their family?

"Let's get this over with." John steered Annie toward an array of sweaters in all sorts of colors displayed in the store windows. "I have a surprise for you later."

"You do?" She looked tired already, and the shopping had just begun.

"But first we must purchase presents in various shades of pastels."

Annie bristled.

CHAPTER THREE

"YOU GUYS ALMOST READY? IT's time to go," Tom shouted. He was extremely punctual, so the perpetually-ten-minutes-late status of his family drove him nuts. Even when they started getting ready to leave ten minutes earlier than usual, they still ended up pulling out of the garage later than they should have. There was always a problem with a jacket, or a poopy diaper, or a Sarah clothing crisis. Tom ushered Nicky into the van and buckled Alex into his car seat.

Sarah jumped in, last to enter as usual. "Okay, I think we have everything."

"I think so too. Let's get this over with and wish Uncle Rectum a happy birthday."

"That's not very nice."

"He's not very nice."

"Oh well. Let's make the best of it."

They drove through downtown Naperville on the way to Rich's house. Naperville was a blend of sprawling subdivisions and painted Victorians. It still had a downtown, which was unusual for large Midwestern suburbs. For most, a mall had taken over as the hub of many areas. It was a "Pleasant Valley Sunday" kind of place. While the Andersons were contemplating where they were going to move, it actually scared Sarah to think of living here. Everything seemed a little too nice. She grew up in Chicago, and the western suburbs were foreign lands populated by faceless women driving mini-vans. But the house had four bedrooms, decent square-footage, and a big backyard—all things that they couldn't afford in other areas. Once they moved there, she realized there were, indeed, "Napervoids" cluelessly motoring around, cell phones stuck to their heads, but they were a very small minority. Most of the people were quite normal.

Each subdivision had its own character. Theirs was about five minutes outside of downtown. It had colonial houses and large trees. It was a place where neighbors brought gifts over for newborn babies, delivered homemade lasagna while your kitchen was being remodeled, and offered beer and conversation while the kids splashed in a sprinkler.

They drove south on Washington Street, past the Woods of Bailey Hobson.

"God, those are gorgeous homes," Sarah said, gazing at the multimillion-dollar, three-story, walkout basement architectural masterpieces to her left. She was very good at living within their means, especially after she quit her job to be home with Nicky, but she did suffer from "house envy," probably from all of those HGTV shows she watched.

"Wonder what they do for a living?" Tom said.

"I don't know."

"Well, whatever it is, it probably takes two salaries to afford it."

"Right."

Going to this party had made Sarah a little queasy. She was neither the loudest nor the most successful member of Tom's family. This relegated her to the position of adjunct relative, there when the clan got together, but not a necessary ingredient to the recipe. Tom's father had four brothers and two sisters, all of whom had two or more children, so the assembly was overwhelming. At gatherings, she spent most of her time bobbing in and out of the various conversations, taking in bits and pieces of dialogue without actually contributing anything, or chasing after Alex as he climbed up and down the stairs… up and down…up and down.

When they arrived at Aunt Gert and Uncle Rich's house, the door was open. "Hey kids!" Aunt Gert sloshed towards them with a vodka tonic in her hand. The lime was bobbing from side to side, a dinghy in rough waters.

"Hi, Aunt Gert."

"Kids, what's the difference between me and a Christmas tree?"

"What?"

"Nothing. We both love to get lit up! Merry Christmas!" She raised her glass.

"But Auntie, this is Uncle Rich's birthday party," Tom said.

"Whatever."

Tom went off to chat with Uncle Roy, inevitably about Notre Dame football, the family's official past time. Tom's father, Jack Anderson, graduated from Notre Dame in 1962, a fact he was more than happy to tell anyone within hearing distance. Tom's four uncles also attended the university, taking their lead from the family's patriarch, Patrick, Tom's grandfather. Tom's two aunts, however, did not go to any college. Their father thought it was a waste of time to educate females.

Each of the uncle's houses had various Notre Dame memorabilia on display, ranging from Uncle Rectum's ever-present Fighting Irish flag, which greeted all who entered his house, to Jack's lithograph of "Touchdown Jesus" that hung above the family room fireplace. Among them, they owned the entire souvenir shop (mugs, footballs, towels, coffee table books, bumper stickers, automobile flags). Being that today was a Game Day, the Anderson men were outfitted in the various ND sweaters, football jerseys, and sweatshirts.

Tom, however, was the first of the cousins not to attend Notre Dame, opting instead for the University of Chicago. This incensed his father in two ways. One, Tom wouldn't grow up to be a "Notre Dame man" (perish the thought), and two, the University of Chicago was a better school than Jack's beloved alma mater, so all feelings of his collegiate superiority went straight out the window. Not wanting to totally alienate most of his family, Tom pretended to root for the Irish on Saturdays and owned one, very worn Notre Dame sweatshirt. Being a gentleman, he resisted the temptation to wear his U of C sweater to the party today. Needless to say, Tom became the aunts' favorite boy, and they secretly prayed for his success at school and afterward.

"Mom, I'll be in the basement." Nicky found his cousin Jack III and went off to play. Sarah and Alex made the rounds, greeting everyone, and accepting the usual comments about how cute the baby was. They made their way into the kitchen, where, most of the female relatives were sitting, including Marjorie, Tom's older sister. The ladies made room for Sarah at the table.

"Let me take him for a little bit." Aunt Margaret lifted Alex. "Come here, big guy.".

"Great. Thanks," said Sarah.

"Ugh. I can't believe it's only two weeks until Christmas. I still haven't done any shopping," said Cousin Jennifer. Cries of "me either" and "tell me about it" circled the table. "How about you, Sarah?"

"I'm almost done. I only have one or two more gifts to buy."

"Figures. You're Missy Organization," said Marjorie. Her mother used to say she was pleasantly plump, but there was nothing pleasant about the way she jammed her enormity into her clothes, which fit her like sausage casing. Today, she was stuffed into a lilac sweater and khaki Dockers. She wore Poison perfume, which made Sarah nauseated. Little Peter, spawn of hell, was her clone, right down to the same cadence in his voice. He and Nicky were only four months apart, but it might as well have been forty years. They had nothing in common but mutual torment, which made family gatherings delightful. It was just a question of who would be hurt first and who would play the victim. More often than not, Peter performed his "Who me? I don't know what happened?" routine, while Sarah got ice for Nicholas. Fortunately today there were plenty of kids to keep both of them occupied and away from each other.

"Well, not really. I still have to bake for Nicky's Christmas party at school, wrap all the presents, finish my own baking, do the menu for Christmas dinner…"

"I had the most terrible week." Marjorie cut Sarah off. "I let Diane borrow my car Sunday night. Hers was in the shop. When I got in to drive it to work on Monday morning, it had a flat. Now the rim's bent too. I'm drivin' on a donut in a snowstorm."

"Oh, that storm was bad this week," Aunt Mary interjected.

"Sure was," said Cousin Ann.

"Anyhow," Marjorie busted in. "Then I get to work, and the system crashes. I can't use my computer, and I lose my entire hard drive. Then I get a call from Peter's kindergarten teacher, asking me to come in for a conference. Well, I can't just leave work at any time. 'But he's been kicking kids in his class,' says the teacher. I ask her, 'What did they do to make him kick them?' And that's just Monday. Then I pick up Peter from after school daycare, grab dinner at McDonald's, give him a bath, and get him to bed, then find a sitter for tonight and tomorrow. Then Tuesday, I had to work until ten o'clock, so Michael had to pick Peter up and drive him to indoor soccer class. And that was only Monday and Tuesday. After the party, Michael and I are driving to Alpine Valley for a ski weekend.

I haven't had a chance to breathe all week. I wonder what it's like to stay at home all day? Must be nice eating bon bons while watching TV."

Eyes darted around the table. Sarah excused herself. "I'm going to check on Alex and Nicky." No surprise, she found Aunt Margaret sitting on the stairs with Alex. "I'll take over. Thanks so much for the break."

"Sure. He's a great kid."

"Hey, where have you been?" Tom emerged from the family room. "The game's starting."

Sarah welcomed the quiet during the ride home. Alex fell asleep, and Nicky was reading an Arthur book. "Tom, don't forget that Nicky's Nativity Pageant is Tuesday."

"What time?"

"Seven o'clock."

"I'll check. Seems like I have something going on that day." Tom felt the daggers Sarah shot at him with her eyes. "Could you check my phone? Under calendar." He pulled it out of his jacket.

"Let's see," Sarah found Tuesday. "What's Global Kick Off?"

"The launch party for the global project in June."

"Can't you get out of it?"

"No. It's my next project. I'm on the leadership team."

"Too bad. If you are on the leadership team, then reschedule it. How many times do you get to see your kid play a shepherd?"

"I'll see what I can do."

"Okay." Sarah began conceptualizing Christmas dinner as they continued the drive home. Just had turkey at Thanksgiving. Won't cook a goose. Chicken's too informal. Maybe Beef Wellington. Or crown roast? She had always wanted to try that. Sarah felt it necessary to one-up herself in the culinary department each party she hosted. And since this was the first Christmas dinner at their house, she had to deliver a showstopper. "Tom, what do you think about a crown roast for Christmas dinner?"

"Aren't those hard to make?"

"I'll figure it out." Because cooking was a big part of her job description, every meal Sarah served for company was made from scratch. It helped her psychologically deal with the fact that she didn't bring in a check. "We can start out with English Stilton Cheese soup, a spinach salad, then the roast with double-stuffed potatoes, asparagus with Hollandaise sauce, and hot cinnamon apples. And for desert, a lovely Dobish torte with an assortment of cookies."

Sarah imagined her family sitting at the table, amid china, crystal, and a magnificent centerpiece of red roses, holly, and candles. She enters, carrying the lovely bit of pig to exclamations of "Oh, how beautiful!" and "My, I didn't know you could make a crown roast!" Smiling, she lovingly places the creation in front of Tom to carve. Oh yes, it would be a Norman Rockwell experience. "I wonder how you carve something like that? Doesn't matter. I'll ask the butcher."

Each year, Christmas consumed Sarah. She loved the decorating, especially making Tom get up on the roof to put up the lighted Santa and sleigh. She stayed on the lookout for the trace of snow that inevitably fell on Christmas Eve right as you get out of Midnight Mass. (Okay, it only happened once fifteen years ago, but it was forever engrained in Sarah's head as how Christmas Eve should look.) She delighted in Christmas cookies, although her fondness of sweets extended throughout the year. Her Santa collection included statues from all over the world and from almost every time period. Her mom and dad had bought her first one in high school when she was studying *Twelfth Night*. He was called "Lord of the Misrule," and it was he who reigned over the Twelfth Night Festival in Shakespearean England. Ever since, Sarah acknowledged the Twelve Days of Christmas by never taking down her tree until after Epiphany was over. It just wouldn't be right.

"Oh yes, this is going to be a magnificent holiday feast, worthy of the Whos in Whoville who love their roast beast." There was no stopping her now. "Maybe I could teach Alex to say 'God Bless Us Everyone.' That would be too cute."

"Sarah, he's not even two yet."

Ignoring him, she went on. "Tom, would you play the piano so we could sing on Christmas Day?"

"I haven't played in fifteen years."

"Do you remember anything?"

"I think I played 'Hark the Herald Angels Sing' once."

"Great. You have two weeks to brush up."

"Okay." He replied with more hesitancy than agreement.

After dinner, they could retire into the living room, hot chocolate in hand, for the singing of carols and other Christmas merriment. Sarah smiled at the perfection she would create.

At approximately three o'clock in the morning on December 22, shouts of "MOM. M—O—M!" woke Sarah. She got up, almost walked into the bedpost, and shuffled to Nicky's room. "What's up sweetie?"

"My head hurts. I can't sleep."

She bent down and checked his forehead. "I'll get the thermometer. Be right back." Sure enough. One hundred and two. "Let me get you some medicine to help bring your fever down and help with the pain."

Nicky sneezed and looked at her through watery eyes.

"Let's get you some decongestant too."

"Will you stay with me?"

"For a little bit. I'll be right back with your medicine."

"Thanks, Mom."

Sarah re-tucked him in and put a cool patch on his forehead. She stroked his hair and sang softly to him. He fell asleep fairly quickly, but Sarah stayed with him awhile longer. It was so rare to be up with Nicky during the night. Sarah looked down at him—somewhere in between little and big— and remembered when he was first born. The awe and fright of it all! The nurse came in the second morning to give her the "good news" that she was going home that afternoon. "Okay thanks," she had mumbled in a state of shock. *What do you mean, go home? I'm quite happy where I am now, having someone else cook meals, shipping the baby off into the nursery at night, and taking naps whenever I please. Who's going to take care of the baby when I get home?*

Sarah couldn't believe it had been six years since then. People tell you to enjoy the time when the kids are little because it goes by so fast, but you never believe them, especially not when you are sleep-deprived. She bent down and kissed Nicky. And in those quiet moments, suspended between day and night, Sarah knew how lucky she was.

Then she remembered that it was less than three days until Christmas.

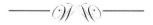

"I'm sorry Tom. We can't go tonight. Nicky is doing a little better, but he is far from okay, and now Alex has a fever." Sarah said.

"But it's Christmas Eve."

"His fever hasn't broken. The doctor said we should keep him in."

"It's only an ear infection."

"A double ear infection. He was in so much pain, he was up three times last night."

"Maybe I should take Nicky, and we'll go."

"What?"

"That way Nicky doesn't miss out on the party or on Santa."

"Nicky has a bronchial infection."

"Oh, come on. He's not that bad."

"How would you know? You've been sound asleep while I ran from room to room with Tylenol, nebulizer treatments, and ear drops at god-forsaken three in the morning."

"Don't be that way."

"What way? The way that says my husband doesn't want to spend Christmas Eve with me and our children?"

"I never said that."

"Sure you did. Maybe not in so many words. Why can't you just accept the kids are sick and that we have to spend Christmas Eve here? You know what? Just go. The boys and I will play some games and watch 'Rudolph.' We don't need you here anyway."

"Oh, please."

"You cannot accept the fact that children get sick, usually at the most inopportune times, and that you just have to deal with it. You're not the one taking care of them day in and day out. You get to leave. And now you want to leave us on Christmas, of all times!"

"Cut it out! You're getting crazy."

"I have been stuck in this house for almost two months straight. When one got better, the other one got sick. And where were you during all of this? Out of town, working late, or at some business dinner leaving me to handle everything."

"It's not like I have been going out drinking with the boys. I've been working my ass off!"

"You haven't been around for the last six months. And now you want to leave us again—on Christmas Eve."

"I'd come back."

"Why bother? The kids haven't seen much of you anyway. What would be different? Do you know what it's like to be asked five times a day 'When's Dad coming home?'"

"Are you finished? You really should have pursued the theater. That was a nice bit of melodrama."

"I have had no help, Tom, none. No help putting up decorations. No help shopping or wrapping. No help with school Christmas parties. You missed Nicky's Nativity Pageant. It broke his heart. Kids remember those kinds of things." By now the tears were coming so strong that Sarah had to take several deep breaths just to get the last sentence out.

"My schedule should clear up after the first of the year. I'll be home more then."

"Don't kid yourself. Once this project ends, another will come."

"No, really. I'm one of three project managers on the next one, and it won't be as intense. I'll be able to help. Tell me what I can do."

"I can't rely on you. You are always stuck in meetings or called out of town or some other crap. This is never going to end. I guess I should just resign myself to that. But what I cannot allow you to do is break up my family on Christmas Eve."

Nicky ran into the kitchen. "What's wrong, Mom?"

"She's okay," Tom said. "She's just tired."

Nicky gave his mom a hug. Sarah kissed him on the head. "I'll be okay. Alex will be up soon from his nap. I'm going to rest for a couple of minutes."

"Okay. Dad, will you play Legos with me?" Nicky started toward the family room.

"Sure. I'll be right there." Tom turned around. "Sarah?" But she had already gone upstairs.

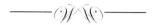

"C'mon, Sarah. I didn't go."

"Do you want a medal?"

"It's Christmas."

"Oh that's right. Time of good cheer, peace on earth, and good will toward husbands?"

"Very funny. Obviously the baby didn't notice, but I know Nicky knew there's tension."

"I tried. It's kind of rough pretending we are one big, happy family when you would rather spend Christmas Eve with your Mommy and Daddy and the throngs instead of us."

"I apologized. So what am I supposed to do?"

"If you'll excuse me, I have to try to throw Christmas dinner together. Might as well just serve cereal. It's all the boys will eat when they are sick anyhow."

Sarah went into the kitchen. What a disaster! She was a fool to think that anything would work out the way she expected, and Christmas was just the latest in the line of failures. She looked in the freezer for some sort of main course. Sarah hadn't been able to go shopping since the boys were ill. Tom was working late all week, so even going at night wasn't an option. Now she was stuck trying to figure out a festive dinner for seven with whatever was left in the fridge.

Sarah stood there, dumbfounded, unable to make a decision. Of course, there wasn't much to choose from. Where did her crown roast vision go? Thrown to the wind like everything she attempted. When she tried to keep the house clean, the boys trashed it. When she tried to create a festive holiday, the kids got sick. When she tried to escape for one measly hour, Tom called and said he had to work late. She was tired of trying.

The phone rang.

"Hi sweetie, Merry Christmas!"

"Oh mom!" It was like opening the floodgates. Sarah recanted the stories and sobbed on the phone. "…and God knows what I'm serving for dinner…and…"

"Honey. Honey? It will be okay. We don't care what's for dinner. We just want to spend the day with you."

"But we have to eat."

"You know what? I have some chicken kievs in the freezer. Do you have any stuffed potatoes?"

Sarah sniffed. "I think so."

"Good, let's just throw those in the oven. I'll bring a vegetable. You make a salad, do you have any?"

"Not even in a bag."

"Okay, I'll bring a salad too. You have cookies from our baking day right? The boys didn't eat all of them yet?"

"Yeah, they are still around."

"Good, arrange them nicely on a platter and serve them with ice cream. The boys will love that for dessert."

"But what about…"

"Hush. It will be just fine. You get the boys dressed, and we will be on our way to put everything together."

"You know you are the greatest, don't you?"

"Sarah, I had little ones once too. I know what it feels like."

Patty Williams came bearing grocery bags of food and a myriad of things to make Christmas dinner. By the time they were done, the table was set, a poinsettia sat in the middle flanked by candles, the napkins were folded like stars, and there was eggnog in a punch bowl.

Sarah looked around and smiled, the first real smile she had shown in days. "Damn, you're good."

"Years of practice. I was constantly flying by the seat of my pants."

"Never looked like it."

"Good." Patty poured Sarah some wine, and they joined Tom and Mark in the living room.

A thunderous thud rang through the air. Never one for doorbells, Greg burst over the threshold, curly dark hair peaking out from the white fur trim of his Santa hat, left hand filled with shopping bags, right hand balancing his latest creation. A true epicurean, as his abdomen size would attest to, Sarah's little brother was master of all things lasagna. His repertoire boasted at least six, including a delightful vegetarian with spinach and plum tomatoes, heavenly mushroom with creamy béchamel sauce, and a very tasty Mexican, with frijoles negros and jalapanos. Today, on this most traditional of holidays, he thought a pan of classic with meat sauce was appropriate. He brought several bottles of Chianti Classico, a firm believer excellent food deserved the perfect complement of wine or why bother?

"Ho. Ho. Ho. Sarah, would you take this? Cooking instructions are on the card attached to the top." Sarah took the lasagna into the kitchen. "Let me put these bags down. Mom! Dad! Merry Christmas!" He pulled Patty and Mark into a huge bear hug and, upon release, scanned the room for the boys. "Where are the rugrats?"

Sarah returned and hung up Greg's coat. "They're a little under the weather."

Her brother noticed Sarah's swollen eyes. "Are you sick too?" he whispered.

"Overwhelmed and sleep-deprived. Minor breakdown earlier. I am completely unprepared for today. Mom had to bring over food and all kinds of stuff."

He ruffled her hair. "Don't worry about anything. I'm here." Greg spread open his arms and hugged his sister. "Merry Christmas, booger brain."

"Right back at ya, pig guts."

Although two years younger, Greg passed Sarah in height when she was twelve and he was ten and in girth when he turned fourteen. He remained much larger than she, even during her pregnancy, which made Sarah exceedingly happy. Greg's large brown eyes anchored a perpetual look of amusement on his face, no matter if he was enjoying a great meal or sitting in the front pew at church. Life was his playground, and he was out for recess.

Needless to say, he had many friends, all of whom hung out at the Williams' house, particularly on summer weekends, playing foosball, ping pong, and pool, the triathlon, as they called it. In the summer of 1983, verbal challenges for bragging rights escalated into a full-scale tournament of twelve teams competing for two tickets to Great America amusement park courtesy of Patty and Mark. At that time, it had the world's only double racing wooden roller coaster, made better for that season only because you could ride the red coaster track *backwards*. This, indeed, was a coveted prize.

Word of the Williams Invitational spread through the neighborhood. There were more spectators than anticipated, so Mark and Greg moved the ping pong and foosball tables outside for maximum viewing capacity. Patty served lemonade and soft drinks, along with plates of cookies, brownies, and crispy rice treats. On the last night of the three-day tournament, Mr. Jenkins from next-door even brought over his old-fashioned popcorn machine. It was better than the Fourth of July.

Tension was high. Competition was fierce. Joey Dickinson and Bob Faldo played Greg and Sam Newson in the finals. Sarah was torn. She knew she should support her brother, but she had always had a secret crush on Bob, even though he was two years younger and had beaten her and Gina on Friday. Joey and Bob won pool. Greg and Sam triumphed in ping pong. It was foosball for the championship and amusement park tickets. The score teeter-tottered, every goal answered by the other team. The yard fell silent. Corn ceased popping.

The score was tied nine to nine. The ball was flying around the foosball table. Sam made a phenomenal side shot, but was blocked by Bob. Joey powered the ball straight up the middle, but Greg got there in time, blocked the shot and tried to pass the ball to Sam. Bob stole it and slammed in the goal. Joey and Bob won the Williams Invitational. Sam threw the foosball across the yard, pegging Neil, who had been eliminated on Saturday, in the chest.

"Easy." Greg patted Sam on the back. "It was a great game."

The competitors shook hands. Mark awarded the victors their tickets to thunderous applause.

At Christmas dinner, Patty said she ran into Bob the other day. He was in finance, apparently. "The first thing out of his mouth was 'Remember the Williams Invitational?'" Laughter circulated the dining room. "Oh, that was so much fun. You should have seen it, Tom."

Tom wiped his mouth. "Sounds like it was great." Clearly, he had heard the story before and had no desire to once more.

"Can we have a Williams Invitational?" Nicky asked.

"Maybe someday, honey. We have to get some game tables first," Sarah said.

Mark and Patty looked at each other. "Greg?" Patty asked. "Would you help us out?"

They went outside. A few of minutes later, the three carried in a huge present wrapped in Santa-face paper and plopped it in the foyer. "Merry Christmas!"

The boys rushed over and tore open the paper. Sarah mouthed "What in the world?" to her mother, who feigned ignorance with a shrug of her shoulders and a grin.

"Sarah, come over here." Tom moved over slightly to let his wife rip off the last shreds of wrapping paper.

"A ping pong table! Oh my god! Ping pong's my favorite!"

"Don't we know it. How many hours did you spend

practicing in the basement?" Mark nudged Tom. "You should have seen her. Pretty good for a girl."

"Hey, I heard that."

Patty rolled her eyes. "Anyhow, we figured with Nicky getting older, you might want to start teaching him."

"Let's set it up after dessert." Greg rubbed his stomach. "There are cookies to be had."

CHAPTER FOUR

With Johnny Mathis singing in the background, John and Annie sipped mulled wine and decorated a huge Douglas Fir. By the time they were done, the tree glistened with white lights and silver tinsel. Most people didn't use real tinsel much anymore, but John and Annie loved the nostalgic touch it gave their tree. They stepped back to admire their work.

"Marvelous," John said.

"What time is it?" asked Annie.

"It's almost four o'clock. We should get going."

"You're right. Let me just go upstairs and touch up my makeup."

They were on their way to Annie's parent's house. It would be a small gathering, just her parents, them, and her almost ninety-year-old grandparents. They had long lifelines in Annie's family. For most people, that would be a good thing. Annie thought it would be just her luck that she would live until one hundred, completely alone (no one in John's family had survived past sixty-five), with no children to bring her nylons or Juicy Fruit gum in the nursing home. Her only hope was that she would be healthy enough to live on her own. Maybe she would buy a big, old Victorian with John's life insurance money and live as a crazy old lady with cats and purple hair.

"Merry Christmas, dear." Marian McDonnell greeted

her daughter with an air kiss and a brandy. "They're in rare form tonight. Get ready." Everything about Marian's parents irritated her, not just as they got older, oh no, she had felt this way as long as she could remember. "Grandma wants to help me in the kitchen, God forbid. Her hands are so shaky that all the china would be good for after she was done is a mosaic. I told her to go sit down with Grandpa."

"I'll help you, Mom, but first I want to say hi to them." Annie walked down the hall.

"Merry Christmas, you two." Annie bent down to give them hugs. They were the cutest little people she had ever seen, sitting on the sofa, holding hands, and watching *It's a Wonderful Life*. Annie glanced down at their cupped fingers. What a fabulous thing to be married so long and still crave such close physical contact.

"Hiya honey. Happy Holidays," Grandpa said. "How's things?"

"Oh, okay. How about you?"

"Good. Good. We've been watching the movie here. Your mother made us sit and get out of her way. You know how she is. Can't help her with anything. Has to do everything herself. Oh well. I'm sure dinner will be good. She's a darn good cook."

Annie smiled. "That's true. I guess I should at least offer to help."

"You go ahead. Where's that husband of yours?"

"Hi, Grandpa Bill, Grandma Mary. I was unloading the presents. Merry Christmas!" John came into the family room.

"Hello, handsome," said Grandma. "Always good to see you."

"You too." John kissed Mary on the check.

"Hey young fella." Bill got up to shake John's hand. "Happy Holidays."

Annie's grandparents were role models for marriage. Her

parents were the poster children for couples' therapy. They had been married a year or two shy of forty years, but how? She was an only child, so Annie wondered why divorce was not an option. It wasn't like there was a huge family to break up. Marian had never respected George, that much Annie knew, but why they stayed together was a mystery. Maybe, subconsciously, her mother felt she had to do the exact opposite of her parents? Or maybe no one else would marry her? Was George the first guy to come along and Marian couldn't wait to get out of the house?

Annie had never heard the story of their courtship or of her father's proposal. They did not speak of it. Her grandparents had told her repeatedly of how they met at a picnic, and how Grandpa was so taken with Grandma that he knew he must escort her home on the streetcar that night or he would lose his heart forever. How she chose him over two other suitors because of the twinkle in his blue eyes. How they hung out drinking moonshine and playing cards until the wee hours of the morning before Marian was born.

When Annie asked about her parents' story, her mother just waved her hand saying "Oh, we met on La Salle Street. You don't want to hear about such ancient history."

"Actually I would. I'll go ask Dad."

"Don't bother. I'm sure he doesn't remember anything anyhow."

"Mmmm, smells good in here." Her mother's kitchen was in perfect order. If Annie were cooking, there would still be dishes in the sink, discarded potato skins in a heap on the counter, and assorted herbs and seasonings strewn about.

"Thanks. Beef Wellington." Marian was putting together a salad.

"Yum. What can I do to help?"

"Nothing really. Everything's under control."

Quel surprise. "Where's Dad?"

"Oh, he's at the hardware store trying to get an extra strand of lights for the tree. The middle went dead last weekend, and he jerry-rigged something or another together, which actually worked for awhile. Of course, they chose Christmas Eve to go out completely. I tried to tell him last weekend to get new ones, but he wouldn't listen."

George McDonnell was a great dad. His cheering face was present at every one of Annie's softball games. He just wasn't very good at being a husband. He gave into Marian early on in their marriage and got mired in the precedent he set. Now, despite wanting desperately to yell back at her after almost forty years of submission, George found it easier to revert to his familiar position of "nag-ee" and be done with it. After all, he had his escapes. Golf provided him with ample opportunity to get away from Marian for more than four hours at a time in the spring, summer, and fall (weather permitting, of course). During winter, he tinkered and putzed around the house, fixing this and that. A cabinet door here. A clogged drainpipe there. Christmas lights became his specialty. He carefully intertwined them on the branches, making sure each light stood up like the old-fashioned candles once did in Victorian days gone by. The effect was spectacular; it was as though the McDonnell Christmas tree glowed from the inside out. The problem was that it took him four hours to put the lights on. By that time, Marian, who never was very patient, had decorated the entire house, both inside and out.

Imagine George's dismay when he plugged in his masterpiece an hour before Christmas Eve was to officially begin, only to see half of the tree lit! He sprinted out the door, coat-tails flapping, only to come back one second later to free the scarf that almost brought about his untimely demise. Marian could envision the headline in the paper: "Local man strangles himself in quest for Christmas lights." Lovely. Fortunately, he reacted fast enough and left the house, muttering.

"Ah. He returns! Merry Christmas, Dad." Annie gave her father a hug and helped him off with his coat.

"Can you believe it? On Christmas Eve, of all nights! I hope I can fix it before dinner."

Annie took his cap and hung it up on the peg in the front closet.

"Thanks, dear. Merry Christmas." George kissed Annie on the cheek.

Despite the worry, the McDonnells achieved Christmas success once again. George's lights were easily fixed (okay, not so easily fixed, but he persevered), and Marian's dinner won raves from all who were at the table. The rest of the night passed pleasantly enough with the gift exchange and eggnog.

"Merry Christmas," John and Annie mumbled to each other, rising from bed, covers strewn. Today, they would face the holiday onslaught. But first, they were going to the latest possible Mass (at noon) to avoid the crowds, John told June. He just did not tell her which crowds. Who could take issue with them attending Mass on today of all days? Then there was lunch to be eaten, traffic to drive in, and, oh, by the time they could get to June's house, it might be almost four o'clock.

"Four o'clock! You'll miss Santa! When will I serve dinner?" June said.

"Whenever you want to. Don't worry about us, Mom. We will get there when we can. It will be fine." June would not dare to contradict her favorite child.

"Yes…I suppose…Try to get here earlier."

What did it matter? Annie wondered. Ham could stay

out for hours. June Jacobs was master of the potluck. Annie wasn't sure June even knew how to produce an entire meal from appetizer to desert. She had never eaten one in her house. Every time the family got together, June would draw up a menu and assign each female one part of the meal. Annie always received the green bean casserole. June could have been serving tacos, but Annie would still have to bring green bean casserole. Clearly, she had no faith in her daughter-in-law's culinary ability. True, Annie didn't get a chance to cook much during the week because of her hours, but on the weekends, she and John sometimes spent an entire day in the kitchen preparing meals for the upcoming week. In fact, last weekend, they made a pot of pasta sauce and meatballs, all from scratch, while listening to Sinatra.

"Perhaps I will find Valium in my stocking." Annie put her coat on and wrapped her scarf twice around her neck. "Hey, John! Are you sure you don't want a scarf? It's handy protection from the elements, and you can hang yourself with it too."

"Just get in the car. Let's get this over with."

"Ho. Ho. Ho."

CHAPTER FIVE

CHRISTMAS. TOM'S BIRTHDAY. THE SUPER Bowl. The celebrations at the Anderson's dragged on until February. Since when did "the holidays" start at Halloween and refuse to leave until Groundhog Day? Despite their illnesses, the kids managed to have a good Christmas. Of course, it's easy to have a good time when everything is done for you. Sarah searched her brain, trying to remember what that was like. She couldn't. Now she had to start planning Alex's second birthday party.

Tom might have been a bit uncomfortable, but she didn't care. Sarah had had enough of him and his job and was tired of hearing how swamped he's been or how he couldn't stand the thought of another corporate dinner. Poor baby, so bored with all that gourmet food prepared by a chef and enjoyed with a glass of wine. Let's see. What did she eat tonight? Mac and cheese. What year of Merlot would complement that?

Her insides were churning. Even when she tried to sit completely still, inside her body was quivering. "I feel like I've been run over by a truck," she told Tom. All she could do was sit there, staring at herself in the full-length mirror next to the dresser. Where was she? The woman in the mirror looked incapable of mustering up even a smirk. She couldn't move. Couldn't get up and change her clothes. Couldn't brush her teeth. Couldn't sleep no matter how exhausted she was.

"Last night I couldn't get back to sleep after Alex yelled for you." Tom was putting on his pajamas in the walk-in closet. "I laid there for three hours. I should have gotten up and gone to work. That would have been more productive than going over and over what information Laurie dropped at the end of the meeting Wednesday. I am still trying to figure out what optimizing our organization really means."

Sarah wanted to pummel him. After five minutes of intense glaring while he babbled on, the words no more than the sound the adult's voices made in the *Peanuts* cartoons, he finally made eye contact with her.

"You still hate me, don't you?"

"I never said I hated you. I merely despise you right now."

"Oh, is that all? Maybe you should go play some ping pong." He chuckled. He still could not imagine his wife being good at any game that required hand-eye coordination, no matter what her father said. "I know I would go nuts if I were stuck here with the kids all day. You need to get out of the house."

Sarah wasn't sure how to respond. When he said it, their sweet, wonderful children sounded like monsters.

"Why don't you go shopping or something?"

"Oh, for the love of God, Tom, the last thing I want to do is go shopping. I had enough of that at Christmas."

"Does anything make you happy anymore?" Tom made a little noise of disgust.

"Happy? That's a novel idea. What makes me happy?" She thought about it for a very long time. "I don't know."

"There must be something. What about before we had kids? Is there anything you miss?"

"Let's see. I miss sleeping until nine o'clock. I miss cooking whatever I wanted, not worrying about who will eat what, or not making veal piccata because there's not a snowball's chance in hell that Nicky will eat it. I miss thinking only about myself for one full day." Sarah began sobbing.

"Hey!" Tom said, wanting more than anything for this situation to be over. He really wanted to go to sleep. "When's the last time you read a book?"

"1990."

"C'mon, smart ass."

"I'm not kidding. When do I have time to read?"

"Make time."

"And when would that be? At midnight?"

"Wait a second." Tom checked the calendar on his phone. "I am not primary contact tomorrow. I could take the kids. You go and buy a book or something. Give yourself some time away. That should help give you some perspective."

Why did she feel like one of his employees? Who cares? Tom had offered to take the kids for an entire day. She would be free.

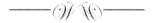

"Mom, where are you going?" Nicky grabbed a snack from the cookie barn.

"Didn't you just eat breakfast?" automatically came out of her mouth, then she remembered it was her first day off in six years. "I'm going out. Bye, sweetie."

He looked like a blank computer screen with "Does not compute" scrolling across the top. "Where?"

"Out."

"Can I come?"

"Nope. Be a good boy. I'll be back in a few hours." Sarah bent down and kissed him on top of his head. He still stood there as she walked to the garage, baffled by her temporary abandonment. Sarah, on the other hand, was quite joyful. She got into the van and slipped in a Springsteen CD. Ah! No little forming ears to worry about. She turned the volume up.

Downtown had several bookstores, but first she went to the coffee shop for a caffe mocha and some decompression. She took a deep breath, trying to remember what she learned in the yoga class she took her senior year of college about deep breaths cleansing the soul. She thought it might ease the pain of impending reality if she could be one with the universe. While studying for the comprehensive exams, which if she failed would deny her the English major she worked so hard for, she ended up in the hospital with a colitis attack. So much for yoga.

"I WANT TO GO HOME" bellowed from a table behind Sarah, in an ear-splitting pitch so high, she was baffled how she, but not the dog chained to the lamppost outside, could hear it. "NO. NO. NOOOOOOOO." The little girl started crying. Then wailing. Then yelling. Crying. Wailing. Yelling. The entire place was turning her way now. The mother was sitting there talking on her cell phone, all the while the child, no brat, had her attack. Sarah picked up her half-finished beverage and ran for the door, determined not to allow someone else's child to ruin her day. Sarah shook her head, her ears still ringing from the shrill noise of the coffeehouse beast.

Reaching the bookstore, she finished her mocha and happily trod inside. Sarah went straight to the Literature/Fiction section. She read the names as dear to her as old college classmates, touching each as she made her way down the aisles. She decided on a lovely leather edition of *Jane Eyre*, another out-of-control household. Turning left, Edgar Allan Poe's face glared down at her from the poster above. She and her mother were just discussing him the other day.

"Do you still have *The Raven* from your horror phase?" Patty needed one of the lines from the poem. Poe was the theme of that day's crossword puzzle. "You went for six solid months reading nothing but scary stories. Lovely way for a ten-year-old to pass the time."

"Can't find it. I wonder what happened to it?"

By the time she was done, Sarah had amassed five novels, including a best of Poe anthology, and a set of bookends. In the checkout line, a bookmark caught her eye. "A room without books is a body without a soul." It said the quote was from Cicero, CVI-XLIII BC. Maybe she would do the math to figure out what year it was from, as if she could remember Roman numerals anymore. Sarah grabbed it and proceeded to the counter. She dropped her credit card trying to put it back into her wallet on the way out. She thought this only happened when the kids were distracting her. Apparently, she really was a klutz. Putting her package on a table next to the door, Sarah picked up her credit card and slid it into its proper ranks of plastic. She noticed a flier on the table. "New for spring! Classics Book Club. English majors and laymen alike. All welcome to dabble in a little analyzation. Free. Choose to speak or not. No pressure, just your attendance required. Tuesday nights at 8 p.m. First meeting on March 20." It was on the most horrible piece of lime-green stationary. Sarah took one and threw it in her bag.

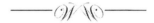

Getting out of the house was miraculous for Sarah, so, naturally, she wanted to do it more often. Maybe once a month for a book club meeting would be good for her and could be manageable with Tom's work schedule. She was also hoping it would also motivate her to read something a little more advanced than Dr. Seuss, the current novelist du jour in the Anderson home. Alex liked to hear Nicky practice reading, then laugh when he made a mistake, which sent Nicky upstairs crying. How do brothers know the precise way to hit the other where it hurts the most? It's like they have emotional radar screens that hone in on Achilles Heels. After sufficiently making a scene, Nicky would come downstairs and promptly trip Alex the first time he took a step anywhere near him.

Alex had turned two last month. The party went well, except for Marjorie thinking it was cute to smash Alex's face in his cake frosting. She lacked the foresight, however, to notice that much of the lettering and swirls of icing were dark blue. So there he sat strapped into his booster seat, a Musketeer with a frosting mustache and goatee, unable to seek revenge upon his aunt. The blue did not come off his face for two days. Sarah made a mental note to invent ways to torture Marjorie on Peter's birthday.

The weather had taken to punishing all who inhabited the Midwest, where there must be an unwritten law stating "no sun shall ever rise during February in the Chicagoland area."

"Oh, it's so depressing," Patty Williams said to Sarah on the telephone that morning. "As if it's not bad enough that we are already chomping at the bit for spring, then Lent starts, like we haven't atoned enough by just living through another Chicago winter."

"There hasn't even been much snow this year, except for that one big storm right before Christmas. The boys haven't been able to go sledding since. They are going crazy." Sarah liked watching Tom and the boys playing in the snow. Inevitably, a snowball would come sailing near her head when she popped out to ask if they wanted hot chocolate. Sarah would shut the door and count her blessings she was not out there with them. The skybox (also known as the family room) suited her just fine.

"It's so gray. If I don't see sun soon, I'm going into hibernation for two months. Wake me up when my daffodils pop." Patty yawned.

"Now that football is over, there's nothing even to watch on TV."

"Your father has been watching golf just so he can look at the scenery and pretend he is there. The Bob Hope Classic was on last weekend. I couldn't get him off his chair. He kept repeating 'Must go to Pebble Beach. Beautiful. Sunshine every day.' Oh well, I've got to run. Have to go to the post office. Let's hope spring is around the corner."

"Dinner!"

Tom put Alex in his high chair, while Sarah put the chicken in front of Nicky. They sat down, prayed, and began the meal.

"I have an idea," Sarah said.

Alex pointed and yelled.

Sarah recognized it as early caveman's language for "May I have more bread, please?"

She got him a crescent roll. "Butter?"

Alex nodded his head and smiled.

"Mom, can I have more juice?" This time it was Nicky.

"What's the magic word?"

"Please."

"Good job. Yes, you can have some more juice." Sarah grabbed his glass, poured, and returned to the table.

"Are there anymore potatoes?"

"Yes, I think so." Sarah went to the stove, brought the pot over, and spooned a heap of mashed potatoes on Tom's plate.

"Can I be excused?"

"Nicky, how can you be done already? I've barely started. No. Sit and engage in pleasant conversation until everyone is done, please."

"Hey, Sarah. Weren't you saying something?"

"I was? Oh, that's right. I would like to institute Family Reading Time."

Nicky was the first to utter his displeasure. Sarah knew it wouldn't go over well with him. He was mandated by his teachers to read aloud for fifteen minutes each day. Achieving this seemingly simple task would be more like ascending Mt. Everest on a llama.

"Nicky, you're supposed to read every day anyhow."

She stopped him after the second "Y" in "W-H-Y-Y-Y-Y" escaped his mouth. "It's going to be fun. Listen, I am going to join a book club, so I'll need extra time to actually read the novels we will be discussing. I think it would be good for all of us."

Tom gave her an "Oh, good God" look, but he did not want to make fun of her in front of the kids.

Her husband had been true to his word, sort of. Once the first-of-the-year project was up and running, which, of course, took until March, he was home by six o'clock every night for dinner. Of course, he worked from seven-thirty until ten o'clock every night. But he did attend Nicky's First Grade Spring Program and parent-teacher conferences. There was hope.

CHAPTER SIX

NNIE DID THE COMMUTER WALK/RUN into the train station. This week could not be over fast enough. She should have taken the three work days in between Christmas and New Year's off like the normal humans, but Annie was trying to purge her mind and plunge herself into something else besides being void of pregnancy. Work was the obvious choice, so Annie returned on December 26 ready to go. But she was the only one.

Although physically present, Annie's staff was on a mental vacation. When she asked her assistant, Donna, to start updating the general press list and to make the necessary calls confirming contact names, Annie received only this reply. "You're kidding, right?"

Now granted, these unusually brazen words were spoken after Donna had consumed a bathtub margarita while lunching at the Mexican restaurant two doors down from their office building. "It was fabulous. The burrito was like six inches high, at least, stuffed with shredded beef and, you know the cheese that is named for that rat-like dog, tomatoes, sour cream, guacamole, and refried beans. I feel like I am going to burst. Everyone went. You should have been there."

Evidence of the fiesta was everywhere. People walked around, fooded-out zombies, recapping stories of the trio that went from table to table playing requests. "Man, they must have played 'La Bamba' twenty times. I think it's the only Mexican song anyone knows." Tim appeared to be editing press releases, but every time Annie walked by his cubicle, the page still read "Chicago Youth Orchestra, Add Two."

Annie stopped in front of her assistant's desk. "Excuse me, Donna. Did you get a chance to start on the list updates?"

"I left ten messages. I have received no replies. I'm sorry. Everybody's out for the holidays." She tried her best to look professional through her glassy eyes.

"Thanks anyhow." So what if Annie was the only person in the office, no in the country, who wanted to work? Annie closed her office door behind her. What could she do? She, herself, had left several voice mail messages and received no replies either. Annie looked over at the piles of paper stacked on the file cabinets. This was as good a time as any to organize.

The project proved much larger than Annie anticipated, so she arrived at Union Station only ten minutes before her train departed. Light on riders for the commuter trains, this gave her plenty of time to get to the gate, maybe even pick up something to drink, as long as the checkout line did not have more than one person ahead of her. What should she do for dinner? The thought entered her head as she passed the ticket booths. Maybe she could phone something into that little Italian place across the street from the train station. Veal parmigiana? Too heavy. Maybe capellini with tomato-basil sauce. That sounded good. And some of those garlic breadsticks. John really loved those.

Annie grabbed a Diet Coke so she would not fall asleep on the train and end up in Aurora. She searched her briefcase for money while glancing over at the magazine rack next to the cash register. There it was, in huge white letters "HAVING A BABY AFTER FORTY," with smiling photos of Madonna (forty-three!) and Geena Davis (forty-six!). Annie grabbed a copy and ran to the train, forgetting the Diet Coke on the counter. She found a single seat in the crow's nest and put her monthly train pass in the clip to her right. Annie quickly turned to page eighty. "Mid-life Moms," she read. "In the past decade, the number of U.S. mothers giving birth after forty has nearly doubled, to more than 94,000 in 2000." Wow! Ninety-four thousand women! "However…fertility rates drop fifty percent after thirty-five…ninety-five percent after forty…A dentist postponed having kids so she could build up her practice…decided to try at thirty-eight…artificial insemination…four miscarriages…fertility drugs…$40,000…adoption…Ovaries don't care what you've done; they age…women over thirty-five have a higher risk of miscarriage, gestational hypertension and other difficulties…only a thirty percent chance of success within the first five cycles of in vitro fertilization…IVF, which costs $15,000 per cycle…myriad of fertility drugs…inseminations…$120,000 in bills."

Annie's head was spinning. She plopped the magazine on her lap and stared out the window, not seeing any of the houses as the train sped past. Afraid she was going to hyperventilate, Annie forced herself to take two deep breaths. They started when she was thirty-five. Her fertility was already down to fifty percent. The old bat was right—damn her! She had overheard June talking with John's sisters on Christmas Day.

"So, are John and Annie ever going to have kids?" Joy asked.

"Well, it's no surprise they can't." June said. "They should have started years ago. But, God forbid, anything gets in the way of her career. Now they are paying the price."

"What do people without kids do, besides work? I'd have so much free time on my hands, I don't think I would know what to do with myself," Julie chimed in.

"She wouldn't be able to handle it," June said.

Annie had dismissed their conversation as more cattiness, courtesy of the three witches from *Macbeth*. After all, this was coming from a woman who named all of her children "J" names. No major brain trust here. The thought of her being correct about anything was dismal enough without this black-and-white proof on her lap. Annie held her pelvis, fully aware of its emptiness. She managed to get to her car before the tears came.

John came home shortly after eight o'clock. Annie was sitting at the kitchen table with a glass of Pinot Noir.

"Hey, fancy meeting you here." Coming closer, he saw her eyes were red and swollen.

"Hi," said Annie feebly.

"What's wrong?"

She threw the magazine across the table. "I can't take it anymore."

"I know celebrity journalism has gotten out of hand in recent years, but—"

"Stop! Read it! I really screwed up, John. I didn't know...I just didn't know. I thought we had time. Would have been nice to know this five years ago. But no, all I saw were 'Woman gives birth at fifty.' All of those articles encouraging us to 'have it all.' Now here I sit without a damn thing I can do about it. You can't turn the clock back, can you?"

John picked up the magazine and skimmed the article.

Annie slid a pile of papers in front of John. "I found this information on the web after I came home. I think we should call tomorrow to make an appointment." The top read "Mitchell Adams and Associates. Specialists in Reproductive Health." "They are right at the hospital. A new fertility unit just opened there. Last year, I think."

There. It was finally out.

"Hey, you've been in here for awhile." John came into the office. Annie was staring at the computer screen. "Lots of work today? Are you preparing a pitch for a new client?"

"I want to be ready for whatever the doctors tell us. I've been surfing the 'Net. I found a good site on ….on infertility."

"Now, don't go jumping the gun. We don't know anything yet."

"I'm not jumping the gun. We have a problem. I'm just trying to get a handle on it."

"But you don't know what the problem is. Don't get your head filled with superfluous information that doesn't apply to us."

"I'm trying to become informed. Did you know that people who have problems conceiving after two years of trying are considered as having fertility problems? That's us, John, no matter if you like it or not."

"Not until we have confirmation from the doctors."

"Did you fill out your part of the questionnaire yet?" Annie looked up at him.

"Not yet."

"Could you get on that, please? We have to turn it in Friday."

"Yes, I know. I'm trying to catch up on e-mails. I'll work on it after I am done."

"Thanks."

Annie was revitalized by the knowledge they were going for their first consultation with Dr. Adams. John was just anxious. Infertility was constantly creeping into his psyche, forcing its way to the forefront no matter how he tried to block it out. All he had to do was walk into Andy's office and see the picture of Joey, smiling, posing with a bat just above his right shoulder. "You might never have a son, you know," a small voice would whisper in his head. "You'll never be able to teach him your curve ball."

Friday morning, the Jacobs entered Mitchell Adams and Associates Center for Reproductive Health and came out several vials less blood in their veins. They were asked how many different forms of birth control they had used in the past and whether or not they had any sexually transmitted diseases. Annie had a Pap smear. John ejaculated into a cup while looking at pornography in a white, sterile room. He left with his head down, unable to look at the nurse to whom he handed the specimen. They were going to test for vitality and good composition. John was certain his sperm would wind up at the mid- to lower-half of its class, just like he had ended up in undergrad. Maybe all his sperm needed was a kick in their little tails.

John joined Annie back in Dr. Adams' office. She reached out to hold his hand. They would hear the results of these initial tests soon, but they should prepare for more specific exams in accordance to Annie's menstrual cycle. They received instructions on how to monitor Annie's Basal Body Temperature and how to use ovulation-predictor tests, making sure to record the results on a chart.

"I can't believe we have to do this."

"Just try to relax, Annie."

"How? In less than an hour, everyone in Dr. Adams' office will know we just had sex."

"It's okay. We are married." John tried to laugh, but all that came out was a chortle.

"Oh, you know that is not the point."

"I guess it is the only way to test what they need to."

"Post-coital testing? Is nothing sacred? Oooh, let's see how John and Annie mate. Will his sperm travel well through her watery cervical mucus? The gun fires. And they're off! Here comes Dick, sperm number one. Woah! Number one hits the cervical mucus wall hard and is laying there flat on his tail. Sperm number two, Peter, approaches the wall, and ...is he? Is he? Yes! He's in! The crowd goes wild."

"Yeah, we can only hope. Well, come on. Our appointment is for four o'clock. We should probably start..." John could not finish the sentence. They were used to sex on demand by now, but this was pushing it. Intellectually, he understood the test's process, but he felt like they might as well be making love in a zoo cage with hundreds of people watching through the bars.

At least they could do it at home, and then go to the doctor's office. Could you imagine having to do it there? In some sex room? But, it would not be called that, of course, it would be the "coital area." You are sitting in the pristine rooms of the Center for Reproductive Health. Sharon, the nurse, calls your names and nods at the door over to the left. You open it and are suddenly enveloped by Barry White music. For reasons unknown, there is a disco ball hanging in the middle of the room from the ceiling. Undoubtedly, there is a complete bar to your right. Magenta shag carpeting cushions your path as you make your way to the heart-shaped bed. John bristled. He looked at Annie. She was staring at the bed. Who would have ever thought making love to her husband would turn into "Come on. Let's get this over with?" She heard that on one of the talk shows, but not usually followed with "so we can get tested at the fertility doctor's."

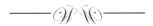

John came into the library. Annie was on the chaise, a cup of chamomile tea in her hands, a feeble attempt to calm herself.

"Hey." He sat on the sofa.

"Hey." Annie stared into her cup.

"Annie, please don't take this the wrong way, but I am worried about you. All you've done since we heard is sit here."

She looked at him, eyes bloodshot and puffy. "At least when you know, you can accept your fate and start working on the problem. I can't do that, John, because there are no answers. No one knows why I can't get pregnant. How can both of us test normal? How is that possible?"

The work up confirmed Annie's fears that their nightmare was real. Somehow, she was hoping the doctors would say, "Oh, Annie. It's just a low sperm count. Here's something for John to increase it. You'll be pregnant in no time." Instead, all she received was the same bafflement from the doctor and the recommendation of another series of tests. Surreal words floated in her head. Insemination? Assisted Reproductive Technologies? These were not just test results. They were the end to her motherhood dreams. She would never conceive a child normally now. That was evident. Why didn't he understand?

"You can't lock yourself in here all weekend."

"I'm sorry I am not reacting the way you would like."

"It's just a rough spot. We'll talk to Dr. Adams and figure out what is most likely to work for us."

"Yeah, why don't we just take bets on our chances? Hell, it's just a crapshoot, isn't it?"

"He said there are a few procedures we might be able to try depending on the results of your next tests."

"*My* tests? I heard the tone in your voice. You think it's all my fault, don't you? Waited too long? Let's see. Your mom says I am too selfish to be a good parent, right? Not good enough genes for her Johnny."

"She never said that."

"On Christmas, she told your sisters I was too obsessed with my career."

"I never heard that."

"Well, it's true."

"Listen, my mother would love us to have kids. Her grandchildren are her life."

"Whatever."

"I don't want to talk about my mother. I'm talking about you. Do you plan on leaving the library anytime soon?"

"Yes, as a matter of fact, right now." Annie stalked out of the room.

"Where are you going?"

"Out." She grabbed her purse and slammed the door.

Annie drove around on autopilot. How was she supposed to act like she was fine? She didn't even know if a baby could live inside her now. She might never be able to talk to her growing stomach or have it listen to Mozart like Jessica at work did. She might never feel her baby kick.

Mr. Always Happy with little frickin' bluebirds singing around his head. Why couldn't he show some sort of emotion, some hint that this bothers him at least a fraction of how it does her? Tired of driving around aimlessly, she pulled up to a bookstore. Maybe she could find some books that could help her out. Here's one. *Experiencing Infertility*. Annie brought it over to a corner chair and started reading.

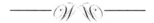

John was fixing the powder room fan when Annie returned. She went through the mudroom, careful to notice that he never looked up when she came in. She was unpacking her book when a vile sort of green piece of paper fell from the bag. What the hell was this? Classics Book Club? Tuesdays? Whatever. She threw it into her junk drawer.

Hello to you, too, John thought as he adjusted the motor.

He could not believe Annie was gone for three hours with no explanation. She was not the only one this affected. She didn't have to hear "Shootin' blanks there, partner? Don't worry, it will come in time," from the ass-in-law, Julie's husband. His mother brought it up again at Christmas. "Annie is an only child, isn't she? Her mother and grandmother too, right?"

"What does that have to do with anything?"

"Some women are breeders, John." June nodded her head in a pseudo-sage-like way. John wanted to strangle her.

He screwed in the fan cover. Although Dr. Adams said it was standard procedure to run more tests on the female, he also told John that about fifteen percent of all infertile couples never receive resolution. Could be him. Could be Annie. They might never know. He turned the fan switch to "on." It worked. At least something did. No matter what he said, he could not make Annie happy. He thought if she heard something positive, it would give her hope, but that just pissed her off more. What did she want? He had spent most of his life preventing pregnancy, not fantasizing about it. Raising children had always been a female responsibility in John's mind, especially since his father died when he was so young. He wasn't even sure he wanted kids now after being married so long already. Annie, on the other hand, made it very clear from the beginning that she wanted children. What was he going to do?

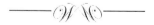

Annie made herself a vodka tonic, took out her new book, and assumed the position on the chaise, *The Wall* playing in the background. Here she could embrace her misery, not hide it. It was the only way she might get some of it out of her system.

John came in. "I fixed the powder room fan. Should work well now."

There was no response.

He sat on the sofa's arm, facing her chaise. "Annie, I don't know what to do. I'll go crazy if I let myself sit and think too much. I've got to get up and do something."

Annie put down her book. "I hate being alone, John. I just hate it. All those hours hiding in my room when I was growing up, with my mother on one side of the house and my father on the other. We came together only for meals, really. I spent most of my time reading *Little Women*, wondering what it would be like to have sisters."

"It's not all it's cracked up to be, believe me."

"Well, you have extraneous circumstances. As I got older and all hopes for sisters vanished, I envisioned myself as Marmee, the benevolent mother, offering bits of wisdom to my children at just the right times. Now, all I can see is me sitting alone, reading about families, just like when I was a child."

CHAPTER SEVEN

"Welcome to the first meeting of the Classics Book Club. Tonight is merely an introduction, most likely a reintroduction for most of you, to the workings of the masters, those tales that have lasted through time and still resonate in our souls." Edwina Hipplewhite was a retired high school English teacher who mostly dressed in florals. She rolled her "r"s, though she clearly hailed from the Midwest. "I am delighted to see such a fine turnout."

Six people, plus Edwina, were tucked away in a small room of the community center building. Edwina shut the door so her students would be better able to focus. "Before I tell you what the first selection is, let us see who you are. Please stand up, introduce yourselves, and offer a few sentences about what you do, where you live, et cetera. You, dear, you start." She pointed to the leftover flower child to her right.

"Hello, everyone. I'm Spring. I used to dabble in poetry, but now I own a juice bar in northern Naperville." She had long, straight brown hair, parted in the middle. Spring was thin, skeletally so, and her little white tee shirt hung loosely off her shoulders, barely meeting the top of her jeans.

"Nice to meet you, dear. You next, sir."

"Uh, hi. I'm Thaddeus. I'm a computer programmer and live in Naperville." His eyes darted around the room nervously.

"Well, darling, how is it that you decided to come over and join our side of the brain for a little while?"

"I've always loved reading. I wanted to study literature, but my father made me focus on something more practical…"

Edwina sniffed, cutting him off.

"No offense, ma'am."

"And you?"

Sarah struggled at what to say. Every time she told anyone she was a stay-at-home mother, they rolled their eyes and dismissed her. "Hi, I'm Sarah. I live practically down the street from here." She stared to sit down.

"Wait, what do you do, dear?"

"I'm a stay-at-home mom," Sarah mumbled and sat down quickly.

"How lovely." Edwina smiled. "How old are your children?"

"Six and two."

"Wonderful. I bet they are blessings."

"Sometimes."

They continued around the room. "I'm Catherine. I'm temporarily unemployed, but I have an audition tomorrow. I'm an actress."

"Good for you. Perhaps you would honor us with readings from our selections?"

Catherine was all too happy to assure Edwina she would love to help out any way she could, hoping her performance would do the works justice. She tipped her head, humbly.

Rounding out the group was Rosemary, whose occupation was never mentioned in her haste to sit back down and take the attention off of her, and Larry, the local newspaper columnist who often quoted great works of literature in his editorials.

Edwina clapped her hands. "Oh, you are a delightful bunch. What fun we'll have! Well, let's get down to business, shall we? A caveat. I want you all to know that I proposed organizing this club long before Oprah decided to resurrect hers and focus on similar subject matter. Now, I love Oprah dearly, but

I am not a copycat. Enough said. Now, my darlings, our first selection is a novel ever so near and dear to my heart."

The door burst open. Everyone jumped in their seats.

"Excuse me, is this the book club?"

"Why yes."

"I'm sorry I'm late. There was a problem with the Burlington Northern line, and my train sat for forty-five minutes before we left Union Station."

"How inconvenient," Edwina muttered, eyeing the intruder.

All six bibliophiles stared at the beautiful woman winding her way to the only empty seat, her briefcase held unusually high so as to not hit someone square in the head as she passed. She was dressed all in taupe. A print scarf tied her straight blonde hair back into a ponytail.

"And who might you be?" Edwina tried to pull the focus back on herself instead of on this latecomer.

The woman stood in front of the open chair, her butt blocking Sarah's face. "My name is Annie Jacobs."

"Hello, Annie. And what do you do for a living? You see, we just finished introducing ourselves before you came."

"Oh. I'm vice president of Jones and MacGregor downtown. A public relations company. But I live in Naperville, not too far down Washington from here."

The exact opposite direction of Sarah's house. Figures, Sarah thought, right before Annie plopped down next to her and let out a huge sigh. The workers are all the same. Everything has to stop because they are late. Can't order dinner because they have a phone call. Can't make it on time to the Valentine's Day party or manage to send the paper goods ahead of time. What are the kids supposed to eat on? Wipe their mouths with?

"Well, welcome to the club, Annie. My name is Edwina Hipplewhite, and I was just about to tell everyone what our first selection will be. It is…are you ready?" Edwina was so excited one would have thought she was announcing winning lottery numbers. "*A Portrait of the Artist as a Young Man* by James Joyce." Edwina scanned the room for reactions.

Thaddeus, Larry, and Catherine nodded approvingly. Sarah searched her memory and retrieved a file that said read it in college, was pretty good. Annie and Rosemary smiled. And Spring, poor Spring, well, no recognition registered on her face.

"I thought this might be an interesting choice, as most people enjoy this book, and the writing style lends itself to conversation." Edwina sat down for the first time that hour. "Besides, it is not too long, so it should be quite manageable to read in one month's time. Wouldn't want to start you out with *Ulysses*, would I? You would never come back!" Her hearty laugh pushed Edwina's entire body two and fro. "It's probably been awhile since you have thought about our dear Mr. Joyce, so please allow me to review some information with you. *A Portrait of the Artist as a Young Man* is Joyce's semi-autobiographical novella of Stephen Dedalus. It is an interesting study in that as the protagonist ages and matures, so does the writing style. Joyce uses symbolism and eventually moves to stream-of-consciousness prose, which is always a treat. I suggest you consult some study guides during your reading, such as the one I have assembled here."

Copies of "Studying Joyce the Hipplewhite Way" floated around the room. "Well, my dear ones, I believe our time is up. I look forward to joining you on our great adventure with Joyce next month. Be ready to discuss the work when we next meet. Good night, all." And with a flourish, Edwina Hipplewhite was gone.

Annie needed a diversion, so this book club thing would do as well as anything else. She and John were in for a long haul. If there was not something to look forward to, Annie would surely jump out of her skin. She discovered the flier at the bottom of her junk drawer. Maybe reading something besides medical journals would be constructive. The pelvic ultrasound showed no blockage in her fallopian tubes. Unexplained infertility was the final diagnosis. Dr. Adams said one in five couples who experience fertility issues have the same thing. He also urged them to put their names on the in vitro fertilization waiting list, since they had little over a ten percent chance of ever becoming pregnant without treatment.

"It can take up to a year before your slot comes up," he said. "In the meantime, you can try IUI, intrauterine insemination. This procedure places sperm in the reproductive tract during ovulation. We can put Annie on some ovulation-induction medication to build up the number of eggs she is producing. But I have to warn you. Couples with unexplained infertility have the worst chances of becoming pregnant. Of course, that does not mean there is absolutely no chance of conception, but it can be more difficult. Deborah will go over everything with you. Let us know what you decide." He ushered them out of the door.

The physician's assistant, Deborah, was skilled at handling couples whose worlds had been shattered mere minutes ago by her employer. She guided John and Annie into the conference room, offered them herbal tea and seats in leather chairs. She left them alone for just the right number of minutes, enough time for the couple to compose themselves, but not enough for the full effect of the situation to come bearing down on them.

Deborah came back and poured herself a cup of mint tea with a hint of tarragon. "We need to discuss your options. Here is an information packet you can read when you have the time." She slid the folder across the table. "Inside, you will see sections on the various reproductive technologies available to you. These include insemination, in vitro fertilization, and using donors and/or surrogates. Usually, most couples begin with insemination and, if necessary, progress to IVF, undergoing evaluations along the way. Do you have any questions?"

Annie looked at John, then at Deborah. "Yes, I have a question. If you have all of this fabulous technology, why can't you give us a real answer? How will any of these even work if you have no idea what the problem is?"

John nudged his wife.

"I can understand your feelings, Mrs. Jacobs," Deborah said. "It is especially difficult for couples with unexplained infertility, but I can assure you, we can help guide you through each procedure until we find one that is successful."

"Thank you." John wanted to step in before Annie started blaming the P.A. for their problems. "What is our next step?"

"You're quite welcome, Mr. Jacobs. Take as much time as you need to read over the materials and digest all of the information. Then give us a call so we can formulate your plan." She rose from the table and shook their hands. "Very nice meeting you."

John and Annie drove home from the doctor's office.

"Of course, out of all the ways to be infertile, ours has to be the most difficult." Annie remembered a button she wore with pride freshman year of college. It was black with white letters that read "Why Be Normal?" What she wouldn't give for a chance at normalcy now. It was a simple request. She was not asking to be the Mother of God at the time of the Second Coming or anything, just for a sweet baby of their own that would have John's quirky smile and her eyes. Now the doctor was telling them the only way they might have a family was to mix her eggs and his sperm in a petri dish—creating some sort of genetic omelet—and hope that fertilization occurred.

For the past two months, the Basal Body Temperature Thermometer was always on her bedside table. Annie and John had arranged their schedules to work from home on her alleged fertile days (if they really existed), so they could copulate at the optimum moment. Last month, John was on a conference call when Annie burst into the office screaming "Now, John!" So much for soft music, candlelight, and ambiance. She was already on their bed naked when he entered their bedroom. "Let's go! Let's go!"

Annie began reading the packet as soon as they got home. After starting the "Defining the Terms" section, she threw it across the family room, annoyed at the patronizing tone. Or maybe she was a little hypersensitive by this time, every page reaffirming that she was, in fact, the freak of nature she suspected.

CHAPTER EIGHT

ANNIE WASN'T ALWAYS INFERTILE. BEFORE this, she and John had managed to live quite a pleasant life. They met in their senior year of college, after the serious partying and goofing off was out of their systems, and it was time to figure out what lay ahead for them. After John got over Melanie.

John was going to spend spring semester in Rome. He was anxious to escape the alienation that had occurred after the break up. John and Melanie were a part of the same social circle, so independence also meant separating from his buddies because their girlfriends had sided with Melanie. John was the black-hearted bastard who confirmed the suspicions of Melanie's entire sorority that true love did not exist.

As he settled into his seat on the airplane, a woman walked through the aisle with the largest carry-on John had ever seen. He tried to duck, but was too late and got biffed right in the head with all fifty pounds of it.

"Oh my goodness, are you okay?" A little stunned, it took awhile for him to respond. She kept talking. "I'm so sorry. I was hoping this wasn't too big—I guess it is—but I needed room for all of the things I don't trust to check, you know, like my maps, Rome guidebook, glasses, makeup, *Dante's Inferno* (I was reading it to get in the mood), address book so I can write post cards…"

"It's okay. I'm fine." He rubbed his head.

"… my journal so I can record memories and…"

"Miss? Please stop."

"What? Oh, I'm sorry. It's just that I talk too much when I am nervous, and this is my first time abroad."

"You'll be fine. It's my first time too. Where's your seat? Let me carry this thing for you."

"Thank you so much. I'm really sorry I hit you with it."

"It's okay. What seat are you in?"

"27A."

"Well, I don't have to carry this too far. You're here in the window seat." He was in 27C. John put the enormous bag in the overhead bin.

"I hope it doesn't fall out and label you again," said the woman.

"Me too. At least I know to get out of the way now." John smiled. He was looking into the most beautiful pair of blue eyes he had ever seen. They had green flecks that made them look almost turquoise. He had seen that color only once before while on a glass-bottom boat trip in the Sea of Cortez during a family vacation to Cabo San Lucas, Mexico.

"Hi, I'm John Jacobs." He offered his hand to shake.

She smirked. "I'm Annie McDonnell." She couldn't contain herself and started laughing uncontrollably.

"Excuse me?"

"I'm sorry. I can't help it."

"What?"

"John Jacobs Jingleheimerschmidt," Annie began to sing. "His name is my name too. Whenever I go out, the people always shout 'There goes John Jacob Jingleheimerschmidt.' Dah dah dah dah dah dah dah dah." She stopped when John didn't seem amused. "I'm sorry, but I just spent the summer taking care of a four-year-old with a penchant for Barney. They do that song a lot on it. Stuck in my head. It's really quite maddening."

"I'm sure it is."

"Bet I'm not the first one to do that to you, huh?"

"Nope."

"And here I was thinking I was the cleverest person on the plane."

They chatted companionably throughout the flight and shared a taxi to the Rome Center, where, as it turned out, Annie would be studying also.

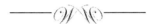

John, Annie, and the rest of the Rome Center students, thirty in all from three different universities, were ushered through the tourist must-see attractions during their first week abroad. Their crash-course included the Colosseum, the Forum (but nothing funny happened on the way there), and Vatican City, where Annie readied herself to join the protesters she was certain would be demonstrating against the Church's policies on women's roles, or lack thereof. But there were none. At first, Annie was indignant, wondering loudly why no one seemed to care about this issue.

John embarrassedly pulled her aside. "Could you please stop? People are watching."

"Who cares? Give me one good reason why women are barred from saying Mass?"

"I don't have any. All I know is that this is Pope territory, and I don't really feel like getting kicked out, okay?"

"I've been waiting my entire life to have my views heard."

"Write a letter, then. Don't go psycho in front of St. Peter's. Have some respect."

Annie did not know how to respond. It was the first time anyone ever silenced her like that. Usually her friends just let her do her Annie-thing, agreeing with her while she ranted on about various injustices. Women's rights. Apartheid. Cruel English professors. This guy had some guts. Annie acquiesced.

After the mother of all tours, as they dubbed their Italian baptism, the students began focusing on daily living essentials, such as eating very thin crusted pizza folded in half and locating the nearest American Express office.

"This is too much to absorb," John said as he and Annie walked down Via Condotti in search of espresso.

Annie thought it would have been a sin not to try the bitter Italian liquid, even though she was no coffee lover.

"That looks interesting." John pointed across the street to number 86.

"Caffe Greco? Why does that sound familiar?" Annie stopped to look up the name in the *Guidebook to Rome* that never left her purse. She read quickly. "Oh my God. Oh my God."

"What is it?"

"I can't believe it. We have to go in. Do you know what this place is?" Not stopping for an answer, Annie continued. "Caffe Greco is where all of the writers and artists hung out, like James Joyce, Ibsen, Byron, Keats, Shelley, oh my God."

"Cool." John remembered the names from various English classes, but, truth be told, he found them unintelligible.

"Let's go." Annie pulled John across the street.

They sat down at one of the marble-topped tables. The windows were adorned with red damask drapes. Annie stroked the table reverently. "I wonder if they ever sat at this table, pondering life or arguing about art? The Romantics were good at that."

"Really? And here I thought they only cut one album and wore red leather suits."

Annie decided to hold her tongue. "It is amazing sitting here, in a place where they all came, maybe drinking espresso too? Who knows?" She closed her eyes, trying to make contact with the literary souls she was sure surrounded her. John's voice brought her back to the present.

"We are sitting here in a city with thousands of years of history. We certainly don't have anything like it back home. Well, my dear Miss McDonnell, let us raise our cups in a toast. To our months in Italy. To drinking in every adventure that lies before us."

They clanked demitasse cups and chugged the bitter liquid. Maybe it was the excessive caffeine pouring through her body at double time. Or it was the heavily perfumed scent of dark-roasted coffee beans. Maybe it was sitting in possibly the oldest coffeehouse in Europe with this man to whom she felt oddly connected. But Annie always remembered that day as the first time she truly felt alive.

The weeks progressed. The students became acclimated, and life now centered on classes at the Rome Center. One of particular interest to Annie was "Shakespeare" taught by Jonathan Byrd, who had trained with the Royal Shakespeare Company in Stratford-upon-Avon, but she was a bit disappointed. Although he was a classically trained actor, Byrd spent an awful lot of time focusing on sexual innuendo in the Bard's works for Annie's taste.

John preferred his drawing class taught by starving artist Paolo (no last name), who looked exactly how you think a starving artist named Paolo should look. Rumpled shirt, worn untucked. Slip-on shoes. No socks. Long, curly black hair. Earring. Perpetual five o'clock shadow. This mystified John. How was that achieved? It was presumed Paolo shaved at some point, so how did the stubble reappear by nine o'clock when class began? Did he draw it on himself with his charcoal for effect? John wouldn't have been surprised. But, no matter, it was cool walking around Rome, sketch books in hand, drawing whatever sight caught John's fancy.

Since he had no idea what he wanted to be when he grew up, John gladly exchanged his role of ordinary college student for budding European artist, right down to attempting his own five o'clock shadow. Unfortunately, all he could muster was a three-fifteen sporadic stubble. Needless to say, John shaved the next day and resumed his usual clean-cut, all-American boy look. He was more at home in a golf shirt and khakis and would never be caught dead wearing his shirt over his pants. John developed his own preppie-artist thing, which, as oxymoronic as it sounds, somehow worked for him. He was quite the talk of the third floor of the Rome Center, where the girls lived.

"How did it go? Last I saw, you and John were quite cozy." Samantha was talking through bubbles of toothpaste overflowing from her mouth. Annie, two sinks down and with the same rabid-dog reflection in the mirror, pricked up her ears.

"Nothing." Jackie was combing her hair. Annie was certain she was going to pull part of her brain out through her tress follicle, she brushed so furiously. "Not a damn thing."

"Can I use your brush?" Samantha's hair fell right into place. "What happened?"

Jackie gave her an irritated look. "I'm not sure. We were getting along great, I thought, then, BAM, he says he has to go."

"I heard he is getting over a massive break up." Linda reached over Samantha and squirted some minty green gel on her toothbrush.

"Really?" Jackie gave up fighting her hair, pulled it into a ponytail and fastened it with a rubber band.

"Didn't you know?" Sally was sucking in her cheeks, applying blush with a large black brush. "John used to go out with that girl Melanie. Remember her from homecoming? For like years." Sally moved to eyeliner. "I heard she thought he was going to marry her and everything. That's what Ginny's cousin Amanda told me."

"He seems nice enough." Linda put in her right contact.

"Who knows?" Jackie pulled up her bra straps and smoothed her magenta shirt over her jeans. "Who needs him? Come ladies, let us conquer Rome today. Tonight, we will seek out men named Tony, Joey, and Giuseppe. See ya later, Annie."

The girls packed up their toiletries and went back to their rooms.

Notorious break up? John had never mentioned it to Annie. Of course, it was not like they divulged their deep dark secrets to each other or anything. No, they hung out a couple times a week, eating pasta or going to museums. Stuff like that. Annie had made a wonderful friend. Well, at least she thought he was a friend, but yet there was a certain, she did not know how to describe it, oh, what the hell, she was falling in love with John. It sounded so trite to go off to Rome and find the man of your dreams. Annie thought it reduced her existence to that of a romance-novel heroine. But if he was recuperating from a recent break up, what were the chances John would think of Annie as more than a buddy anyhow? She was probably a pal. Or maybe the rebound girlfriend? Or worse, the Rome fling. Annie was getting too far ahead of herself. There were no indications of anything other than friendship, she was sad to say. Annie would have to settle for that.

There were only five weeks left in Italy. Annie awoke slowly on April 14, her twenty-first birthday. Every year since she could remember, her father had greeted Annie with a bouquet of variegated tulips, symbolic of her "beautiful eyes," he always said. After presenting her with the flowers, George would launch into a rendition of "Thank Heaven for Little Girls," in a mock-Maurice Chevalier accent. Humming, her father would extend his hand, and Annie would join him in a Fred Astaire-Ginger Rogers dance routine, twirling around the kitchen. Last year, George tried to dip Annie, but tripped over her foot instead, and they landed with a whack on the kitchen floor.

"Oh for goodness sake." Annie's mother walked over the laughing pile of them, shaking her head.

This would be the first year they would not dance together. All of a sudden, Annie missed home. Maybe she could call later, but with the time difference, it was difficult to coordinate. She took a shower and went downstairs for breakfast.

"Annie, there's something for you at the reception desk." Mark walked by, swatting her with his newspaper.

"Thanks." She went to pick up her package, bumping into John on the way. "Hey."

He was carrying his sketch pad. "Hey yourself."

"I guess something is up there for me." Annie gestured toward the large item covered with paper at the front desk.

"Special occasion?"

"Um," Annie put her eyes down and mumbled. "It's my birthday."

"Well, Happy Birthday, Miss Annie. What could that be?" John glanced at the package, wondering himself who sent Annie flowers. "Go on, don't let me stop you."

Annie thanked the receptionist and started walking to her room.

"Let's see who sent them." John followed her.

"John, what are you doing?"

"Just curious. I love presents." John lied. Had Annie had

met someone else while she was here…or…what if she had a boyfriend at home? They had never discussed it. "Open it."

"Okay, relax." What was up with him? Annie tore the paper. It was a huge bouquet of white variegated tulips, sitting tall amongst beargrass greenery. Annie misted up reading the card.

"Who are they from?" John's heart was beating fast.

"Happy Twenty-First Birthday to my darling Annie. With all my love," Annie read. John looked like his eyes were going to pop out of his head. "Dad."

John took a deep breath. "Isn't that nice?"

"Yes, it is." Was he nervous? Who did he think the flowers were from?

"Well, um, I'm sure you have big plans for tonight." John walked toward the door.

"Actually no. I have a nine o'clock class tomorrow morning."

"But you have to celebrate your birthday."

"I don't feel much like…"

"It's your twenty-first. Come on." John lightly punched Annie in the arm. "I know! How about you and I hit the town after classes end?" Standing there with his light-bulb-just-went-off-over-his-head smile, John was irresistible.

"Oh, okay."

They stood there, both trying to suppress the silly smirks taking over their faces.

"I'll be here at two o'clock, okay?" John broke the silence.

"Sure. Where are we going?"

"It's a surprise."

"What should I wear?"

"You look great in anything. I'll see you tonight." John shut her door quickly, whistling as he walked to his room. He had finally figured it out. Annie was the reason John kept declining the other girls, not his break up with Melanie. When he saw those flowers, butterflies erupted in his stomach, but they magically disappeared when "Dad" sung out of her lips. John had a date with Annie McDonnell. On her birthday, no less. He'd better make this good. John turned around and bolted downstairs. It was ten o'clock. He only had four hours to create the perfect birthday present.

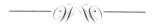

There was a knock on Annie's door at exactly two o'clock. She checked out her hair in the mirror, smoothing down the right side that jetted out slightly above her ear. Although John had picked her up several times during the last two months for one of their adventures, Annie's stomach somersaulted when she opened the door.

John took out one long-stemmed red rose from behind his back. "Happy Birthday."

Annie smelled its blossom. "It's lovely. Thank you."

"Shall we go? After you, senorita." John held the door open for Annie.

"Thank you, sir."

"This way, please." John guided her to the left as they exited the Rome Center.

They processed awkwardly down the streets, their stilted conversation resuming to a normal cadence with each fountain passed, every shop traversed, until stopping at Piazza di Spagna.

"Birthday lady, I give you the Spanish Steps." John gestured with his arms and bowed.

"Get up, you goof." Annie tapped him in the head.

The area was alive with people. French, German, and Russian was being spoken around them. In fact, there were so many people, one could barely see the actual stairs themselves. At the top was a church.

"The Trinita dei Monti," John said. "built by the French in 1495."

Annie shot him a quizzical look.

"I did some research. Come on. Let's get a better look." They were careful not to land on a hand or a foot of a fellow tourist as they ascended. "Did you know this area used to be called er ghetto de l'inglesi, the English ghetto? A ton of writers hung out here while they were on their Grand Tour. Probably the same ones that got their espresso at Caffe Greco. It's just down the street. Can you believe it? We never came far enough down that day."

They reached the top of the Spanish Steps and looked out at the crowd below. Easels hid wannabes, furiously working on their masterpieces. Children ate gelato, trying not to drip chocolate on their shirts. People intent, it seemed, on reading their books, but whose eyes really followed every passerby. Small clusters of two or three engaged in conversation. Lovers gazed only at each other, oblivious to the circus surrounding them. Amateur photographers, lenses extended, worked on the perfect shot.

"Would you like to see the church?" John said.

"Definitely."

"I hear there is a sculpture by one of Michelangelo's students in there."

"You are a font of knowledge."

"Not really. That one I got from Paolo."

"Ah, Paolo with no last name."

"Yes."

"I half expected to see his face pop out from behind one of those easels down there."

"Glad not. He would probably nag me about my portfolio. It's due in a week. I've got a lot of work to do. Never mind that. Today is for you. Come this way." They entered the church.

"This is fabulous, John. Thank you so much."

"But wait, there's more." John led Annie to a pink building situated to the right of the Steps, his hand falling around her shoulders.

"What is this, tour guide?"

"This, my dear lady, is the Keats-Shelley House. Keats died in this very establishment. If you want to feel at one with deceased authors, this is probably the place for it."

She could not believe he had taken the time to find something related to English literature in Rome. "You are awesome." Annie hugged him.

"Anything for Miss Annie on her birthday," John said softly, stroking her cheek.

They kissed underneath the plaque marking the building. "Come on. Let's go in." John took Annie's hand.

When they returned from Italy, John and Annie graduated from their respective colleges and began the arduous tasks of planning a wedding and finding employment. For Annie, the previous summer's internship, in which she created a public relations plan for a start-up orchestra's premier season, parlayed itself into a full-time position with that company. Harry Jones, CEO of Jones and MacGregor, was on the orchestra's editorial advisory board. He was impressed by Annie, gave her his card, and told her to give him a call after she graduated. She did and became a PR assistant.

It was not as easy for John. John was a business major with no minor, no focus. He graduated with very general qualifications to do practically nothing. John searched, but there were no openings for undetermined talents.

Seeing as he had to do something to fill his days, John took a floor sales position at a local golf store, selling expensive clubs to hackers, as if any amount of graphite could save their games. One afternoon, when the store was empty because all potential customers were out on the links, John was putting around the practice area. His mind traveled back to Rome and those magical months with Annie. Then Paolo's scruffy face invaded his thoughts. That bastard said John he was a terrible artist. Well, maybe terrible was too harsh, Paolo told him while reviewing his portfolio. He was sub-par on a good day and lacked passion. John replied by spitting venom at the little man who went from cool to pathetic. "I lack passion? Well, at least I know what my last name is. What's the matter, Paolo, no man want to claim you as his son?"

Paolo was speechless, which was rare, as the starving artist enjoyed pontificating to his students on a daily basis. And then it hit him. Nothing made him happier than silencing people he deemed wrong. The heavens parted, and a ray of sunlight shone on John's sandy head. He would go to law school and fight for the wronged.

John decided on Northwestern. Annie was happy for him, but knew there was no way they could afford it on her beginner salary of $19,000 after they were married. Help came in the form of June Jacobs, who blubbered on about how proud she was of John and how she could not wait to tell everyone her son was studying to be a lawyer. June, red-faced and tear-stained, offered to take out a home equity loan to pay for John's graduate studies. He, emphasis on he, could pay her back after he signed a contract with one of the large firms downtown, which June was certain would hire her Johnny. He started law school in the fall.

The Jacobs were married on a beautiful May day, one year after their return from Rome. Annie carried a bouquet of white variegated tulips held together by a satin cuff. Mike, the best man and friend of John's for some twenty years (one of the boys who lived behind his family), said he had never seen two people so perfectly suited for each other. Everyone but Marian McDonnell cried, but seeing as she paid the bill, Annie could not have cared less.

After returning from their honeymoon, the couple focused on their careers. On Saturday nights, they would go out to dinner and drink red wine. The conversation would inevitably settle on the "when we have kids" talk.

"Wouldn't it be cool to be able to take the kids to Williamsburg when they are studying American history?" John would say.

Annie would continue. "I can't wait to see their eyes when we go to Disney World."

But, no matter how good that sounded, it never seemed to be the right time. When John hinted at starting a family, Annie told him now wasn't good because she was working on an account that, if she did well on it, would guarantee her a promotion. When Annie thought it might be the time, John was working on a big case. It yo-yoed back and forth like this, and, before they knew it, they had been married for almost thirteen years and were childless.

Their IRAs and 401(k)s were in place. They had vacationed in Australia, Aruba, and returned to their beloved Italy on their tenth anniversary. They had pursued their careers with a vengeance and were finally in places where co-workers actually listened to them, rather than giving them the managerial equivalent to a pat on the head.

They had just moved into their dream house, a five-bedroom, four-bath English Tudor in the Hobson Woods area of Naperville, surrounded by mature trees and bordering a river. John and Annie fell in love with the house the moment they saw it. It had a traditional layout and rooms that actually had walls, unlike many of the others they had been shown with their soaring, two-story family room ceilings and borderless first floors. Annie liked parameters for her living space. She felt comfortable with four tangible walls around her.

This house also had formal living and dining rooms, rather than one large great room. John liked the idea of serving cocktails in the living room at dinner parties. It suggested an era when everything was not so casual. John loved his suits, thought wearing them was like putting on your uniform to get into work mode. They made him sit up straighter and think more clearly.

Although John was nostalgic for decades he had never lived through, he was definitely smack into the twenty-first century when it came to his favorite place in the house. The family room was a shrine to the God of Electronica. To make sure the room did not look too *Metropolis*, the equipment was nicely stored in built-in cabinetry, and a Victrola was tucked into the right corner.

Annie's favorite space was down the hall from the family room and to the right. The library was decorated in Old English paneling shipped here from a manor home in East Sussex that was being destroyed. A suit of armor, passed down through generations of the McDonnell family, guarded the French doors. Annie could not believe her mother had no use for it. "All of that metal. What an eyesore!"

Large, burgundy leather furniture surrounded the stone fireplace. The built-in bookcases held great works of literature. Jane Austen. James Joyce. Virginia Woolf. Christopher Marlowe. Photos of John and Annie's travels dotted the shelves. Annie holding a koala. John holding a strawberry smoothie on the beach. John and Annie holding each other in front of the Colosseum. Annie's chair, a chaise lounge, was flanked by an eighteenth-century tea table, the only true antique they had purchased, in a nook opposite the doors. The audio speaker system was always set on WFMT, the classical music station. This was not just a room; it was a sanctuary.

The house had various other required rooms, like a kitchen that flowed into the family room and upstairs, a master suite and two very empty extra bedrooms.

Everything they wanted to do was done, and now it was time to start a family with no regrets, no "would haves" or "should haves." Unfortunately, nature had not complied with their perfect plan.

CHAPTER NINE

SARAH FOUND A BENCH IN front of the local college's gymnasium where Nicky took swimming lessons every Saturday morning. It was a decent spring day, even for Chicago in the first week of April, with plenty of sunshine and a light breeze. Sarah had abandoned her winter parka, donning instead a light fleece pullover. Tiny purple crocuses peeked out of the ground around the trees, checking if it was safe to come out. The smell of impending spring lilted past Sarah's nose. She breathed it in most willingly. It had been a long winter.

Alex was at home with Tom, building Duplo spaceships and crash-landing them to earth. She opened *A Portrait of the Artist as a Young Man* and began reading the first sentence of Chapter Five.

"Oh, yeah. Did you get my message? I know. Me too." Another mother sat on the opposite bench talking on her cell phone. Despite great efforts at concentration, Sarah could not read. Didn't anyone believe in quiet time anymore? There were reasons phone booths were not found on every block before cell phones made aural invasion a part of daily life.

After attempting the same sentence five times, Sarah walked around the building. She sat down at a picnic table under a budding tree, the college's soccer field, football stadium, and baseball diamond before her. Sarah sighed and began again. Something moved in her peripheral vision. A mass of blackbirds were flying and landing on the soccer field.

She watched them ascend in formation, reach a seemingly agreed upon height, then swoop down to the grass. Sarah was mesmerized. The birds' patterns rivaled any Blue Angel's. Her stomach leapt as they soared high into the sky, then cruised, wings fully extended.

"Howard called me into his office today. It seems the new system is doing really well. Everyone is pleased with its progress."

Sarah was folding laundry. The dutiful wife she, feigning interest in Tom's latest project, while incapable of contributing a well-put-together sentence of her own. Discussing today's *Winnie-the-Pooh* episode, no matter how sweet, did not seem appropriate. He had become so serious. She had become so dowdy. Where was the couple who talked at dinner for so long the night of their first official date they almost missed the movie?

"It has gone so well that they would like us to implement it at the satellite offices and train everyone how to use it."

"Congratulations."

Tom hesitated. "They want me to go to Boston for awhile."

"Oh? How long? A week?"

"Two months."

Sarah's mind spun with questions, but all she could manage out of her mouth was "What?"

"I'm sorry. I just found out this morning. It's not optional. I'm the project lead."

"How is this going to work?"

"I'll be there during the week, fly home on Friday nights, and fly back out Sunday."

"Two months of that?" Sarah was used to the occasional two- or three-day business trip, which usually left her depleted and asleep by nine-thirty each night. Now she would have to multiply that by ten?

Sarah felt nauseated, although she could not tell if it was from Tom's news or from staring at blackbirds for almost a half an hour straight. Flight school was over. The birds had begun looking for food in the soccer field. Back to the reality of survival. The Carillon chimed eleven o'clock. Time to pick up Nicky.

Two weeks into Tom's pseudo-relocation to Boston, Sarah established modified bedtime rituals to reduce the amount of times she had to hear "When is Daddy coming home?" and "Ou Dada?" from Nicky and Alex respectively. "Ou Dada?" was a new one. Sarah was, at once, delighted by Alex's first sentence, yet dismayed at its subject. She tried teaching him "Ou est mon pere?" in an attempt for the little one to sound continental rather than temporarily fatherless. It failed for obvious reasons, but the tot did latch onto "pere" and enjoyed repeating it until his mother's ears rang.

Sarah even began enjoying mini-stabs at independence, like leaving her makeup bag on the bathroom counter all day. After all, who would it inconvenience? Making half the bed was much easier, to be sure, but slumbering with only Tom's pillow was not optimum. Sarah usually went upstairs around nine o'clock, afraid to fall asleep on the family room sofa with no alarm or adult to awaken her. Every night, a little shiver prickled the back of her neck after she shut off the kitchen lights. She was convinced she would see a face staring back at her through the window. Sarah had seen *Scream*. She knew how it worked.

Just before Tom came home on Friday nights at around ten o'clock, Sarah allowed herself to relax, knowing he could always wake her up if need be. Besides, she liked knowing he was home safe, even if it was in a half-awakened haze.

They rose each Saturday morning, an hour earlier than necessary because Tom was on Boston time, where upon Sarah endured a thirty-minute diatribe on the innerworkings of the Boston office: what was organized well (only one-quarter of all areas! imagine that!), who was inefficient (nearly everyone), and how his system would be a godsend. He was a hero, Tom was, Lord, God, and Messiah all rolled into one.

"I am really glad it's going so well." Sarah jumped in when Tom yawned.

"Then on Thursday, I was in this meeting…" Thirty more minutes.

Sarah thought her head would burst. "Enough, please."

"Excuse me?"

"Please stop. I am interested in your work, but you have not asked me anything about the boys' and my week."

"I'm sure the boys are fine. Let me just finish…"

"…your self-inflated view of your role at Icon Systems? Wouldn't want to build up your ego anymore, would we?"

"I am trying to share my week with my wife. Isn't that what you always want? This has nothing to do with my ego."

"It most certainly does. How ever did the Boston office survive without you? Don't kid yourself. It's all about your ego, which, by the way is growing daily… like a tumor."

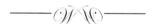

That conversation was the longest of the weekend, other than exchanging mumbles each time they clumsily bumped into each other. Sarah gave Tom and the boys plenty of "quality time" while she cleaned the house, balanced the checkbook, and made roasted turkey with all the trimmings.

Offering to help did not occur to Tom, as he was exhausted from last night's flight. Sarah had planned Tom's favorite dinner Friday morning, thinking he might enjoy a homemade meal since he ate out every night. She had already taken the turkey out of the freezer, so now she had no choice but to make it. Sarah would have rather gone out for the day, maybe taken a walk by the river. She needed to get out of the house, which was evident by her rather violent chopping of onions and celery for the stuffing that grew louder each time "good to be home" fell out of Tom's mouth. He had already made his wishes known, and the kids were happy enough just sitting beside him while he watched some basketball. Her acting out went unnoticed.

That night, Sarah washed off her makeup before getting undressed. How does anyone survive being a stay-at-home mom? Is it possible to emerge with any sense of self after denying so much of who you are day after day?

"Could you please move this? I don't have any room." Tom handed her the makeup bag.

"I was not finished. This cleanser goes in there too."

"I'll go use the kids' bathroom to brush my teeth."

"Fine."

Balancing the laundry basket filled with dirty sheets and towels on her hip, Sarah's calendar hit her in the face as she flung open the basement door. The seventeenth of April, circled in red with BOOK CLUB written underneath, was eye-height and staring her in the face. How had she missed it? She must have passed this door a thousand times this week. She still had several pages of *A Portrait of the Artist as a Young Man* to go, plus the time she needed to ponder the piece instead of adopting Cliffs Notes' opinions as her own. She dropped the laundry basket. She didn't even have a baby sitter. Maybe she could call her Mom. Where was the bloody phone?

"Alex? Have you seen the phone?" He looked out from behind his tower of stacking cups, shrugged his shoulders, and placed the blue cup on top of the red.

For the next twenty minutes, Sarah retraced her steps throughout the house, searching for the telephone. Everything she did ended up in the shiter. Why should this be any different? She checked in their bedroom. One lousy night a month. Was that so much to ask? Sarah looked in Alex's crib. Damn Tom. She should have known better than to believe him. "Oh, sure. No problem. I'll be here to take the kids." She eyeballed the powder room.

Sarah knew she should be grateful for what she had. She heard it frequently in church. Wonderful. Now she was miserable and ungrateful. It was just that there were so many people living amazing, fulfilling lives, while here she was mired in her sameness. Day after day, diaper after diaper, the life sucked out of her by the vacuum called motherhood. She attempted to make forays into the world outside her home. Occasionally, she was even successful, but usually only for groceries or driving Nicky to t-ball. When she attempted anything of a social nature—getting together with friends from college or going to breakfast with the bus moms—she was Cinderella sans the fairy godmother. Oh, no. You cannot go to the ball. You must stay here and take care of your vomiting child. Go back in now and rinse out that bucket. Too bad, but you have no baby sitter and your husband's all-important job must come first. POOF! Your book club disappears. Sarah could feel her face flush. Where the hell was that phone? She let out a primal scream. Alex started to cry. She ran over and picked him up.

"It's okay, honey. Mommy is really frustrated that she cannot find the telephone. I'm not mad at you." Sarah hugged him and stroked his hair. "I love you very much." She put him down and walked into the kitchen. Sitting down at the kitchen table, she felt something jab her behind. It was the phone.

"Alex? Did you put this here?"

"No." Of course, she could not put much stock into his response, since "no" was his third and favorite word.

"Please don't play with the telephone, honey. Mommy needs it." Sarah dialed her mother's number.

"Hello?"

"Hi, Mom."

"Hi, honey. What's up?"

"Can you take the kids for me tomorrow night? I'm sorry it is such short notice. I have my second book club meeting, and I forgot all about it. Tom was going to stay with the kids, but obviously that is out of the question."

Patty could hear the disdain in her daughter's voice. "It's hard when they are out of town, isn't it? I used to envy your dad's job. Thought he was on some great adventure that I was missing out on."

"Tom is. I've always wanted to go to Boston. Not only that, but apparently he is the toast of the Boston office. The golden child. Wonder what it is like to receive praise for a job well done?"

"Maybe you two can arrange a weekend out there. Instead of him flying home, you could go there for a few days."

"With my luck Tom would be too busy, and I'd spend the entire time stuck in the hotel, waiting for him to finish reading e-mails."

Ignoring the negativity, Patty plodded on. "You would love it. There is a fabulous little Italian restaurant right by Paul Revere's house. Your dad and I could take the kids for the weekend. I remember when your dad was sent to New York for a month when you kids were small. I was so lonely and exhausted. I began resenting every word that came out of his mouth during our daily phone conversations. How dare he support us and have fun at the same time, while I was stuck slaving away in the house, chained to two small children. I thought his life was full of important corporate stuff and martini lunches, while mine consisted of poopy diapers and never-ending laundry."

"When was this? I don't remember."

"Oh, you were only four. Anyhow, I can take the kids tomorrow night. Would you like me to come there since it is a school night?"

"Would you mind? Hey, why don't you and Dad come over for an early dinner so we can visit a little before I leave? I would love some adult company."

"Certainly. And Sarah? Please try to be patient. This is for a finite time period. It will all be over soon, and things will get back to normal."

"Whatever that is."

Sarah took a deep breath. Maybe she could read tonight after the kids go to sleep. If she could stay awake.

CHAPTER TEN

*J*OHN AND ANNIE WALKED UP the steps to the house in which he and his sisters grew up, "Excessive Estrogen Manor." It was a three-bedroom, two-bath raised ranch, meticulously manicured on the outside. A goose statue sat to the left of the stairs next to a flower pot that always contained some sort of pink flower, except for last fall, when June had to settle for a very light purple mum.

Everyone would be here today. John's sister, Joy, had married Geoff, who wished his name were spelled "J-e-f-f" like most normal men, but since he was stuck with it and with all of the associations with the toy store mascot giraffe, Geoff was hell bent on naming his children distinctive, but not goofy, names. His efforts at originality were thwarted, however, when he learned through Joy that there were three Caitlyns and four Sophies in the twins' mini-gym class at the park district.

John's other sister, Julie, was wed to the ass-in-law. John had called him thus almost since their first meeting and, consequently, could never remember his real first name. Annie had to remind him it was Ralph every time they saw them. Julie and the ass-in-law begot three children—Boston, Madison, and Austin—all of whom were named for the cities they were conceived in. Annie wished them no more children, not from any jealousy, but because she could not stand her future niece or nephew to be called Downer's Grove, their current place of residence.

"Hello, John, darling." June gave him a kiss on the cheek, then wiped away the bubble-gum-colored lipstick off of his face with her handkerchief. Annie slid in behind John just in case June temporarily lost her mind and tried to kiss her too. Of course, that would be ridiculous. In all of their fifteen years of marriage, June had never kissed her. Not even the social "welcome to my house" peck on the check most people offered, sometimes even to strangers. The only time they had physical contact was on their wedding day, when the photographer forced June to put her arm around her daughter-in-law for the family photo. To this day, that picture still made Annie a bit queasy.

"Oh, hi, um, Annie." June gestured for Annie to come in.

"Hi, June. How are you?"

"Fine, thank you. John, I've got to show you my new toy. It's in the basement." June took her son by the arm and escorted him downstairs, leaving Annie in the foyer, green bean casserole still in her arms.

The house was unusually quiet. Annie supposed everyone was in the basement. She walked into the kitchen, which was painted a light blue and had mauve hearts on the boarder above the oak cabinets. A huge hen with two fake eggs sat in the middle of the kitchen table. Various other fowl were strewn about. The curtains were blue gingham checks with small pink hearts to echo the boarder.

Annie put her dish into the refrigerator, which was covered with grandchildren photos. The twins smiling on their tricycles. Austin suited up for the Naperville Youth Football League. Boston dressed like a snowball from last year's Christmas pageant. Madison, red and wrinkly, in her newborn picture. Annie liked the kids. They provided a welcome distraction from their mothers' insipid conversation. There was one photo she had never noticed before, in the upper left-hand corner of the freezer. Who was that? He looked familiar. Light brown hair. About eight years old. Was that John? Then she paused, trying to guess if any of John's siblings were also there as children, but all of the other photos were current. That must be the spot June was saving for their child some day.

Annie walked down the hall and descended the basement stairs. The room ran across the entire footprint of the house and was recently remodeled to accommodate entertaining June Jacobs' grandchildren. It was stuffed with Tinker Toys, Legos, Barbies, Barney, ping pong and pool tables, pint-sized kitchen equipment, and a playhouse. There was also a small kitchenette and college-sized fridge stocked with soft drinks and those juices in the funny silver pouches with their own straws. Shelves housed about thirty board games, running the gamut from Candyland for Caitlyn and Sophie to Risk for Austin.

John felt a kinship with Austin, the only boy among the cousins, and made sure to play a video game or toss around a baseball with him every time they saw each other. Annie was certain a trip to Home Depot was next on the list.

As soon as she stepped on the bottom stair, Annie could see June's new toy—a fifty-inch television. A video game unit was hooked up to it, Annie saw, because Austin was playing Super Mario. Mario's nose was as large as Annie's head. He reminded her of Peter Luger, her first supervisor at Jones and MacGregor, back when she was an intern. He looked almost exactly like Mario, complete with enormous nose and goofy little black mustache. Luger had constantly harped at Annie to find new, fresh angles for their clients. He was convinced that since she was young, Annie would be able to plug him into the youth market.

After a particularly long meeting with Peter harping on the aforementioned point, Annie snapped. She made an eight-by-ten copy of a Super Mario advertisement from the newspaper. She whited out the copy and replaced it with "Please replace my pacemaker wiring with plugs into the youth market." Annie received applause when she entered the lunchroom, but Peter was not amused. He complained to Harry Jones, who saw the prank as just the spark he was looking for and took Annie under his wing.

The sisters saw Annie come down the stairs.

"Hi. We thought you might be ill." Julie hit Joy on the arm. She turned around.

"Oh no. I was just putting the green bean casserole in the refrigerator."

Julie and Joy shot each other knowing looks.

Annie tried to engage them in conversation. "How are you?"

Joy launched into her litany. "I'm exhausted. The girls were up at two this morning. Sophie had a nightmare, and, of course, woke up Caitlyn too. By the time I got them back down, it was about three. Then I couldn't fall back to sleep. You know how that goes."

Julie nodded. They both looked at Annie.

"I can only imagine."

The sisters looked around the room.

"Excuse me, will you? I need to ask John something." Annie made her way across the basement, giving kisses to the kids along the way. "How is it going?"

John was explaining how to use the new television's remote control to June. "Oh, this remote is a bit much for Mom."

"I'm no good with electronics. I don't even use the dishwasher much unless you kids are here," June said.

"Some remotes are more complicated than necessary," Annie said. She sensed she was intruding.

"Hi, Auntie Annie." It was Boston, the former snowball.

"Hi, sweetie. What are you up to?"

"Would you play restaurant with me?"
"I'd love to."

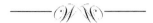

After a dessert of June's famous apple pie, which won first place in the church bake-off in 1980, the adults sat sipping coffee and, in Annie's case, tea. The kids went downstairs to play.

"What do you think? This is as good a time as any," John whispered to Annie.

She squeezed his hand under the table. "You do the talking."

"Excuse me, everyone. Annie and I have something we would like to share with you."

June put her hand to her mouth and let out a little "oh." The rest looked up. Annie knew what they were thinking. Her stomach ached.

"Annie and I are…"

"Oh, thank God!" June looked upward and crossed herself.

"No, Mom. We are not pregnant."

Signs of disappointment rippled around the table. No one but June dared to speak.

"What?"

"We're not pregnant. That is what we need to talk to you about. Annie and I have been seeing a fertility specialist."

"Oh, sweet Jesus! Not my son!"

"Mom, try to relax."

Annie shifted from side to side in her chair, wishing she was anywhere but here right now.

"We have been diagnosed as having unexplained infertility." They all looked at John as though he just spoke in Greek. "You might not be familiar with this since obviously none of you have dealt with this before. We have been trying to conceive for more than two years. When that didn't happen, Annie suggested we see a specialist. For the last several months, we have gone through several series of tests." John bit his lip. "Unfortunately, the doctor has found nothing, no reason why we cannot have a baby."

June sat at the head of the table, staring at John and Annie, shell-shocked. "D...D...Does this mean you will never have children?"

"Not necessarily," said John. "Annie and I are trying to figure out what our course of action will be. Probably some form of...it's called Assisted Reproductive Technologies, like insemination or in vitro fertilization. We aren't sure yet, but we wanted you to know because you are our family, and we would like your support."

"Oh, dear God. It's really that bad?"

"Yes, Mom. It is."

"And you both tested normal still?" June looked at Annie, who raised her head for the first time since John started talking. "Yes, June."

"I'd be happy to donate some, um, you know, to help you out," Ralph said. Julie punched his arm.

"Of all things, Ralph! I'm sure John's sperm is more than healthy enough for Annie." June was getting red. All this talk; she was not used to such things.

Annie shot Ralph a look that said if you utter a single word I will personally beat the living crap out of you.

"Would anyone like more coffee? I'll go make another pot." Ralph excused himself and went into the kitchen.

They all got up from the table. June immediately went to John, hugging him and patting his head like he was a wounded puppy. Julie went into the kitchen to help her husband. Geoff went to check on the kids.

Joy came over to Annie. "I am very sorry you are going through this. If you need anything, please give me a call."

Annie searched Joy's face for any sign of sarcasm, superiority or delight. All she saw was something she had never seen Joy exhibit before—concern. "Thank you, Joy. I appreciate that."

There must be a full moon tonight.

"Honestly. I cannot believe you brought that up at the dinner table." Marian McDonnell rinsed off the dinner dishes before she put them in the dishwasher.

Annie placed two plates on the counter to Marian's left. Dirty dishes always went on the left, got rinsed in the sink, then put into the dishwasher on the right. Marian had laid down the rules for cleaning up after dinner when Annie was eight. They were not to be deviated from, or Marian's system for kitchen clean up perfection would come to an abrupt halt. Same held true for appropriate topics for dinner conversation.

When all else fails, discuss the weather, Marian told her daughter years ago. Annie felt like she lived in a Jane Austen novel. It wasn't like they were entertaining guests; it was just her, John, and her parents. When she was a teenager, Annie worked hard to suppress blurting out "Hey, guess what? I lost my virginity last night." during Sunday dinner, just to watch the expression on her mother's face, even though she had been a "good girl" until well into college.

"I thought you should know, considering most parents your age are interested in becoming grandparents."

"Me, a grandmother?" Marian bristled. Having to spend all that time dealing with baby diapers and crying infants? She had had plenty of that with Annie and did not wish to revisit those days. When Annie was two, she walked over to the marble-topped, mahogany-legged urn stand in the dining room and shook it until Marian's Baccarat crystal vase, a wedding present from Aunt Harriet, came crashing down around her. That vase was irreplaceable. Then, on top of that, Marian had to take little Annie to the emergency room to repair a cut on her hand from trying to pick up a piece of broken crystal. The cut was so deep they could not stop the bleeding. It stained Marian's Persian rug, a souvenir they picked up on their trip to Turkey. She took it to several cleaners, all with no luck. Maybe if she had brought the rug in sooner, but not three hours later. All that time wasted in the emergency room. You would have thought she cut off her entire hand with the commotion the girl generated. They even brought in a plastic surgeon. What a nightmare!

"Well, I am thirty-seven. Certainly you had to wonder what our plans were. John's family asks us practically every time we see them."

"No, I really hadn't." Actually, Marian was surmising the feasibility of Annie becoming president of Jones and MacGregor. Now that would be something she could tell the ladies at the club! While they driveled on about whose grandchild made the basketball team or which one was learning clarinet, she could casually slip in her little tidbit and shut them up cold. All their daughters did was take care of kids. They had no accomplishments of their own to boast of, constantly living vicariously through their children. "So, how's work?"

Annie threw down the towel she was drying the counter with. "Screw work. I am telling you we are starting infertility treatments, and you ask me how work is?"

"Well, you didn't mention the office once today. Usually you have some anecdote about an account you are working on."

"I think I have been a hair preoccupied with this little issue of not being able to have a child. Call me wacky, but that takes precedence over what new account I am representing."

"Don't yell, Annie. I am sorry you are going through this, but it is not the worst thing that could happen to a person."

Annie stared at this woman in disbelief, wondering how her own mother could not at least try to understand her pain.

"It's not like you have cancer or something. You *can* live with this."

"Yeah? You try to live with it. Oh, I forgot. Not being able to have children would have been ideal for you."

"It was different then. Women had to stay home with their children. There was no choice."

"Oh, how horrible. Imagine your life of domestic servitude."

"Lower your voice, please. I wish I had the options you grew up with. I was an executive secretary before you were born. I managed twenty women in the pool."

"Moving up the corporate ladder was more important than having me?"

"You are blowing this out of proportion. Anyhow, maybe there's a reason you can't conceive. God may have other plans for you. Maybe your destiny lies elsewhere."

"What does God have to do with this? For your information, Mother, I've wanted a child ever since I was five years old playing with my Baby Tenderlove. Why would God do this to me?"

"We cannot presume to know what God has in store for us."

Annie stormed out of the kitchen and into the family room. "John, we need to leave."

"Annie, what's wrong?" Her father rose from his chair.

"Your wife doesn't think the fact that I cannot have kids normally is a big deal. She makes it seem like I should be grateful not to be saddled down with that stress."

"Oh, Annie. Your mother sometimes speaks…"

"…out of her ass. And frankly, Dad, I cannot deal with this right now. I'm sorry, but I need to get out of here."

John got up and shook George's hand. "Sorry about this."

"Not your fault."

Annie was already starting the car by the time her father closed the door behind John.

"God, I hate that woman. You know, throughout my whole life, I've called her 'mother,' never 'mom.' 'Mom' never felt right, and now I know why. 'Mother' fits."

George went into the kitchen. Marian was putting the last piece of roast in a Tupperware. "What did you say to her?"

"Nothing. I just said infertility is a problem you can live with, not like cancer, where you have to get..."

"Marian! You have the compassion level of a flea."

"But..."

"I'm going to the driving range. They installed new lights, you know. I'll be home whenever." George left the kitchen. That should give Annie enough time to calm down. He would call her later to smooth things over. George skipped hitting balls and went straight to the bar. He couldn't understand it. When he met Marian, she was so poised, so polished. Smart, too. George shook his head and ordered a martini.

CHAPTER ELEVEN

"CAN YOU BELIEVE THIS RAIN?" Rosemary entered Room 204 of the community center, dripping. "Of course, I pick today to leave my house without watching the Weather Channel." Her black raincoat was so wet it sagged on her shoulders, and damp curls stuck to her head. The effect was that of an overgrown Shirley Temple after being tossed into a pool.

"It's not like an umbrella is very helpful on days such as this." Larry looked sympathetic. "It was raining horizontally when I came in."

"Oooh, that's the worst." Spring was unpacking her book, paper, and pen from a vinyl tote bag with large magenta flowers on it.

Sarah was frantically reading the last few pages of the novel. She had been up until midnight and managed to finish most of it.

Thaddeus sat, looking up, analyzing the ceiling tiles and wondering why whoever constructed this building chose the pattern he did.

Catherine moved one of the chairs back a bit from the others and sat down.

"Oh, hello darlings." Edwina Hipplewhite appeared, shaking a red and black umbrella with signatures of famous artists scrawled across. "It is not a fit night for man nor beast, or woman, as the case may be. Ah, Catherine, my dear, perhaps you would favor us with a selection from *King Lear* to refocus our minds from the weather to writing. A sort of literary barometer, if you will."

"Nothing my lord." She sounded more like Penny Marshall than a Shakespearean actor.

Edwina looked around the room and decided to take the bait. "Nothing? Nothing will come of nothing. Speak again."

Catherine sighed, her shoulders dropping more with every slight word. "Unhappy that I am, I cannot heave My heart into my mouth. I love your Majesty According to my bond, no more nor less."

"So few words, so much emotional content, eh, class, or shall I say group? Although I must confess, I was hoping for the speech when Lear is wandering through the storm, his fool by his side. Oh, I cannot resist. Indulge me, will you?"

Heads nodded. Sarah smiled, always appreciative of a good tragedy. *King Lear* was her favorite Shakespearean play. Thaddeus looked like he was about to partake in a guilty pleasure. Just before the performance started, Annie slid into the chair between the door and Sarah.

Edwina ruffled her red hair and pulled out the sides speckled with gray back with her fingers, creating a makeshift, wind-blown look. When she was certain she had the attention of all seven, Edwina began.

> *"Blow, winds, and crack your cheeks! Rage, blow!*
> *You cataracts and hurricanoes, spout*
> *Till you have drench'd our steeples, drown'd the cocks!*
> *You sulph'rous and thought-executing fires,*
> *Vaunt-couriers of oak-cleaving thunderbolts,*
> *Singe my white head! And thou, all-shaking thunder,*
> *Strike flat the thick rotundity o' th' world!*
> *Crack nature's molds, all germains spill at once.*
> *That makes ingrateful man!"*

The class applauded. Catherine looked like she was going to cry.

"Thank you, darlings, thank you." Edwina bowed. Then she caught Catherine's eye. "My dear fellow thespian, are you all right?"

She cleared her throat. "Ah, yeah, I'm okay."

"Oh, but I can see you are not."

Catherine scanned around the room. They were all staring at her, which would normally be pleasant for one such as she, but not today. "Please. I'm sorry. I do not mean to be rude, but I really don't want to talk about it."

"Certainly, darling. I just hate seeing a lovely young woman such as yourself in distress."

Thaddeus shifted uncomfortably in his chair. Spring stared large, brown puppy eyes in Catherine's direction.

"I'll be okay. I should be used to this by now."

"Used to what, dear?"

"Rejection. I know I would have been perfect for that part. I nailed the audition. I don't know why…"

Edwina made her way through the seats. "Excuse me, darlings. I hate to see one of my people upset." She sat down next to her. "Who knows why they did not choose you? Do not even attempt to guess." Edwina put her arm around Catherine's shoulders. "You know, a few old students of mine are starting a theater company here. Let me give you their numbers after class. Here's a hint. If you cannot get an audition right away, offer to help out any way you can. Stuff envelopes. Work in the box office. Usher. People are more apt to give those who are familiar to them a chance." She gave her a little squeeze. "Don't you worry."

"Thank you, Mrs., er, Miss Hipplewhite. I'm sorry, which is it?"

"Oh, Miss, my dear. I have no time for husbands. They prohibit you from developing your true essence. Call me Edwina, darling."

She walked back to the front of Room 204. "Do forgive me, will you? Now, let us get down to Joyce. I trust you have all finished. The main character, Stephen Dedalus. Are you familiar with the story from mythology? Greek mythology, of course, Roman being slightly different. Thaddeus, darling, can you give us a synopsis of the Dedalus myth for it is very important in deciphering the overall theme of this wonderful novel."

"Em, okay." Thaddeus hesitated and adopted the same posture he had in high school twenty years ago, slumped in his seat, eyes down to the floor. "Dedalus and, em, his son, um...I can't remember his name."

"Icarus," Sarah interjected. Everyone looked at her, impressed.

"Excellent, dear." Edwina smiled.

Little did they know her knowledge of Dedalus and Icarus came from *Hercules* on Toon Disney. Sarah received their glances and nods of recognition nonetheless. It was nice emoting pseudo-intelligence.

"Yes, Icarus. Thank you. Um..." Thaddeus continued. "They were imprisoned in a labyrinth. There was no way out. All exits by land or sea were blocked. The only escape was by air, so Dedalus constructed wings. He and Icarus flew out of the labyrinth, but the son did not listen to his father when Dedalus told Icarus not to fly too close to the sun."

"Oh, that's right. Icarus is the one who burns himself because he got too close to the sun." Rosemary snapped her fingers.

"Yes. As a matter of fact, I used the Dedalus/Icarus story every year as a reminder to my high school juniors, warning them of the dangers that could occur if they did not mind their parents." Edwina smirked, then rolled her eyes. "As if the connection even dawned upon their thick skulls. Oh well. So let us begin our conversation with reasons why the Dedalus imagery is so crucial to *A Portrait of the Artist as a Young Man*. Spring, dear, what is your view on this topic?"

Sarah felt wonderful discussing literature again after all these years. It was her favorite part of school, even high school, when Miss Shaden would have them arrange their desks in a circle and talk of imagery in *Moby Dick*. Sarah could not believe it when she realized she could major in literature in college, English literature no less, the best kind. Never mind the questions from others on how she would parlay this major into a career.

"It's about as useful as a philosophy major." Buck Howard snarled while sitting across from her at lunch in the dining hall.

"That's not true." Sarah readied herself to defend her passion.

"Well, what do you plan on becoming? Oh, wait. You can be a librarian and spend your life with your face shoved in and around your precious books every single quiet, lonely, boring day."

"I could teach." Sarah refused to cave. "At least I am doing something I love. Something that fulfills my soul."

"Hey, I have a higher purpose too."

"Oh yeah, what?"

"The almighty dollar. That's right, chickey babe. What literature major can get you that?"

"Money is not the only thing that matters in life. Last night, you were complaining about accounting and how you practically fall asleep each time Professor Goodwin opens his mouth."

"But I'll be damn happy when I am the CFO of a big company, sitting back in my corner office with a kick-ass view."

Sarah shook her head. He did it, too. Not quite CFO, but vice president of accounting, she had read in the alumni magazine two years ago. What had she accomplished?

"Well, dears, that about wraps it up for this month. Enjoy our next selection and come back in four weeks with oodles to say. Ta ta."

It was only nine o'clock. Unwilling to surrender her literary frame of mind quite yet, Sarah decided to take a walk, searching for a bookstore. The streets, damp and translucent from the previous hour's rain, still bustled with diners retrieving their cars. She glanced left on Main Street and another thought invaded her mind. Caffe mocha. That was it. Once the beloved beverage entered her thought process, there was no stopping her. She turned left and sprinted the two blocks, careful not to slip on the wet pavement.

She settled down into a comfortable brown chair near the coffeehouse's window. Three college students were having a debate on what Sarah was sure was some sort of fascinating current event, until the entire place heard the man with the fuzzy blond hair and goatee scream. "Everyone knows Betty is hotter. Veronica was a bitch."

Her eyes met with, what was her name? She had sat next to her tonight. What's her name was juggling a cup and her briefcase while trying to put change in her purse. Annie. That was it.

Annie was in the habit of avoiding new acquaintances so she would not have to explain "the situation," but now that Sarah from the book club had made eye contact, she supposed she should go over and make small talk.

"Hi." Annie lifted her cup. "Grande nonfat chai. My newest addiction."

"I'm a mocha person. Interesting meeting tonight. I thought Edwina was going to skewer Thaddeus with her umbrella, or shall I say, 'parasol,' when he made that remark about *Pride and Prejudice* being a chick book. Would you like to sit down?" Sarah gestured at the empty chair across from her while she took a sip.

"Um, sure, thanks. You're right. She postured like some goofy old hen. Of course, I tried to get my husband to read it when we were first married with no luck. Then we watched the BBC version, and he loved it." Annie smiled.

"Oh, the six-hour one? That was fabulous, wasn't it? The way Darcy was so tortured and awkward when he asked Elizabeth to marry him."

"Or how he looked at her so adoringly while she was flipping music pages for Georgianna when she was playing the piano."

"I wish someone would look at me that way. Guess that's reserved for courtship."

"Or BBC period productions." Annie looked at the ring on Sarah's cup-holding hand. "How long have you been married?"

"Almost nine years. How about you?"

"Fifteen."

"Wow! You must have gotten married young."

"A year after college graduation. We met in Rome during our last semester."

"Sounds romantic."

"I guess."

"Do you have kids?"

There it was. The million-dollar question. Here comes the pity party. "No." Annie quickly added, "and you?"

"Yes. My oldest is six and my little one just turned two."

"That's nice." Annie stared at her cup.

Not wanting to discuss her family, Sarah tried to change the subject. "I can't wait to read *Pride and Prejudice* again. I think it's been since high school."

"College for me. I wrote many a term paper on dear Jane Austen." *All the while thinking how cool it would be to name my little girl Elizabeth Bennet.* Annie thought it best not to utter those last words aloud.

CHAPTER TWELVE

J OHN WALKED INTO MURDOCK AND Stoddard at nine-thirty on Monday morning, significantly late for a breakfast meeting with Andy and Craig. What usually took him thirty minutes to drive (forty on high-traffic days), ended up an hour and fifteen minutes, most of which were spent stuck on the expressway less than one mile away from his Midwest Road exit.

"Half day?" Valerie the receptionist greeted him.

"Very funny. Accident on Midwest Road, right at the top of the ramp. I sat on I-88 for an hour."

"Yikes. Mr. Murdock and Mr. Stoddard were looking for you."

"I figured."

John poked his head into Andy's office on the way to his own in vain. He knew the meeting was well over by this time. Neither Andy nor Craig was to be found. Great. He had worked all these hours to impress them and could not even make one stupid meeting. Andy sounded okay when he called him from the car, but John could tell Craig was making annoyed noises in the background.

He set his briefcase on the desk. Starving, John went to the lunchroom for some coffee. A box of donuts sat on the table. Salvation! He opened it with anticipation, only to gaze at an empty box. Who was the idiot who took the last donut and left the box? People were such slobs. It reminded him of something

Annie would do lately. She was so immersed in this infertility stuff, she was incapable of doing anything else. The house used to be in good order between the two of them sharing chores. Now, laundry overflowed in the hamper. Dark rings encircled the toilet bowls. Three stacks of mail sat unopened on the table in the foyer. The house had not been vacuumed for weeks.

John went back to his office and checked messages. There were ten e-mails and six on the phone. He did voice mail first. "Hi, John. It's Maggie in H.R. I checked into our health insurance. I'm sorry, but Assisted Reproductive Technologies are not covered. I even called them to see what I could finagle, but I was stonewalled. If you have any questions, please feel free to contact me."

Still holding the phone with his left hand, John smacked his forehead with the receiver. He hated having to tell Maggie about their problems, but he needed to know if insurance would pay for any of the procedures. He replayed the message to make sure he heard everything correctly, then deleted it.

How were they going to afford this? Annie said in vitro fertilization costs almost $10,000. $10,000! Who has that kind of cash lying around? Maybe he would get some bonus money if they won the Biotech labs case. Oh, shit. Where was that deposition? Maybe Matt had it.

"So what do you think?" Sarah pitched the Boston long-weekend idea to Tom. "Don't you think that sounds like fun?"

Tom processed the last ten lines of dialogue that had sprung from Sarah's mouth. "You want to come out here?" After last weekend, he was surprised they were even speaking.

"That's what I just said. Are you reading e-mails while I am talking to you? You sound distracted."

"No."

"Well then, do you want me to come or not?" Dead silence on the other side of the phone. "You know what? Forget it. I should have known better than to think you and I could have some time together. God forbid, I get to go anywhere."

"You misunderstand."

"Enlighten me."

"I was amazed you wanted to leave the kids. That's all."

"What, don't you think I can exist without them? I did so for twenty-five years, you know."

"Relax." Tom cut Sarah off before she would take them down a path he was unwilling to travel. "Of course, I would like you to come. Do you have any dates in mind?"

"How's Thursday, the twenty-second?" Sarah said, flipping the calendar page.

"Hmm. Oh, no, that's not good. Management dinner."

"Why don't you tell me when you are available?"

"How about the twenty-eighth?"

"Nope. I have to make cheesecake for the First Communion family mass."

"Okay, what about the following week?"

"Let's see. That looks open."

"Okay, me too. I'll put you in."

"Do you remember how to spell my name? I mean, it's been so long since we have been together for more than one day. S-a-r..."

"Yes, I think so. S-a-r-a-h. You are the one I stood with at the altar reciting some vow. What was it?"

"I'll call for plane tickets."

"I will clear my schedule. Well, talk to you tomorrow. Have a good night."

"You too."

Tom hung up the telephone and plopped down on the

standard-issue, residence-inn sofa, his home base for the past four weeks. It was industrial at best, but he didn't care. All he required of a living space was a small kitchen where he could make oatmeal in the morning and an Internet connection. Tom put his feet up on the coffee table. He wished Sarah would get a job, but she was too entrenched in mommyland to ever make that leap. If he even mentioned daycare, Sarah went ballistic. His mom worked, and it never affected him. He went to Peter Pan after school for two hours, that was all. A certain amount of independence is good for kids. They have to grow up sometime.

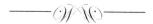

"I don't care how much it costs, John." Annie was livid at even the inference that insemination and in vitro were expensive. She had made her decision, and she was going to stick to it. "I'll sell stuff if I have to. That stupid suit of armor could pay for half, probably."

"We have to know what we are getting into financially." John was torn between wanting a child and choking on the price tag.

"What good is a family heirloom without anyone to pass it down to?" Annie yelled. She ran over to the suit of armor, shaking it to see how easily it would come apart to fit in a box.

"Easy. You are going to break it."

Annie kept shaking.

"Stop!" Visions of hundreds of years of family history crumbling on top of his wife's head sent John running across the room. He grabbed Annie's hands.

"Let go of me. What are you doing?"

For an instant, John thought Annie might begin shaking him with the same voracity as the armor. "Relax. It won't be worth anything if it is broken."

Annie let John's words sink in and sat down on the sofa, head in her hands. Her body was ticking, a constant countdown that would not cease. After a few minutes, she looked up at John. "I do not intend to have cost stand in my way. We'll take out a loan if we have to."

Maybe the center offered payment plans.

Sarah sat at Gate C20 in O'Hare Airport, delayed for an hour because a dense fog had rolled into Boston. Good old Logan Airport, constantly besieged by snow, hurricane remnants, fog. Tom's flight was never on time. Who had the bright idea of putting an airport on a very small island off any city on the East Coast? That was Boston, or so she was told. Tom had complained about the streets, literally paved over cow paths and running every which way, lecturing anyone who would listen on the precision of Chicago streets that were laid out in a grid. Getting from Point A to Point B was easy. There were no surprise twists or turns. No time wasted back-tracking. If she insisted on coming, she would see.

Sarah was afraid Tom was enjoying his temporary freedom a bit too much, and her presence would remind him his independence was fleeting. He seemed to discourage their weekend together, saying at least one negative comment about Boston per telephone conversation, but Sarah would not be deterred. She wanted to see how he had structured his life without them. And, honestly, she wanted to get away.

Sitting there waiting to board, Sarah gradually relaxed, the delay having little affect on her spirits. On the contrary, it gave her more time to herself. Mocha was but thirty yards away, and *Pride and Prejudice* was in her hands. All in all, it was quite pleasurable. Sarah was even beginning to overcome the guilt of leaving the children. She knew it was healthy for her to separate from them, healthy for all three of them. Nicky and Alex needed to know she had other roles besides being their mother, as Tom had harped on the phone yesterday. What were they? Oh yes, wife, although that was a stretch as she and Tom mitigated their long-distance relationship. Maybe that should only count for half a role. What else? Dishwasher? Cook? Laundress? Butcher? Baker? Candlestick maker? All of these were just household jobs. A maid? No, servant because she was not salaried. Was that all she was? Sarah shook her head to dispel the negativity and began reading.

"I'm sorry if I offended you a few weeks ago." That was it. Marian McDonnell was not one to admit wrongdoing, conveniently working in "if" for her absolution. Annie didn't know whether to be appeased or disgusted. Marian was the only person who would dare to handle Annie in such a public location as afternoon tea at The Drake Hotel, under the guise of an easy commute for her daughter—Annie was already downtown, she could easily take a late lunch—hiding among this genteel crowd, most of whom sat blissfully unaware, spreading clotted cream and strawberry jam on tasty scones.

Annie stared at her mother.

"I was surprised, that's all. I didn't even know you were trying. More tea?" Marian picked up the floral teapot, holding its lid to avoid more unwanted attention. Before Annie could answer, Marian grabbed her cup and refilled it. "Oops, I forgot to pour the cream in first."

"It doesn't matter." Annie snatched the cup back. "How could you not have known? I told you we were starting a family three years ago."

"Did you? I never remember. Time goes by so quickly. It's been three years?" Marian fiddled with her pearl earring.

"Come off it."

"I thought maybe you'd changed your mind, considering how well work was going, and I am certainly not the kind of woman who nags her daughter about such things."

There was no use arguing. Annie helped herself to a petit four, wondering what would emerge from her mother's mouth next. It only took one bite of the small cake to receive her answer.

"So, what do you plan to do about this?"

"Well, we are weighing our options. I'm on ovulation boosters."

Marian scanned the room, hoping no one heard.

"Oh, please, Mother. No matter which procedure we attempt first, we need those, so…"

"Why do you need a procedure? What about adoption? There are so many kids who need parents. When I was growing up, you either had kids or you adopted."

"This technology didn't exist then. John and I thought we would explore ways to have our own child first."

"Why would you put your body through all that?"

Annie shook her head. She should have known her mother would never understand. "Because it is important to us."

"Important to have a child or to pass on your genes? It's expensive, isn't it? I read somewhere about it costing thousands."

"Yes, but…"

"How are you going to afford it? Does your insurance cover it?"

"Well, I'm not sure. John is looking into it," Annie lied. She would not give her mother the upper hand.

"The article said most of the time it is out-of-pocket. What is the success rate?"

"What?"

"You could be throwing your money away for not much rate of return."

"This is not an investment, Mother, it's a child."

"How do you know your doctor is credible?"

Annie pushed back her chair, hands in the air. "What's with the rapid-fire questions?"

"I'm trying to ensure your emotions don't cloud your reason."

"God knows we would not want to show any emotion. What are you? A cyborg?" Annie checked her watch. "I need to get back to work. Thanks for tea." She sprinted out of the room.

She must get it from George's side, Marian sighed, taking a small bite of cucumber sandwich, aware of the eyes upon her.

Annie hailed a cab, but decided to walk off the urge to purchase a set of boxing gloves and mount her mother's photo on a punching bag, insufferable woman. Didn't she understand anything? The technology exists, why not use it? How dare she question them. As if she made all the correct choices in her model existence, married to a man she could never appreciate, attending her charity luncheons with other fifties throwbacks. Annie tried calming herself down, taking deep breaths, only to have her swollen breasts ache upon every heave. She picked up the largest chai they had—if it came in gallon jugs, she would have bought it—and went back to the office.

Why did her daughter always jump to the conclusion she was trying to thwart her? Marian was merely pointing out practical issues that must be considered if Annie was going to undertake this situation. This was not something to rush into like the time she found that little street kitten with the big chunk missing from its left ear and brought it home. If one is to engage in pet ownership, one must ready the household, not let the little scamp run amok, tearing down draperies and relieving itself on the kitchen floor. Oh, how Annie cried when she and George took it to the Humane Society Shelter. Of course, she was lucky it did not end up the victim of a most unfortunate accident after the damage it caused.

Marian wished Annie would remember that actions have ramifications. She tried to impress that upon her while Annie was growing up, but it did not seem to sink in. Marian winced. It was the same speech her father had delivered to her the day she came home from the doctor with a positive pregnancy test, sure the child was George's.

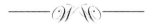

Tom met Sarah at the baggage claim. He would have preferred for her to retrieve the luggage first. That way, he could have picked her up where the cabs and limos met their clients. This would have spared him the hassle of parking, but Sarah insisted on him coming into the airport. She was independent in so many ways, yet caught up in proper gender roles when she saw fit. Sarah expected Tom to help her carry luggage, even though every airport has perfectly large enough carts on which, he was certain, she could fit however many bags she chose to bring. It was only three-and-a-half days. How many could there be?

Tom was watching the first-arriving luggage ride the carousel, the same disinterested look across his face as when he watched Nicky on a real one. His displeasure could only be enhanced if his son asked him to ride with him. Tom had no time for frivolity. He would have rather been building a tree fort with his son. Now that was time well spent, although once the project was done and the goal achieved, Tom would move on, never to participate in the battles of Davy Crockett. Sarah worried that he thought of their marriage in the same way. They had the two kids they agreed upon when they were engaged. Goal achieved. Onto the next thing?

Tom turned and saw his wife approaching. "Hi. I haven't seen your things yet. What did you bring?"

Sarah flipped out her right hip, indicating the carry-on slung over her right shoulder. "Just this and the garment bag."

"How was your flight? Delayed as usual, I see."

"Only an hour. It wasn't too bad."

The garment bag made the turn. Tom picked it up and motioned toward the exit. Sarah was finally in Boston.

"Sarah? Sarah. C'mon. Wake up."

Had she actually slept through the night?

"We should get an early start if you want to walk the Freedom Trail."

Adjusting her eyes, Sarah tried to focus on the brochure thrust before her face.

"I was thinking we could have a quick breakfast here. I have cereal."

"Sure." Sarah scanned the small map. The Freedom Trail started in Boston Common and snaked its way through the city, various historical landmarks on the way. Old North Church. Bunker Hill Monument. Graveyards. "Tom, did you see this? 'The Old Corner Bookstore building is one of Boston's oldest surviving structures,' according to this. Hawthorne. Longfellow. We have to go."

"I'd like to see the U.S.S. Constitution." Tom placed his socks neatly atop the stack of clothes he had prepared the night before. Although in Boston for some time, he was always in the office and had no time for sightseeing.

"Hmm. Let's see where that is on here. Okay. The bookstore is at one end. The ship is at the other."

"I'm going to take a shower."

Sarah wandered into the galley kitchen. Making coffee would help suppress the urge to check on the boys at her mom's. Maybe Tom was right. Maybe she was obsessed. No, she would wait until evening like normal parents do when they are away from their children. Besides, it was only six o'clock there. Undoubtedly, the house would be wide-awake, cartoon noises battling talk radio for supremacy. She walked around Tom's "bachelor suite," unsure how to act. Clicking on the Weather Channel, she was just in time for the local forecast. Upper fifties, maybe reaching sixty. Seasonal for spring.

Tom walked out of the bathroom, wet towel secured around his waist. "Sarah. Aren't you getting ready? Let's go."

Partly cloudy. Fifty percent chance of rain.

His wife had been on egg-producing hormones for awhile now, in preparation for insemination day. John was never sure whether Annie Jekyll or Annie Hyde would greet him from one minute to the next. It was like PMS multiplied twenty-five times. He opened the door, braced himself, and tiptoed toward the kitchen.

"Hi."

John jumped. "Oh, hi, honey." He pecked her cheek. It was seven o'clock. "Did I miss dinner?"

"Actually, I've been rather busy with my body feeling like my skin cannot hold it in."

"Oookay. Do you want to go out?"

"No." She tugged at her shirt, sure her stomach would burst right through it at any second.

"Would you like me to pick up something?"

Annie shook her head.

"Well, it's either one or the other. It think it's a safe assumption you haven't cooked."

"No, June Junior, I have not. I have failed once again in fulfilling my domestic duties. Perhaps if you wanted that sort of thing, you should have married that Melanie girl. Maybe she would have greeted you in an apron, holding a martini."

"I don't even think she's married, last time I heard."

"You keep in touch?" The mushroom cloud was forming.

"No. No. I talked with Fred the other day. He ran into her in Hilton Head, of all places. They both were there for conferences." Cloud defused.

"I see." Annie went into the kitchen, poured some tea, and fell into a chair, legs straddling the sides.

John followed her, wiping his brow. "So, how was your day?"

"Oh, fabulous, as usual. FMG's quarterly figures are in. The press release needs to get out tomorrow."

"You going to make it?"

"I suppose. I've tried to write the damn thing all day, and all I can come up with is the headline. I should just copy last quarter's and change the figures. Who would know? All of this aggravation for a few inches of copy in the *Tribune*?"

John nodded and opened the refrigerator door. "Any leftovers in here?"

"God, John, is food all you can think of?"

"I'm starving. I skipped lunch. Coke and a Snickers. That was it."

"That won't do for your regimen, Mr. Running Man."

"If I don't eat something soon, I might have to resort to cannibalism." He came up behind Annie, nuzzling her neck.

"Ugh, John, please." She pushed him away, wiping off her neck with her hand.

He bit his tongue and returned to the empty fridge. No matter how hard he looked, no food would appear. "I'm going to call that little Chinese place on 75th. Want something?"

"Sure." She was a disgusting cow anyway, why not load

up on Chinese? John was patronizing her with those kisses, she was certain. They had ceased physical contact after the mandatory, right-this-minute conception attempts proved useless. Besides, Annie ached all over. The last thing she wanted was someone fondling her swollen breasts. She had stopped consuming all alcohol and caffeine, as well as salty, and greasy products to ease the symptoms, but to no avail. All she wanted to do was crawl up into a ball on the library sofa, the most comfortable one in the house.

John put the phone down. "It'll be ready in twenty minutes. I'll go pick it up."

Annie walked out of the kitchen, leaving her husband standing alone.

CHAPTER THIRTEEN

"WAIT UP, TOM." SARAH WAS struggling with her camera, attempting to get an unobstructed view of the bookstore's hallowed ground, an almost impossible feat due to the plethora of pedestrian traffic engulfing her.

"Who was Hawthorne?" A girl with straight brown hair, parted down the middle, walked by holding a map in front of her. It was easy spotting the tourists in Boston. They were the ones trying to inconspicuously fold and refold Freedom Trail maps, while the locals weaved around them. She teetered on platform shoes that easily rivaled anything Elton John donned in years past.

"Some dead guy," the boy next to her replied, his face obstructed by at least one thousand brown springy curls, or was it a dust mop toupee? Sarah wasn't sure. Either way, she wished kids would pay more attention in high school English classes.

The throngs parted briefly. Sarah snapped her photo. Tom watched her, a slight smile on his lips. She was so excited. Anything literary did that for her. A couple of years ago, before the boys were born, they had received an invitation to a Halloween costume party from one of her old college friends. Sarah pleaded with him to dress up as Arthur Dimmesdale so she could be Hester Prynne.

"It would be so much fun."

"But nobody will know who we are."

"I think the big red A on my chest might give it away. Perhaps that, along with the Puritan attire."

"They won't remember, trust me."

"Then it's up to us to educate them. Come on, Tom. It will be a riot. I guarantee no one will be dressed the same as us. But you might need to shave off that cheesy mustache, otherwise people will think you are Father Guido Sarducci instead of Arthur Dimmesdale."

Tom's right hand went immediately up to the small, hairy patch above his lip, stroking it. He was never very good at growing facial hair. "Okay. Okay. You win."

Sarah hugged him. "We are going to have so much fun. You'll see."

Her prophecy came true. They won the Best Costumed Couple Award and a bottle of cheap wine. It felt like so long ago.

Sarah had always had this quirky, idiosyncratic way about her. Now she was up close to the building, attempting to stroke its facade while not looking like a complete buffoon.

"Fabulous, isn't it?" Sarah returned beside him. "Can you imagine? I read the original building burned down, but this is still great, huh?" She looked up at him hopeful he would not dismiss her as frivolous, something she felt a lot when he returned home on the weekends.

Tom placed his arm at the small of Sarah's back, rubbing it gently. "Yes, it is."

She could not remember the last time he showed a spontaneous display of affection. Nine years was a long time to be with the same person. They already defied the marriage odds.

"Are you ready?" Tom smiled at her.

"Yes. Let us forge ahead. To the Old State House!"

The sidewalk was too crowded for them to continue side by side, so Tom went ahead to make a path for Sarah. "Oh, by all means. You go ahead. What happened to ladies first?" Sarah stuck her tongue out at him, just the tip protruding from her lips.

"I thought you might like the view." Tom stuck his tongue out back at her.

"Now that you mentioned it, yes, I have always preferred you at this angle." She slapped his butt.

Sarah and her high school best friend had resumed their acquaintance upon returning home from college. Gina had landed her first real job as a communications assistant for Lucent Technologies. Sarah, secretly jealous and longing for a position of her own, invited her friend out for a drink to celebrate.

"All hail the conquering hero." Sarah bowed as Gina entered John Barleycorn, a mock English pub outfitted with stained-glass windows, a tin ceiling, and, most importantly, ten dartboards across the far right wall.

Gina produced her best Queen Mum wave. "Thank you. Thank you."

"Beverage, m'lady?" Sarah pulled out the stool next to hers.

"You bet. What are you drinking?" Gina sat down, swiveling to face the bar.

"Black and tan. What else?"

"Yuck, too bitter. How about a Pimm's Cup?"

"To a wonderful future." Sarah clinked Gina's glass. "So, how does it feel?"

"Actually, I'm really nervous." Gina set down her glass. "I mean, this is a huge company. What if I can't pull this off?"

"Baloney. Of course you can do it. They wouldn't have hired you if you couldn't."

"Here. Here. Hey, how are your Mom and Dad?"

"They are doing well. Wishing I could find a job, of course. I think they got used to having no kids around after Greg left for U of I."

"He's a sophomore?"

"Junior."

"What's he majoring in?"

"Business, what else?"

"Remember when he set up his own food stand at the football game, low-balling prices to steal customers from the Booster Club's concessions because he didn't think monopolies were fair business practices?"

"Oh my God. My parents had to go to Principal Smith's office. They tried to explain to Greg that the concession stand was a fund-raiser, but he would hear none of it."

"Guess what? I found an apartment."

"Where?"

"Off of Ogden in Lisle."

"Awesome."

"I used my last savings for the deposit and first month's rent. Maybe Mom will float me some money until I get my first check. Signed the lease yesterday."

"Well, that calls for another toast."

In celebration of Gina's personal independence, which happened to coincide with America's, she decided to throw a Fourth of July party. "A barbecue on my very own patio," the invitation read. Sarah didn't see any evidence of a party when she pulled up to what she thought was the correct address. She did not see any patios either, only small slabs of concrete not measuring more than eight by four feet in front of each first-floor apartment. Then she saw Gina step through a sliding glass door, second one from the left.

"Hey! You're here." Gina juggled lighter fluid, matches, and a bag of charcoal in her arms.

"Congratulations on your new place." Sarah decided to hold onto the bottle of wine she brought as a housewarming gift.

"Let me start the fire, then I'll introduce you to everyone." Gina poured a smattering of charcoal into a hibachi grill, doused it with lighter fluid, and ignited.

Sarah supposed the grill was in proportion to the patio. A regular-sized one would have overtaken it, leaving no room for the white plastic chair and matching table sitting to the left of the mini-grill. Sarah wondered if everything in Ginaland was tiny. She was hesitant to cross the threshold for fear of Munchkins, who always creeped her out when she was a kid, especially the coroner who pronounced the Wicked Witch of the East dead.

"Come on in." Gina waved her arm.

Instead of a multitude of dwarfs hiding in Technicolor shrubbery, Sarah saw about ten normal-sized people divided into groups of twos and threes. Gina walked her over to Mike and Tina, as Sarah found out through introductions, who were in a deep discussion of German philosophy. They nodded politely and continued with their verbal expedition. Maybe the Lollipop Guild was not so bad after all. At least they came bearing candy.

Two girls walked by. Gina grabbed them. "Hey, Kate. Nancy. This is my friend from high school, Sarah. I can guarantee no philosophy will pass through their lips. Be right back. Have to check the charcoal."

"So you went to high school with Gina." Kate held onto Sarah's arm. "What was she like? Give us all the dirt."

"Well, um…" Sarah searched for something that would not

bite Gina in the butt later on, although nothing ever happened at Boredom High School anyhow.

"There must be something. Her first boyfriend? Favorite band? Did she sing in the choir?" Nancy came up alongside Sarah's other arm.

"No. No. She didn't sing, thank God."

"Oh, how 'bout it. Gina's got the worst voice ever. I can't even stand it when she sings 'Happy Birthday,' she's so tone deaf."

"You know what? I'll be back in a second. I'm going to get something to drink." Sarah escaped into the kitchen. She bent her head down to examine the contents of the refrigerator. Beer, beer, and beer, all of cheap American origin. Eureka! A six-pack of Newcastle. Triumphant, Sarah rose and was treated to yet another wonderful sight. Standing amid two very handsome gentlemen was another with his back toward her. Dark hair, broad shoulders, nicely sized, not work-out maniacal, sitting upon an excellent torso that slimmed down to what she could only term a fabulous butt, comfortably fitted into faded jean shorts. It was he who registered a certain wave through Sarah's system, although years later, she wondered if the current was caused by him or a real electric shock, since Gina's fridge was fairly old.

One of the men noticed Sarah checking out his friend and made eye contact with her, grinning through large, perfect teeth. Sarah realized she was caught, turned away, and fumbled around the kitchen, trying to find the bottle opener.

"Newcastle. Nice choice."

Sarah turned around. It was the blond. He looked like the guy on the Brawny paper towels package, sans the plaid shirt, thank God, since flannel would have been a curious choice in the middle of summer. Sarah was delighted, albeit somewhat embarrassed, to be so near him. After all, he did see her checking out presumably his friend's, or at least a minor acquaintance's, rear end. What if the dark-haired mystery man turned around and the face of an ape stared back at her? Maybe she should continue the pleasantries with the Brawny man.

"Wish I could find the opener." Sarah held up her bottle, tipping it toward him.

"Actually, I believe it was out on the table by where I was. You might have been too distracted by my friend's posterior to notice, so I thought I'd help you out." Brawny man handed her the opener.

Sarah muttered "thank you," not knowing where to look. Before she knew it, he turned her toward the living room, keeping his hands on her shoulders.

"Hey, Tom. This lovely lady drinks Newcastle too, so you have two things in common. Beer and your butt." He whispered in Sarah's ear. "Don't worry, he doesn't bite, well, only if you're into that sort of thing." He ushered her into the living room. "Tom, I'd like you to meet…what's your name, by the way?"

"Sarah."

"To meet Sarah."

"Hey, you don't look like an ape," Sarah burst out.

"Excuse me?"

"I can't believe I just said that. I'm sorry. Oh, never mind. Let's start fresh." She stuck out her hand. "Hi, my name is Sarah Williams. It's nice to meet you. And you are?"

"Tom Anderson. Damn glad to meet you." They shook hands. The auburn-headed one was Pete. Brawny man's name was Andy. They were fraternity brothers where Gina pledged as a little sister. Frat boys? Wonderful. Fabulous butt wasted on a frat boy. What else was new? No good could come of this frat boy, not after all of the things she heard from Gina about their parties.

"So, Sarah. What brings you to this fine shindig?" Brawny man seemed to be the official mouthpiece.

"Gina and I went to high school together."

"I see. We had some great times with Gina at Delta Upsilon. She was Pete's little sister."

"Not that you remember any of them." Pete laughed, high-fiving Andy.

Sarah began evaluating exit routes. She eyed the room, disappointed the only person she knew was the hostess who was busy with party duties. Might as well settle in for fraternity drunken bash recaps. At least there was good scenery. Andy and Pete monopolized the conversation with tales of Swampwater weekend and garbage cans filled with lime-green Kool-Aid spiked with Everclear, dry ice floating on the top.

"Yeah. And where was our man Tom during all this?" Andy rolled his eyes.

"No need to get into that." Tom excused himself, heading for the kitchen and a new beverage. "Anyone need anything?"

Andy leaned in. "Biggest party of the year, where's Tom? In the library, writing computer programs. Can you believe it?"

"I had a huge project due that Monday," Tom yelled from the kitchen.

"So you miss your last Swampwater? You're whacked." Andy rubbed his stomach. "I'm starving. Wonder how the food's coming?"

What was this? Frat boy misses large party to make homework deadline? Fabulous butt and conscientious?

"That seems almost against the fraternity code." Sarah turned to Tom who returned from the kitchen, bottled water in hand. Light drinker, too? Sarah's hard wiring in her brain almost short-circuited. She might even be able to overlook him being a computer person.

Tom shrugged. "It counted for fifty percent of my grade. I wasn't going to flunk for one weekend of fun."

"Very responsible of you." Sarah nodded her head.

Tom gave her a very nice smile, not too broad and forced, but comfortable within his own skin, a very good smile indeed. There was not an ape in sight.

This was it. This was the day that could change their lives forever. *Don't worry little sweetie, your mommy and daddy will find a way to get you here.* Annie was elated. She was going to be artificially inseminated, and she felt great. At last, no more waiting or preparing. Today, they were actually going to start the process of creating their child.

"This should speed things up. Go straight to the source, my grandfather always said." Annie sat in the waiting area of Mitchell Adams and Associates, bouncing her knees. "Of course, he probably did not mean this exactly."

John flipped around the pages of *Newsweek*, oblivious to the articles. He scanned *National Geographic* and *Sports Illustrated* in the same fashion.

"Mr. and Mrs. Jacobs?"

John and Annie rose simultaneously.

"Right this way, please."

"Sustenance. I need sustenance," Sarah whispered into Tom's ear. Her gurgling stomach won out in the battle of hunger versus history.

"Sssh. I want to listen." They were in Paul Revere's house. Lunch would have to wait.

"Yes, Daddy."

Tom emerged from the tour amazed Revere's house was still there, first, because of the American penchant for remodeling, and, second, because the rest of modern-day Boston was built up around it. How could it be that no construction mishaps had landed on the gray wooden structure?

"Must eat. Starving."

"What? Hunger causes you to de-evolve?"

"Only during PMS week. That looks like a restaurant. Let's go." Suddenly filled with glee, Sarah ran a few doors down to the corner. "This must be the place my mom mentioned. She said it was good. Would you like to try it?"

They went up the two steps into Five North Square. There were only a few tables taken, as it was nearly one-thirty. Four men in suits sat near the window finishing their cappuccinos, the one in navy blue taking extra pains to rid himself of all traces of foam from his mustache before the others had a chance to make sport of him. Catty-corner from them, two women laughed while twirling their angel hair pasta on large spoons. Tom and Sarah were seated three tables down from the women and to the left in a corner alcove that afforded the most wonderful view of old North Square, which the guide map said was the oldest public square in America.

"It smells wonderful in here, doesn't it?" Sarah scanned the room, sophisticated, yet comfortable.

Tom peered over his menu. "What are you thinking of?"

"I have no idea. One of everything? How about some wine?"

"It's the middle of the day."

"So what?" Now what was the name of that wine her brother brought on Christmas Day? Sarah ordered the Chianti before Tom could utter otherwise, along with two bowls of minestrone, remembering that Greg always said you can always tell how good an Italian restaurant is by its minestrone.

"Very good." The waiter bent over. "Did you know you are seated at our famous Table Thirty, sight of many a marriage proposal and anniversary celebration? Are you in Boston for something special?"

"Not really. Sightseeing. Today we're doing the Freedom Trail. We are taking a long weekend. Well, I guess it is special. It's the first time away from our boys." Sarah felt a little guilty. She had not thought about the kids for the entire morning until now.

"That is cause for celebration indeed. I will be back shortly to take your entree order."

Sarah focused on ordering something she would never make at home, nor would the boys ever let pass their lips, choosing mussels, clams, calamari, and shrimp sautéed with basil, garlic, and tomatoes over linguine. Tom had veal cacciatore, opting for rosso over the bianco sauce so it would taste better with his wife's wine choice.

Sarah took a last drink of Chianti and sat back in her chair, a deep sigh escaping her mouth and thoughts of cannoli dancing in her head. They had made it through an entire meal without having to cut someone else's meat or blow on another one's pasta. No spills. No poorly timed bowel movements. No crumbs to sweep up. Well, okay, maybe a few.

"You look content." Tom had not seen Sarah relaxed in so long, he had almost forgotten how attractive she was, hands resting on her stomach, Cheshire cat grin decorating her visage. They had talked during lunch, a real conversation, her complete attention focused on what he said. "This was fabulous."

"It sure was." Sarah smiled at him. Tom reached for her hand. She blushed. Was Tom really looking at her like that, or had some really beautiful blonde sat down behind her?

Sarah was not used to men checking her out anymore. Maybe when she was preparing for Friday nights that summer after college graduation, singing to herself in the mirror with a hairbrush microphone, but certainly not now. Pregnancy had moved her into vessel status. She had great difficulty in achieving any sort of personal sparkle while throwing up twice daily. Before she knew it, Sarah was gone, and in her place was Nicky's mom, wound so tightly, one out-of-sync movement might cause her to out spin even the most whirling of dervishes. After Alex, they decided they would have no more children, barring any future accidents. Maybe it was the wine, but Sarah felt ready to reclaim her body as her own.

Tom squeezed her hand. "I've missed you."

So had she.

CHAPTER FOURTEEN

*A*NNIE BARELY GOT UP THE stairs as the train's doors slammed shut, and it departed from Union Station. She walked through car after car, searching for a seat. Why anyone felt compelled to drone on in a meeting about what the Bulls had become after the championship years was beyond her. Didn't Harry have anything better to talk about? They were supposed to be discussing next year's goals. Of course, Annie did not think she could do much about those either.

By the fifth car, it was clear there were no available seats. Annie was tired of being jostled, so she found a place at the bottom of the staircase leading to the crow's nest and rested her briefcase on her knees. Too tired to read, she eyed the fortunate ones whose behinds rested upon cushions while hers met with straight metal. She wished she were home right now, cooking dinner or maybe picking up one of her children from some sort of practice. Baseball or cello? One of each, what the heck? Just as long as it was not soccer. Annie never wanted to become a stereotype. Never average. Never ordinary. Her mother made certain of that. Where did it get her? Tested like some lab animal, while all of the normal women read *Goodnight Moon* to drowsy babies.

Much like Marian McDonnell, Harry Jones never wanted anyone to become complacent. He greeted every new client announcement with a "Good for you. Now who's next?" Annie and everyone down the food chain had to look elsewhere for positive reinforcement. They were expected to get out there and be hungry. For awhile, Annie relished the challenge. But there were only so many companies to court. So many accounts to be snagged. How many different ways are there to make a corporation look good? Nothing was original anymore. She was no longer the golden girl. Wondering if she could be pregnant kept her brain sleep-deprived and useless, with no worthwhile ideas to dazzle the hierarchy. Annie's head felt too heavy for her shoulders. She slumped and rested it on the train's wall.

At the park a few blocks away from their house, neighborhood children climbed red rigging and glided down kelly green corkscrew slides. She was being pulled toward the swings by a child, a little girl who looked about five years old with curly blonde pigtails and bright blue eyes wearing a yellow dress with a light-brown teddy bear holding a daisy in the middle. Matching yellow socks were cuffed over Winnie-the-Pooh gym shoes. "Come on, push me."

Annie lifted the girl onto the "big kid" swing, for she was definitely too old for the baby swing and had made that quite clear to Annie. "Are you ready, Lizzie? One, two, three. Blast off!" She pulled the swing back as far as she could then let go.

Lizzie laughed. "Let's go slide." Before Annie could slow her down, Lizzie jumped off the swing, landing hard on the wood chips below. She began to cry.

Annie bent over toward her. "Are you okay, sweetie?"

"I want my mommy." Lizzie held out her arms to Annie.

Annie picked her up and held her as she cried. "It'll be okay, honey. It will be okay."

"Let go of my daughter!" A woman screamed as she ran across the park. "What do you think you are doing?"

Annie held onto Lizzie confused.

"Let her go, or I'll call the police." The woman ripped

Lizzie out of Annie's arms, while the girl cried "Mommy" reaching for Annie.

"Ma'am. Excuse me, ma'am." A woman looked down at Annie from the step above. "This is my stop."

Annie stared at her.

"Excuse me, I need to get through."

"Sorry. Fell asleep. Long day." Annie sat down in one of the vacant seats that opened up after the train made the first stop. She closed her eyes again, trying to recapture the scene. She could still smell the Johnson's baby shampoo from Lizzie's golden curls, could still feel the wetness from the girl's tears on her neck.

The telephone was ringing when Annie unlocked the front door. She ran to answer it.

"Mrs. Jacobs?" Annie recognized the nurse's voice from the center. "We have the results from the pregnancy test."

"And?" Annie was shaking.

"I'm sorry. The procedure was not successful. Would you like to make an appointment with Dr. Adams to discuss your other options? I see you are on the IVF waiting list. Mrs. Jacobs?"

It was seven o'clock. A night much like any other, John and his co-council Matt were still working. "I'd better call my wife and tell her I'll be late. I'll meet you in the lobby in ten minutes." John dreaded this. He did not want to hear Annie's deflated voice mumble another "okay, whatever you need to do." At least if he came home at midnight, he would not have to see her crying again. She cried so much, she didn't even bother to put her contacts in anymore. Those stupid glasses made her look like a librarian. John shivered from junior high flashbacks of Miss Gladstone's omnipresent face of disapproval.

Everything he did was wrong. If he hugged her, she told him not to touch her. If he tried to have a conversation, the only things she wanted to discuss were the procedures. It was always about her. Her cycle. Her ovulation boosters. What about him? It would be nice if someone asked how he was. Even when his mom called now, the first question out of her mouth was "How's Annie doing?" Who was he supposed to talk to? It's not like you can bring it up with your friends. "Hey, how about them Bears, and, by the way, I'm infertile."

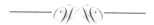

Sarah checked the thermometer outside the kitchen window. Seventy-five degrees. Not a cloud in the sky. No wind. A San Diego day, Tom would call it. He had visited there on several occasions for business, each time returning only to question why the Andersons still resided in the Midwest. Sarah, on the other hand, enjoyed the seasons. Yes, she would concede, sometimes spring came way too late, like in June, but where nature failed in bestowing mountains or even interesting hill elevations, humans took the initiative, constructing a dazzling skyline to adorn Lake Michigan. How she missed working downtown—those buildings, that energy! Each morning, when the Metra train rounded the bend before entering Union Station, Sarah felt a jolt as she and the rest of the commuters plugged into the electricity of the city.

The Old Republic Building sat on Michigan Avenue, just south of the Chicago River, awkwardly positioned among giants. The first time the cab dropped her off for her job interview, Sarah wondered how The Write Group could afford such pricey real estate. After all, the company specialized in providing grant-writing services and other management duties to nonprofit organizations. Visitors were met by Vince, resplendent in his blue uniform with touches of brass, who greeted all who worked there by name with a smile. The gold-leafed elevators, however, revealed the building's true secrets with each ascension. Floor eight. Peeling wallpaper. Stained carpet. This was more what she envisioned sadly enough for such a company, but the location was worth her closet-sized office with its fire escape view. Grant Writers 'R Us would have been a more appropriate moniker.

At lunchtime, Sarah usually headed north, crossed the river, and walked down Michigan Avenue, the Wrigley Building to the west, her destination to the east. Tribune Tower stood cloaked in neo-gothic splendor, a crown resting atop its French cathedral-inspired buttresses. More than one hundred and twenty rocks and bricks from historical sites worldwide were embedded in the walls, which correspondents had gathered from their numerous travels. The Colosseum. The Great Wall of China. St. Peter's. Sarah would choose one each day, touching each crevice, each outline, trying to channel some vibe from distant lands. Afterward, she would sit on the benches a few yards away and imagine what it would be like to go there.

Sarah's wanderlust was never fulfilled, having no luck persuading her parents to allow her to study in Madrid for a semester and possessing no job that paid much more than living expenses until she married Tom. She was pregnant with Nicky soon after, so that was that. Case closed until Alex grew up.

On days such as this, Sarah settled for walking around downtown Naperville with Alex. She often heard foreign languages spoken on its streets and saw photographs being snapped. That would have to do.

First stop, of course, was for a beverage. Alex decided he was thirsty as well, so they sat at an outdoor bistro table, the little one guzzling apple juice, Sarah sipping her mocha frappucino, appropriately cold for those warmer days. She could not bear an entire season without mocha and was ever so grateful when the frappucinos answered her prayers.

The Beach Boy's "California Girls" floated through the air, courtesy of the gray-haired man in a green convertible stopped at the corner. Good for him, out cruising with his music blaring. Who says the kids get all the fun? Lately, Sarah had noticed several cool cars piloted by gray heads. A corvette. A Jaguar XJS. She admired their gumption.

"Well, little buddy, let's go for a walk." Sarah put Alex in the stroller, the frappucino in the cup holder, and set off. Miles of landscaped walkways dotted with covered bridges escorted the West Branch of the Du Page River through Naperville. In the early hours, it lay quiet and serene for power walkers and joggers with headsets. As the sun rose, so, too, did the level of activity, as moms and kids stopped to feed the ducks, play at the park, or roll down Settler's Hill, laughing as they tumbled. Nighttime brought out Carillon concert-goers at one end, and Goth kids shrouded in black lurking under a pavilion at the other. Diners strolled to work off their feasts, pausing at Dandelion Fountain, while five-year-olds threw in pennies for wishes.

Since it was around eleven o'clock in the morning, the path was glutted with ladies pushing strollers. Shorts season had officially begun. Sarah applied her identification system to each as they passed. Woman + stroller + fat anywhere on her body, preferably in the stomach, hips, or butt = physically altered by childbirth = hello, sister. Woman + stroller + size 6 shorts + abundance of energy as she bulldozes over other strollers with her power walking = wonder what it feels like, missy show-off as I gaze down at the largest stomach anyone could ever have and still be human even though I had a baby two years ago = bitch.

Another stroller brigade zoomed past with water bottles in their cup holders. Sarah looked down at the frappucino. She saw a magazine cover yesterday celebrating two new-mom actresses for fitting back into their size-two designer gowns so quickly for some awards show. As if real women need any more pressure. Do you spend enough time with your kids? Are they reading enough? Do they know how to play every sport and musical instrument, plus fully understand art theory? What have you done today that will land your children in therapy eighteen years from now? Heaped on top of this is looking beautiful, yet another entry in the great "To Do" list of life, longer and more unobtainable by the day. So much for enjoying the weather and a relaxing stroll. Sarah would make a salad for dinner. Oh wait, Nicky hated lettuce. A salad for her then. That would mean having to make two different dinners. Forget it. Everyone would get chicken fingers and fries.

"Park!" Alex's little finger came jetting out from under the stroller's canopy. "Park!"

"Good job, sweetie. Yes, that is a park. Would you like to stop and play?"

"Peeeeze."

Sarah tickled Alex's legs each time she pushed the baby swing. "I'm going to get you." He had such a hearty laugh; she could not help but chuckle too. They ran up and down the equipment, scaling rigging, and navigating the suspension bridge. More adventurous than his older brother, Alex wanted to try the tallest tube slide. Sarah put him in between her legs, held him tight, and pushed off, spiraling toward the black squishy mat below.

"More!" Alex clapped his hands with glee.

After about twenty times, Sarah needed a respite. "Honey, why don't you play in the sand. Mommy needs to sit for a second. Go ahead and play for a few minutes, then we'll get going home." It was almost nap time, and laundry in the dryer awaited her return. Sarah breathed in the fresh air once more before heading to the van.

"Alex. Let's go. Alex?" She scanned the sandbox.

"Mama." She felt a tug on her t-shirt.

Sarah turned around. Alex held out a yellow dandelion. "Is this for me?"

Alex nodded. "Uv you."

"Oh, sweetie, thank you." She knelt down and drew him close. "I love you too. Very much."

Annie ripped off her black suit, grateful to be free of the control-top pantyhose she began wearing a few weeks ago. She had tried to push her bloated stomach in, but it refused and resumed its pouchy appearance. She slipped on her stretched-out old workout pants and an oversized tee shirt. She was hideous no matter what she wore; might as well be comfortable. John always said she had too nice a butt to hide in droopy pants, but he did not have an exclusive claim on her body anymore. She had been poked and prodded by every doctor at the center. They had seen angles of her John never dreamed of. Annie was a living cadaver.

She went into the kitchen and filled the kettle with water. Decaffeinated green tea tastes good and allegedly rids the body of toxins. She was extremely mindful of what she ingested. After steeping the tea, she brought her cup in the family room. What a joke! She was the only one in here on a regular basis, and one does not a family make. Even the house was mocking her. Annie sat on the sofa and turned on the television. Maybe she could catch the last few minutes of the evening news.

"Show her how much you care this Mothers' Day with the

diamond solitaire necklace. How will you repay her for giving you the greatest gift?" Images of a man holding his baby in one hand and a jewelry-shaped box in the other flashed across the screen. Children playing in their yard with a couple holding hands looking on. A man secretly watching his wife and baby as the woman sings a soft lullaby and the baby smiles up adoringly at her. Tears flowed down Annie's face. How do you repay her for denying you of the wonderment of parenthood? A shot of Annie opening the door. There is a man in a suit holding an envelope. She recognizes him from John's company Christmas parties.

"Annie Jacobs?"

"Yes?"

"These are for you."

She opens the envelope. Divorce papers.

Annie cried harder now, the pain drilling a hole into her stomach. The phone rang. She could not move to answer it. The machine picked it up.

"Annie? Annie, are you there? If you are, pick up. (Few seconds of silence.) Oh well, anyhow, listen, Matt and I…"

"It's me, John."

"Oh, hi. I wasn't sure if you were home."

"I am. Couldn't get to the phone fast enough."

"Oh."

"What's up?" She sniffed.

He knew it. She was crying again. "Matt and I need to work late tonight on the case. We are going to grab a bite to eat, then continue on for a few more hours."

"Oh, okay."

"So I'll see you later?"

"I will probably be asleep. Hope you get done what you need to."

"Okay. Bye."

"Bye."

This was the pattern of her days lately. Work. Train. Tea/dinner. Cry herself to sleep. One or twice a week, John was there, but he never seemed to want to talk. She tried to give him updates on what steps were next, but he did not hear her.

Annie flipped through the stations. "This Mother's Day, let Mom know you…" Click. "Care enough to send…" Click. "Happy Moth…" Click.

PART TWO

CHAPTER FIFTEEN

A LMOST ONE YEAR HAD PASSED since the Jacobs put their names on the in vitro fertilization waiting list. Another spring decorated Naperville with daffodils and tulips, their beauty wasted on Annie, who instead wondered how she would ever survive the onslaught of new life. She braced herself for the pain that came with each season. On Halloween, she had placed a bowl of candy by their front door with a sign that read "Sorry we are not home. Take as much as you'd like" to avoid seeing preschoolers dressed as super heroes and princesses. At Thanksgiving, members of the Jacobs family had looked at her like she was a three-legged kitten.

"So sorry to hear about you and John." June's sister, Poppy, gave her a half-hearted hug. "I don't understand. A nice couple like you two." She walked away, shaking her head.

Annie put her foot down at Christmas and told John she was going away for the last two weeks of December with or without him. Seeing as he had no desire to partake in another family pity party, he called his mother, who threw a fit as soon as the words "away for the" escaped his mouth.

"No child of mine has ever been gone for Christmas, and it will not happen this year." June had yelled into the telephone receiver.

"Maybe you should have e-mailed her," Annie whispered as she walked past John who was holding the phone out two feet from his head to save his ear. She wasn't sure if what she heard was a teakettle's high whistle or her mother-in-law.

"Mom."

"I can't believe you would ruin our family Christmas."

"Mom."

"Why would you…"

"Mom! Please stop and hear me out. I don't think you realize how difficult this is on Annie and me. Holidays are especially hard now, and we don't want to deal with them this year, okay? I'm not saying forever, just this year."

"You are breaking my heart."

"Yeah? Well, mine's been broken since the first time I heard the words unexplained infertility. I think you can survive quite well without us."

"But John, I never meant…"

"Please don't."

"You know I love you. I never meant to hurt you." June's voice lowered. "I'm sorry, honey."

There was no such battle with Marian McDonnell. Annie refused to speak to her after the Drake tea incident. As far as she was concerned, they were estranged. Marian went about her life as if nothing was wrong, no attempts at making amends, telling herself she and her daughter never talked that much anyway. Annie met her father on occasion for lunch on Saturdays while John put in extra hours at Murdock and Stoddard in hopes of winning one of the co-council seats on a big malpractice lawsuit coming up.

"Hello, my darling." George rose to kiss Annie on the cheek.

"Hi, Dad." She sat down across from him. "Don't you love this place? They have Shepherd's Pie *and* Bangers and Mash."

It was as if a *Wizard of Oz* twister picked up a pub in Ireland and landed it in Naperville. Too bad it did not land on her mother. Annie smiled at the thought.

"Ah, this brings me back." George smirked. "How old were you when we went? Sixteen?"

In Ireland, Annie was dying to see inside one of the many cathedrals on their tour. Unbeknownst to the McDonnells, daily Mass had just begun at the main altar. The only audible sound was the echo of the solemn priest's voice off the stone walls. Teenager Annie opened the large doors and slid in before her mother could stop her.

"Oh, for goodness sakes." Marian could not believe Annie wanted to see another church.

George opened the door for his wife, who went on talking. "You know, if you've seen one church in this country, you've seen them all." Marian's voice bellowed high, crisscrossing through the flying buttresses. The priest stopped the Penitential Rite. The entire congregation turned and stared at Marian, who could only backtrack and sprint down the street, mortified. George and Annie, stumbling from laughter, followed behind.

"So, how is she?"

"Your mother is all right. Doing her usual spring gardening."

"Of course." Annie fidgeted. "Anyhow, how are you doing?"

"I'm okay. Been out on the course twice since the weather has been so decent."

"Has it?"

George looked into the preoccupied, sad eyes of his daughter. "Never mind me. How are you? How are, you know, the procedures going?"

"Right now, we are on pause, waiting for our spot to come up for in vitro." Annie had no idea how many people were infertile too. It was incomprehensible there were kindred spirits plugging along around her, all feeling as isolated as she.

"That's got to be difficult. You were never good at waiting."

"Still not." The server brought over a pint of Guinness for George and water for Annie. "Anyhow, how's the golf game?" Knowing this would expand into a discussion of how high the rough was for this time of year and George's difficulty hitting out of sand traps, Annie sat back in the booth, taking comfort in its familiarity.

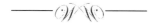

For awhile, life resumed its normal routine, if there was such a thing, after Tom Anderson returned home from Boston. During this reassimilation period, he was mindful to be home for dinner at six o'clock on the dot. After all, he was in Boston for almost a full month longer than was agreed upon.

The summer was punctuated by an onslaught of Alex illnesses. Although none were severe, thank goodness, several fevers, the flu, and a perpetual runny nose stymied any plans the family tried to make, and Sarah was often nursing the little one back to health while Tom and Nicky attended picnics, cookouts, and a minor league baseball game. The book club had taken a summer vacation as well, and Sarah longed for its next meeting, the first Tuesday after Labor Day.

School began, and the pace accelerated. Early autumn, Joe Prescott asked Tom to head the implementation of Icon System's new Human Resources self-service software at a large insurance company about thirty-five miles north of Naperville. Six o'clock became six-thirty, then seven, eight, and sometimes nine. Sarah, Nicky, and Alex ate most dinners without him, and Tom ingested microwaved versions of what were probably very good meals, but were now quite dry. It was exciting being the go-to man on such a high-profile project. He came home every night tired, but invigorated from the challenge. Eventually,

Nicky had stopped asking when Tom would be home, and the words "Da Da" disappeared from Alex's vocabulary.

On one bright April day, Sarah strapped Alex into a large hybrid of red plastic truck/shopping cart. "Are you ready to drive?"

"Vroom. Vroom." Alex spun the wheel.

"Okay, here we go." Anything to please sir toddler so errands could be done in under an hour. The thing should have had back-up lights and beeping sounds, it was so huge. Sarah kept cutting turns into the next aisles too short, banging into the store end-cap displays with large thuds, and making people flinch as she passed. She drove the cart the same way she drove the mini-van, taking the curb right along with her.

While speeding through the main aisle en route to diapers, Sarah noticed a brown and taupe scarf tied around a straw hat, paired with an ecru crocheted purse. It looked like something Annie would buy, only she would purchase it from the real department store, not its scaled-down cousin. Sarah and Annie had become beverage buddies ever since that rainy night and talk of *Pride and Prejudice*, a book club annex of sorts, meeting at the coffeehouse for extended conversation.

Throughout the year, they discussed albatross symbolism in *Moby Dick*, debated whether Poe was a genius or if his laudanum hallucinations would have made anyone as creepy as he was, and why Emily rather than Charlotte Bronte was more well-known. Annie and Sarah agreed on the albatross and concluded Poe was a genius despite his addiction. On Emily versus Charlotte, however, they could not come to terms. Sarah was clearly a *Jane Eyre* person, while Annie's heart roamed the Moors with Catherine and Heathcliff.

Together, Sarah and Annie wondered what Edwina Hipplewhite's house looked like, what Thaddeus did for fun, and how Catherine managed to support herself, for it seemed every first Tuesday of the month brought yet another rejection.

On this particular Tuesday, the ladies settled into a corner spot of the coffeehouse. It was a slow night, only one table was occupied. A middle-aged couple sat near the window, sipping their beverages, staring in opposite directions.

"Well, still no job for Catherine." Sarah inched her backside into a large brown chenille chair and plopped her purse down next to her.

"Poor girl. She probably has a better chance of winning the lottery." Annie paused for a moment. "I wonder if I can set up an audition for her with Bart? He directs training videos for our larger clients. It's not Moliere, but it's something at least." She opened her day planner and jotted down a reminder.

"What, you don't use your phone? Tom wouldn't be caught dead without his. I think he's going to have it welded to his left arm so he's never in danger of losing it."

"Most of my office is like that. I don't like reading everything on screen. It hurts my eyes."

"Me too." Sarah was about to add she even used to write her grant proposals out by hand first, then input them into the computer, but she realized that was so long ago, it was no longer relevant.

"Of course, the squirrels call me a dinosaur."

"Squirrels?"

"The recent graduates that scurry around the office, all bright-eyed and bushy-tailed. They haven't had life kick the shit out of them yet." Annie smirked. "Not that I'm bitter or anything."

"No, of course not." Sarah thought of the youngsters who worked under Tom. They were sweet, all fresh and ambitious. "Little bastards."

"My, my. Miss Sarah! Such language!"

"Aaaah, that felt good. The kids repeat everything. I can't even say 'shit' anymore. I've started using alternative cursing prose, mostly stolen from British slang. 'Bloody Hell' is a good one. It's driving me crazy."

"One cannot suppress the basic human desire to swear. I bet one of the so-called archeological finds in the Field Museum's display is really the cave-painting symbol for 'ass.'"

Two men walked in, one with jeans and golf shirt, untucked, one with Dockers and golf shirt, tucked. Both had messy-funky hair, connoting the early- to mid-twenties. They sat at a table within hearing distance. The dark-haired one stuffed half a huge cookie into his mouth. "So I'm having a hard time with monogamy lately," he said through crumbs.

Sarah and Annie could feigned interest in their drinks, using the silence to eavesdrop.

"Wipe your mouth, man. There's chocolate everywhere. You look like someone knocked your front teeth out." The sandy-haired guy threw a napkin across the table, laughing.

"Better?" He smiled for his friend, who was still laughing, but managed a nod. "I'm serious, dude. I cannot imagine waking up with the same woman day after day after day."

The other guy set his drink down and spread his arms across the table. "Check this out. I'm trying to get my life straightened out. I've been going back to church. I got rid of Chris. It's Sandra exclusively now."

"What? No way."

"Seriously. It's great. I feel like I'm finally on the right track."

"I don't know, man. I don't think I could do that."

"Maybe you haven't found the right woman yet."

"Dude, you sound like my mom."

"But it's true. When I met Sandra, I don't know, it was like a bell went off in my head. It all clicked."

"You sound serious."

"I am. I think I am going to ask her to marry me."

"No way."

"Can you believe it? I think it's time."

"Your funeral, man."

Sarah scoffed. "I'd like to have a dollar for each time that conversation has taken place on this planet. I'd have enough money to send both boys to Harvard."

"Really?" Annie wondered if all men spoke of commitment the way those two did. Was it really such a big decision? "It all seemed so natural when John and I got together, I never even thought of it like John would be the last guy I would ever have sex with."

"You didn't? I certainly did. Well, not with John, of course."

"I suppose." Annie took a sip of chai.

Sarah uncrossed her legs and leaned in close to Annie. "Speaking of jarring, listen to this. Judy next-door told me the other day that her sister's husband came home from work last Friday and announced flat out he did not love her anymore. Apparently, he had been having an affair for six months and was leaving her to live with his mistress that very night. Can you imagine?"

Annie gasped. "She never even knew about the affair?"

"No. Judy said the husband was home every night to tuck their kids in. It wasn't like he was working late every day or anything."

John flashed into Annie's mind. Not possible. He was working late to score brownie points with Andy and maybe even a partnership. More money made IVF more palatable, especially to John. Sarah was still talking.

"Poor woman." Sarah leaned back in her chair. "So what did you think about Rosemary's comment about Virginia Woolf?"

Focus, Annie. "What was she thinking? Virginia Woolf was

one of the greatest literary minds of the twentieth century. Maybe she didn't read the whole thing."

"It took me awhile to get used to her sentence structure, though."

"There was some study done awhile ago on the average number of words used in sentences, comparing novels from early 1900s to now. I think it was something like twenty or thirty then to seven now. It's crazy." Annie picked up her chai. She was herself again, at least for a few hours a month, without the Scarlet I emblazoned across her chest.

"Oh, hi, Mom." John answered the phone while towel-drying his hair. They had slept in this morning.

"Hello, dear. Listen, I don't mean to be a nosy Nellie, but I had to call you as soon as I got in from church." June was flustered. "I never heard about this fertility business before you and poor Annie brought it up. Then, I'm sitting at Mass, saying an extra prayer for you, by the way, when all of a sudden, who starts talking about it but Father Brown. Can you believe it? Anyhow, I'm afraid it's not good news, dear. Not good at all."

"What do you mean?" What did she do? Tell the whole church? John threw the towel into the sink.

"It was Pro-Life Sunday. People were out in front of church selling roses, small pins, that sort of thing. Father Brown said there is a whole new issue for us to be aware of. Do you know what he said?" June paused for dramatic affect.

It was a long enough halt in verbiage to indicate she expected some sort of response. "No. What?" was all he could muster.

"Reproductive technologies, that's what! Can you believe it?" No pause this time, thank God. "Father said many eggs are fertilized, then only certain ones are implanted into the woman, and the rest are destroyed. That's abortion, John."

Dr. Adams mentioned something about freezing some embryos after harvesting in case the first IVF did not work, but he never thought about it like that. "I'm not sure, Mom."

"But it is, dear, whether the baby is created inside a woman or a test tube, it's still a life."

John leaned against the vanity. "What else did he say?"

"That the church frowns upon insemination and is definitely against in vitro fertilization. Aren't those the two things you were doing?"

"Yup." He rubbed his eyes.

"Whatever you do, please think about this. Don't do something terrible."

"I'll look into it, Mom. Thanks for calling." He leaned against the vanity, running his hand through his hair. *Shit. Annie is going to pop a gasket.*

Annie sat in the office, researching in vitro fertilization on the Internet, certain the more informed she became, the better her chances of parenthood. Maybe other women with unexplained infertility had limited conception options, but if she just kept accumulating data, Annie would ace this thing. She wasn't an overachiever all of her life for nothing. This was her final exam in womanhood.

A small altar on her dresser showcased various fertility goddesses from the major religions arranged in height order so as to not anger any one of them. She was not about to take any chances. On a whim, Annie had asked June to enroll them in a monthly novena with the Passionists. June's God might not approve of infertility science, but it was her God, too, and hers was merciful and compassionate. Annie wished God had shown some of that kindness three years ago. Then they would not be facing the choice that today made her head spin.

Deborah had told them during the IVF process, Dr. Adams usually fertilizes two to four eggs, implants them, and sees which attach to the uterus. There is no guarantee any will survive, but if all four do, sometimes parents will have to make the choice to terminate one or more of the embryos for the others to have a better chance for a "live birth," a term that made Annie cringe. "This increases your chances of a healthy baby," Deborah had said. They all talked about it so matter-of-factly, Annie did not even question it at the time.

Then John told her what June said. Normally, Annie ignored anything blubbering from her mother-in-law's mouth, but something about what Deborah said did not feel right. *Sometimes parents will have to make the choice to terminate one or more embryos for the others to have a better chance of live birth.* Annie sat back from the desk. They actually asked people so wanting, so craving a child of their own to endure this hell and then get rid of fertilized embryos? How could those words even come out of their mouths? It was the ultimate irony. But it must happen enough times for Deborah to mention it. What about the fertilized embryos created in case a second round of IVF was needed? What happened to them? Annie knew harvesting many embryos at one time was cost-effective, but that really wasn't the point, was it? How does one choose which embryos live?

Annie had no desire to play God. All she wanted was a baby. Guess that was too much to ask. What would have happened if the insemination was successful? All that sperm zooming around trying to connect with the large number of ova she produced for the procedure. There had to have been a higher probability of multiple births with such inherent randomness. What would they have done? All the literature and web sites

KAREN WOJCIK BERNER

discussed the procedures in strictly medical terms. Annie was
Catholic; she could not escape it. The house was one huge
vise, its walls crushing in on her with every turn. Maybe a walk
would help.

Outside was peaceful, the calm before the throngs of future
Peles invaded the soccer fields two blocks down and yells of
"get the ball" went wafting through the neighborhood. The sun
had yet to break through the clouds. The grass was thick with
dew. Poor kids' feet will get all wet. She had been up since six,
on the computer by six-thirty. John had gone for his run at
about seven-thirty. He was in the shower when she left. Annie
missed him suddenly, wishing they were traversing the park
path together, but he had probably ran through it earlier.

She had always imagined herself with two kids. Two girls
running around, giggling and telling secrets. Best friends, like
Jo and Meg. This vision cheered her somehow. Elizabeth and ?.
She never got past being delighted about the Austen reference
to name the other one. Should she go for the full homage?
Why not? Elizabeth and Jane secretly staying up late, reading
books too good to put down.

Annie passed a woman with a double stroller who had
stopped to tie two pairs of Elmo gym shoes that had come
undone. The two boys sat side by side, mucus dripping from
their full noses. It snaked down to the tops of their lips until
joining with large cylindrical lollipops as they sucked them
in and out of their mouths. The snot pop, a uniquely toddler
confection. Annie smiled at the three and bade them "good
morning," her stomach doing a flip as they passed. She would
have at least wiped their noses. Wait a minute. Eating lollipops
this early? It was only eight-thirty. No candy before noon would
be Annie's rule, unless it was Easter, and chocolate eggs were
right there in your basket, well within reach. The twins' mother
tried to move the snot pops so she could wipe their noses.

Unfortunately, this resulted in stereo screams that would wake the dead. In one fast move, a tissue flew past the kids' faces, and the candy was returned before the entire family would be run out of the neighborhood by angry mobs carrying torches.

It would not be so bad to have twins, Annie supposed, manageable even, exhausting, but do-able, but three or four at a time would be a bit much. There had to be an answer somewhere. She headed back home to her computer.

"Oh, hey." John had just finished shaving.

Annie reached into the medicine cabinet and downed two extra-strength Tylenol. The walk had done nothing for her headache. "How was your run?"

"Great," he said, a bit muffled through the golf shirt going over his head.

"Don't forget about the McDonnell family picnic at eleven."

"What time do you want to leave?"

"About ten-thirty."

"Are you sure you want to go?" John doubted Annie's ability to handle large family events where at least one pregnant woman would probably be in attendance.

"I'd like to go for my dad. He never gets to see his side."

"Okay. I'm going to make some breakfast. I'm starving after the run. Want anything?"

"No, not hungry,"

"Suit yourself."

John had not ran since high school, when it was mandatory for baseball conditioning. He started again April first, which greatly amused Annie and prompted her to quip, "It's poetic, really. Only a fool would want to run for miles." She had come into the family room while he was stretching out his hamstrings, one leg up like a pink flamingo. He heard her snicker and plopped his leg down.

"Very funny. I'm getting older. I need to get in shape before it's too late."

"Knock yourself out." Annie loathed anything that led to excessive sweating.

The health benefits were only half of it. John enjoyed the solitude running afforded. It cleared his head, gave him perspective. He controlled the pace. He controlled the distance. He released the guilt.

This was one of the rare occasions Annie's immediate family attended the yearly McDonnell picnic. Marian was never fond of George's relations. She busied herself fussing over the food table, arranging and rearranging fried chicken, potato salad, and fruit, cleverly looking a part of the event without having to talk to anyone. This was good, especially since Annie had no wish for mother-daughter conversation on such a lovely day.

"Annie bananie!" Her cousin waddled over. She was very pregnant and red-faced from the spring sun.

They hugged. Annie pulled back to look at Lilly, putting on her best false smile, which she had earned from years of watching her mother. Annie coughed. "Congratulations. When are you due?"

"In two weeks, thank God. I don't think I could last much past that. Anyone pregnant in the summer deserves an award." Lilly tugged at her t-shirt collar. "I'm so hot."

"Here, sit down. I'll get you some lemonade." Annie ran off, all the while repeating an internal mantra. *I will not freak out. I will not hate my favorite cousin. I will be happy for her. I will act normal.* Reaching the coolers, she bent down to find lemonade and let the coolness from the ice refresh her face.

Annie returned with two beverages and a clear resolve to enjoy herself. John was playing badminton with Lilly's husband, Jim, while two little second cousins shagged birdies like ball boys at Wimbledon.

"Oh, thanks so much." Lilly chugged half of the lemonade in one swig. "Oh, that's good. I swear to God, it's like there's a space heater inside of me instead of a baby." She wiped her forehead with her sleeve. "So, how are you? Last time I saw you, we were in charge of water balloons at one of these things."

"We spent the entire day wet, if I remember correctly. Couldn't fit that spigot thingy on the hose to fill them. I should have known not to volunteer for anything requiring motor skills." Annie tried to ignore her cousin's pregnant stomach, but was unsuccessful, seeing as various family members had to say hello to her and rub her belly like she was a Buddha.

"I get that all the time, believe it or not. At least these people are related to me. Strangers come up to me in the grocery store to stroke the belly."

"Oh, you're kidding." After awhile of again repeating her mantra, Annie calmed down and was able to chat without clearing her throat or coughing. This was a chance to ask a real, live pregnant lady what it felt like, to do some field research. "So, how does it feel?" Annie thought the answer would be about feeling as big as a house or something. She was unprepared for what she heard.

"I knew as soon as it happened." Lilly's eyes sparkled. "Something inside of me was different, like a flicker of recognition. It was the most amazing thing. I checked the calendar after my OB/GYN appointment, and, sure enough, I knew exactly when we conceived the baby."

"How?"

"I don't know. I just knew."

How could a microscopic mass of cells register such certainty? Was the baby's tiny soul settling in, readying itself for incubation? Lilly bonded with her baby before she had scientific proof there even was one. Annie excused herself, walked past the volleyball and horseshoe competitions, past the bean bag toss and piñata, toward the huge elm tree near the parking lot. How was this possible? This was no clump of cells, this was a tiny person. If that was true, then how could she or John ever terminate any fertilized embryo?

Maybe there was a way for only one or two eggs to be fertilized at a time. It would be more expensive, but, so what? She wasn't her mother. Not everything was a business proposition. Or maybe they should just prepare one embryo and hope for the best. That's what happened in nature, right?

Annie felt warmth on her shoulders. The sun was making its presence known, its rays burning through the clouds creating a sunburst Annie had never seen before. It was the sort of sun children drew, a yellow circle with lines emanating from every side. She had her plan, and God approved. Now, she only had to convince John.

CHAPTER SIXTEEN

FMG CHEMICALS PROVED EXTREMELY CONVENIENT on those days when Annie could not bear to trudge downtown to work. She could drive a mere twenty minutes, ten with no traffic, to obtain financial figures for FMG's annual report or to help Fred Gordon with his shareholders' speech. Annie used creative scheduling to get that all-important face time with Fred and the others, as well as to book appointments with Dr. Adams or one of his technicians, without anyone at the office the wiser. Maybe she would be able to work out a freelance deal with Harry after the baby was born. She had already started making plans to convert the library into an office, where she envisioned working on her laptop with the baby playing nearby in the portable crib.

Annie shook her head. She had to get back to developing FMG's booth for the fall trade show in New Orleans. Hopefully by that time she would be pregnant and would not have to deal with the fourteen-hour days, nonstop meetings with trade magazine editors, and standing on concrete convention center floors in heels. She was also heading up preparations for the company's soiree to introduce the new emulsifier. A few details needed to be ironed out with the manager of Antoine's, but otherwise things were going fairly well. Her team would be presenting three ideas for party favors tomorrow at nine o'clock.

This morning, Annie and Bob Nolan, one of FMG's marketing managers, attended a "dog and pony show," as they called meetings in which magazine sales representatives schlep the editors on tour with them hoping to leave with a twelve-time advertising rate schedule. Afterward, they went to lunch and batted around ideas for the theme of this year's shareholders' meeting. At two o'clock, Annie had an appointment at the center, a general system check after being on and off super ovulators.

The next day, Annie entered Jones and MacGregor at eight o'clock having had only four hours of sleep. A body idling like a Pacer with the air conditioning on was not conducive to a restful night's slumber. She made some tea, checked voice mails, and headed for the conference room where she was greeted by Ursula, Jennifer, and Christian, all of whom were semi-hidden by a large box on the table.

"Good morning." Annie took a seat and placed her notepad and tea in front of her. "Okay, what do you have for me?"

The three grinned and tipped over the gigantic box, spilling an assortment of toys onto the conference table. Rubber duckies. Squishy balls. Bubble blowers. Paddle balls.

"What do you think?" Jennifer picked up a jar of bubbles.

Christian squeezed a rubber duckie for effect. "Cool, huh?"

Annie looked at each of them, their eyes large and pleased with themselves. "This is what you've come up with? Two months and all I get is this?" Annie tossed a squishy ball across the table. She was in no mood for playtime. Other companies had done all of these before, badly.

"We thought they would be kind of fun, y'know, like a flashback to everyone's childhood?" Christian said.

Annie shook her head. "This is the chemical industry, ladies and gentleman. They probably never played with this stuff as kids, except maybe to figure out what it was made of. They don't remember their youths and certainly have no time to recapture them."

"We just thought…" Ursula tried to defend the team's decision, stopping mid-sentence after making eye contact with Annie.

"We are premiering the product at Antoine's, the incredibly famous restaurant where presidents and movie stars have dined. I think we need something a bit classier, don't you? FMG is a well-respected industry leader. So think about those words: classy, well-respected, elegant. Go from there, okay? Let's meet again on," Annie flipped open her calendar, "on Tuesday. How's that for everyone?"

The three gathered the leftover items from a preschooler's party goodie bag and exited the conference room deflated.

Rubber duckies? Didn't they notice anything about last year's give-aways? Annie went to her office and began tackling the piles of paper on her desk.

Harry Jones peeked his head around the door. "Do you have a minute?"

"Sure, Harry. Have a seat. What's up?" Annie gestured toward the chair across the desk.

"Thanks." He sat down. "Annie, I'm just going to come out with it. You and I have always been straight with each other, right?"

"Yes."

"We have a problem. I ran into Christian after their meeting with you."

"And?"

"He and the others were pretty upset."

"Well, did they tell you what they proposed? I would be upset if I worked for two months and only came up with that."

"You came down pretty hard on them."

"What?"

"They feel they did not receive any guidance from you on this project. You have not been in the office enough for them to ask you questions."

"Harry, that's what cell phones are for."

"Really, Annie. You seem distracted. You snapped at Ursula about the press release." He could see the anger building in Annie's eyes. How dare any junior account executive supersede her and go straight to Harry with personal grievances. "Settle down. I heard you myself. Ursula didn't say anything. You told your team you had confidence in their abilities, then when they showed you their ideas, you shot them down so fast, their heads spun."

Annie could not respond. Maybe if they could discover a thing called creativity.

"You have been extremely tense lately. What's the matter? Is something going on I should know about?"

He was male. How could he understand? She sat there, speechless.

"There's something else. Your yearly review came across my desk earlier."

Great, now Brian Moore hated her too. He was the executive vice president and her direct-report up the food chain, between herself and Harry.

Harry leaned his elbows onto Annie's desk, lowering his voice. "For the first time in all these years, you received a 'Does Not Meet.'" He slid a paper across her desk.

Annie scanned it. Apparently she fell short on every evaluation point. "I'm sorry about all of this. I will try to give more guidance to my team and to be courteous to everyone." She sounded like a robot. "I have been a bit distracted lately." If she didn't tell him now, she could lose everything she worked for. "I am...I mean...we, John and I, are..." Annie sighed and drew herself up straight. "We are having fertility issues. We are seeing a specialist, and I'm on ovulation-enhancement medication. It's really screwing up my system." Annie put her head down, avoiding his eyes. She could not deal with any pity emanating from them. Yes, she was only half a woman. Yes, she was flawed on both sides of her life now.

"My daughter and her husband went through the same thing."

Annie looked up. "Really?"

"It took them five years, but they finally had little Billy. It will happen for you too." Harry smiled. "You know, I've always liked you, Annie. You are very talented. But, unfortunately, I cannot have someone in your position be on the job only fifty percent of the time. Too many things to do."

Oh my God, was he firing her?

"Why don't you take a sabbatical? Take some time off. If you're going through what Danielle did, I know you could use some."

"You want me to leave?"

"I can't pay you, but I can make sure your job is here when you are ready to come back."

Annie started to cry, out of relief or disappointment, she was not sure which.

"Clear your schedule. I'll make the necessary excuses to the team."

"You are taking a sabbatical now? When we need all the money we can get?" John could not believe what he was hearing. When Annie asked him to join her for a cup of tea, several possible conversations swirled around in his head. Maybe she wanted to abandon the whole IVF thing before they wasted anymore money on odds no betting man would gamble on. Or perhaps she needed to get away for a weekend alone. He wouldn't have even been surprised if Annie asked for a separation the way things were going lately. But he never expected this.

"Would you like some chamomile tea?" Annie poured the hot water, seeming more calm right this instant than she had been for the entire three years previous. It was unnerving. "It's not really my choice. Harry suggested it. Besides, it will let me focus on the procedure. Dr. Adams' office called. It's our turn, John. It's finally here."

John did not even hear the last few sentences. He was too blown away by Annie's illogical behavior.

Annie continued. "I want to make sure it goes exactly how it should. I can't be stressed about work."

"We are throwing away tens of thousands of dollars with no guarantees, and now you are going to throw your job away too?"

"I'm not quitting. I talked with Harry. It's not paid, of course, but at least I'll have a job to go back to if I'd like." She could not deal with John thinking she was a failure at work too.

John held his forehead. He was pacing.

"This IVF might be the only chance I get to carry my own child inside of me. I cannot, no, I will not screw it up like I already did by waiting too long to start our family."

"It's not your fault."

"You don't know that for sure."

"Well, you don't know that it is not my fault either. Stop it with the guilt. That's not doing us any good."

Annie started to cry, she couldn't help it, damn drugs. "I thought you would be happy to see how committed I am."

"I can't see anything but your obsession with these procedures. In case you haven't noticed, infertility is our only common bond right now."

"Well, it is a little important," Annie shot back.

"Of course it is, but it's not everything. You and I used to have lives, remember? We used to go out to dinner and to see movies. Hang out on Sundays watching football."

"None of that matters anymore. In the grand scheme of life, who cares if the Bears win?"

John could see there was no reasoning with her anymore. He sat down at the table opposite Annie. "What did Harry say?"

Annie recanted the meeting. John left his teacup untouched and walked out of the kitchen. It did not matter what John thought today. He would understand the minute he held their baby in his arms. He would know, as she did now, that it would all be worth it.

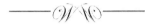

Everything was different now that the IVF was scheduled. As her father had said, waiting was not Annie's forte; she was much better in action. She read the itinerary every day. There could be no errors. Ovulation-inducing medication. Check. Appointments for blood samples to test estrogen levels. Check. Vaginal ultrasound to monitor ovum growth and numbers scheduled. Check. Egg harvesting. Check. Dr. Adams said timing was crucial especially at this stage. If harvesting was done too early or too late, fertilization would not occur. John had arranged to take some days off to be with her for egg harvesting and the embryo transfer. She would be in no shape to drive. Two weeks later, they would take a pregnancy test at the center.

After reading and re-reading the schedule about twenty-seven times, Annie bounced around the house, trying to figure out what to do. John had already cleaned and vacuumed. It was only eleven o'clock, so cooking dinner was out of the question. Reading? Nah, her mind could not possibly focus. She had to get out of the house. Annie decided to call Sarah for an impromptu lunch. She thought she could even handle meeting the baby now, seeing as once the IVF worked, she, too, would have a toddler some day. On the other end of the phone line, Sarah was more than happy to leave six loads of laundry undone in the basement.

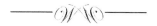

Annie arrived at the restaurant first, after sprinting out of her house, delighted to be elsewhere. She glanced up from her menu. There was Sarah, maneuvering a stroller with one hand, opening the restaurant door with the other. This was complicated by the behemoth blue-and-white-striped diaper bag swung over her right shoulder. Annie rose to help, but was too late. Sarah's foot stuck midway in the entrance, and the door's momentum slapped her in over its threshold.

"Let me get that for you." Annie took the diaper bag, faltering under its unexpected weight.

"Hi. Oh, thanks." Sarah rubbed her back, glaring at the teenaged hostess who watched the incident with a smirk from behind her podium.

Annie ushered Sarah and stroller over to their table, suddenly realizing there was something sitting in the stroller. The usual covetousness had not squeezed the breath from her. In less than a year, she told herself, she would be in the same position. She bent down to get a better look. "Hello, sweetie. I'm Annie. It's nice to meet you." She tickled his tummy.

Alex giggled. "Hi."

"I'll get you a high chair." Sarah scoped the area.

"May I?" Annie unstrapped Alex's safety belt and lifted him up. "Aren't you a cutie? Look at those dimples. Do you know the spider song?" She sat him on the table and scooted into the booth. The toddler mimicked her hand motions as they sang "Itsy Bitsy Spider," Alex joining her for the words' last syllables.

The server delivered the high chair, but Alex would have none of it, screaming "big boy, big boy" as his mom tried to put him in it. "I know you're a big boy, but you need to sit in here so you can eat lunch. Please listen to mommy."

He slid further on the table out of her grasp.

"Honey, please?"

"No."

"Hey, Alex. How about if you sit out here with us until your food comes, then you can go in the high chair? Is that okay, Mom?" Annie tried.

"Sure." As long as he did not make a scene, anything was fine with Sarah. She was so grateful to be out of the house with adult company having a meal she did not have to prepare, she begged God for Alex not to screw this up for her. "Honey, would you like to read a book or color?"

"Col..." was indication enough for Sarah to fish crayons and a Clifford coloring book from the immense bag.

"Okay. Whew. How are you, Annie?" There was a slight awkwardness amidst this melding of worlds. Sarah was surprised Annie was so good with Alex. For some reason, she never associated Annie with kids.

"I'm okay. Had the day off and didn't feel like spending it doing chores," Annie lied. She watched as Sarah unloaded a full dining set up: sippy cup, bib, pint-sized utensils, disposable placemat, and munchables to tide him over until lunch was served. What else was she going to pull out of that thing? Sarah nodded and "um hummed" while Annie spoke, but her friend knew she did not have her full attention, not like after the book club meetings. Sarah seemed focused then; now she just looked frazzled.

The high chair went unused, as Alex insisted on eating his lunch while sitting on his mom's lap. This made it difficult for Sarah to ingest any of her own meal. Annie tried to get him to come to her, but apparently the novelty had worn off and only mommy would do now.

"I know this sounds strange, but would you like me to cut your quesadilla for you so you could pick it up easier? You know, I'll mother you, you mother him," Annie said.

Sarah shook her head. "Thanks anyway. I'm fairly used to this. I don't think you ever get completely used to someone hanging on you constantly."

"Only when you're dating in high school."

"At least I didn't have to feed him Cheerios."

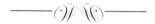

The three walked around downtown after lunch in no hurry to go back home, past restaurants and shops, clothing stores and fountains. Sarah bent over to check on the little one who had fallen asleep in his stroller. "Thank goodness. The whole day has been like at lunch. I'm exhausted." She rubbed her temple with her free hand, still pushing the stroller as they walked. "God, I used to think I was destined for something amazing, something big, like Amelia Earhart, or someone like that."

"I hope not. She crashed god-knows-where and either drowned or was eaten by sharks."

"Oh, you know what I mean. If Tom's not working until ten, he's out of town. All I do is wash underwear, clean toilets, and change diapers. No matter how much I do, there is always more. I sweep twice a day, and I still find crumbs under the table."

"I'm sure it's difficult, but..." Every corpuscle in Annie's body was beginning to throb.

"Nicky treats me like I'm a fool. Alex's diaper leaks diarrhea all over his crib. He woke up at four thirty this morning wanting to play. Can you believe it? Four thirty! Nicky was up twice the night before with dreams of tornadoes. God, I need a vacation! You get an automatic two weeks, don't you? I don't get that luxury."

"Shut up! At least you can have kids." Annie flung her hand to her mouth, hoping Sarah was too absorbed in her diatribe to notice.

Sarah stopped walking, stunned. "What did you say?"

Annie mumbled, "Nothing."

"What do you mean, nothing? What did you say?"

Annie gestured toward the pavilion next to the river. They walked in silence, Sarah trying to process what Annie said; Annie wishing beyond all she had learned restraint. Sarah parked Alex and his stroller by the end of the picnic table and sat down. Annie gazed down the river at the covered bridge, saying a silent good bye to her precious just Annie moments to become Annie the Infertile once again. She sat next to Sarah. "John and I have fertility problems. We have been trying to become pregnant for more than three years."

"Oh God, Annie. I'm so sorry. I had no idea."

Annie blanched. "I didn't tell you because it was really nice having a friend who didn't look at me the way you are looking at me now."

Sarah tried to erase the sympathy and shock from her face.

"I couldn't take hearing you rag on like that. You make motherhood sound so horrible. If it is so terrible, why am I going through all of this?" Her shoulders fell.

"I had no idea…I thought…maybe you chose your career and weren't going to have kids."

"You thought wrong."

"Are you going to…um, what are you…are you seeing a doctor? Oh, I'm sorry. Is that too personal to ask? God, did I say too much? I hope I didn't…"

"Please don't tip-toe around me. Yes, we are seeing a doctor. We have been diagnosed with unexplained infertility. We've tried insemination and are now up for IVF next month."

"Next month? You never said anything this entire time?" Sarah's care-taking side kicked in. "Is there anything I can do?"

Annie bit her lip. "Yes. Please do not treat me like I'm damaged. I get plenty of that from the family."

Sarah reached out to hold Annie's hand, but she pulled away. "I need to go."

"Please don't. I'm sorry."

Annie shook her head and waved. Sarah sat there, dazed. She moved Alex's stroller around so she could see him. His head was slumped over, brown teddy cuddled under his chin. Sarah stroked his cheek. The day they came home from the hospital, Nicky held "his baby," as he insisted on calling Alex, while sitting on the sofa in between his parents. He told him of the many adventures they would have together, playing pirates, knights, and Batman. "It's gonna be great. I'll even let you use the Batmobile." He kissed Alex on the head.

Two-year-olds are not trying to thwart you. They just want to be near you. Six-year-olds are not ignoring you when they watch television. They are focusing on one thing at a time, doing the best they can. It's not a personal vendetta. Sarah started to cry. She threw on her sunglasses so all of Naperville would not know what an idiot she was and headed for the mini-van parked two blocks away.

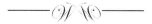

Sarah left several messages on Annie's machine, but none were ever returned. She even tried calling her at work, but was told she was on sabbatical. How would she let Annie know how sorry she was for spouting her mouth off? Maybe at the book club meeting next Tuesday.

Annie did not have the energy to return Sarah's calls. The procedure was only one week away, and she was going to the center every day to give blood samples. This had to have her full attention. Egg harvesting was the same day as the book club meeting, and Dr. Adams suggested she take it easy afterward. Sarah would just have to wait.

———⌀———

After Annie did not show up at the book club meeting, Sarah wrote her an apology letter after tracking down her address on the Internet. She also wanted Annie to know she was praying for the procedure to be successful.

———⌀———

From your hands to God's ears, Annie thought, putting the letter down. Maybe she could join with June's women's group from church who began a month-long novena a few weeks ago. Annie was past praying now. It was of no use before, why waste the time? Their fate was in science's hands now.

———⌀———

Sarah left early Saturday morning. Halfway through her mental "To Do" list—bank, post office, drop off videos, groceries—thunder drummed in the distance. Smoky gray clouds overtook their pale white cousins. Lighting tore apart the sky. The rain, huge drops at first, quickly multiplied, leaping up from the streets. Within ten minutes, Ogden Avenue was flooded near Washington Street. Sarah pulled over, waiting for the storm to subside. About fifteen minutes later, she headed for the grocery store, hoping by the time she was done, the rain would cease completely.

"Did you see that storm?" Sarah walked into the kitchen,

balancing her purse, four bags of groceries, and her keys. "Could someone give me a hand? It's still pouring out there. And you know how much I enjoy doing groceries in the rain. I particularly love the way water gathers on the back door of the van while I am loading the bags, then dumps right on my head when I shut it. Hey, could someone get the phone? Tom? Nicky?" She heard clatter in the basement. They must not be able to hear her. "Hello?"

"Sarah." It was her father. "I need to talk to you."

CHAPTER SEVENTEEN

THEY SAT IN THE CONFERENCE room, Sarah, Tom, and Mark Williams. It was completely white, except for the large cherry table and black chairs they were using. Greg, Sarah's brother, was finally on the way. Mark couldn't get him on the phone until now. Apparently his cell was turned off.

"Would you like some coffee?" A nurse gestured toward the side table. "Water? The doctor will be in shortly."

"We should wait until your brother gets here," Mark said.

"No! I can't wait another minute. It will probably take him over an hour to drive in from the city." They had been at the hospital all night, and Sarah's nerves were ready to burst through her skin. She looked over at her father. "I'm sorry, Dad."

"I know."

The doctor entered. Sarah noticed a green golf shirt under his lab coat. Since when were doctors the same age as her? From what the nurses said, he had a reputation as the best in spinal trauma in the western suburbs. Good. Nothing but the best for Mom. It is what she deserves.

"Hello, Mr. Williams. Mrs. Anderson. Mr. Anderson. I'm not good at pretending, so I am going to tell you like it is. We have worked on Mrs. Williams for about twenty hours now. We have performed every procedure conceivable. Unfortunately, she has not responded. When the tree hit her car, the impact was so great that it, in essence, severed a portion of her spine, leaving no way to repair it."

"What are you saying? There is no way to help her?" Sarah could not process what the doctor was saying.

"I'm sorry, Mrs. Anderson. Your mother is brain-dead. We are getting no responses."

Mark stared at the conference table before him, small tears leaking from the corners of his eyes. "What do we do now?"

"Well, Mr. Williams, there are two options. One is placement in a life-support nursing home."

"Is there any chance she could get better?" Tom asked. But Sarah knew the answer. The look on the doctor's face betrayed him. It was helplessness.

"No. She would live there in a vegetative state."

Sarah gasped.

"No. No. That's not my Patty." Mark looked around the table. He took a deep breath. "Patty and I have Living Wills. We talked about it. You know she would never want to be in some nursing home, hooked up to machines. What kind of life, if you could call it that, what that be?"

"The only other option is disconnection."

George McDonnell donned a visor and flung his golf bag over his shoulder. "You know, you really should talk to her."

"I'm sure she doesn't want me to call." Marian dusted the television, wondering how it could attract so much dirt in only one week. All these electronic devices George insisted upon having, they were constantly filthy.

"You might be surprised." He headed for the door. "I'll be home at six."

She watched as her husband's car pulled out of the driveway, grateful he did not offer to help clean. Last time, he left powder residue in the sink and watermarks all over the faucet. Marian had purified her surroundings every Friday since their first week of marriage, dusting every single possession, washing the floors on her hands and knees, and vacuuming for hours. If a guest would ever see a cobweb dangling from a ceiling corner, Marian would be mortified.

She put down the dust cloth on the side table and sat on the sofa. Her life's routine was interrupted by this estrangement from her daughter, no matter how she denied it. Holidays were not the same, of course, stuck with the geriatrics repeating the same stories over and over until Marian's head spun. Then there was George.

Since she had returned from tea at the Drake, he seemed more distant than usual, rarely speaking at dinner except for the occasional "Would you please pass the parmesan?" when she cooked pasta every second Thursday night of the month. They were never the sort of couple who stayed up into the wee hours discussing the meaning of life or debating social issues, although in their defense, the honeymoon was a short one. Annie was born six months after the wedding, and most of their time was spent setting up house and preparing for the baby. They had achieved a purposeful small talk, shared when dining and periodically throughout the day. That was, until now.

George loved Annie more, that was certain, but it never really bothered Marian, who was grateful he strove to be the model father. Marian was the disciplinarian and schedule keeper. She baked cupcakes for each class party as required. She enforced bedtimes, then curfews. She fed and clothed her daughter. As long as she accomplished those duties, Marian could settle into her own life without guilt. George had played "Chutes and Ladders," attended school talent shows, and drove his daughter to college. One perfect parent was more than most people ended up with. What more did Annie want?

Marian supposed her daughter was dealing with hard times, but she still could not understand why Annie and John did not adopt if they absolutely had to have children and forget this whole other business. She had read an article in one of the women's magazines about infertility treatments. The process sounded painful, emotionally exhausting, and expensive. Did her daughter really want to be a mother that badly? Marian could not imagine it.

While cleaning out the china cabinet drawers, she came across a handprint set in clay and spray-painted gold. "Happy Mother's Day!" Her daughter was so excited when she brought it home. How old was she? Judging by the size, about five. Little Annie ran into her room and got her baby doll Susie. "Some day, my baby is going to get big just like me and bring her handprint home from school. I'm going to hang it up on my wall." Come to think of it, she was always playing house and insisted on bringing Susie everywhere with her, mimicking Marian's every move as they went.

She went into the kitchen and dialed the phone.

Sarah sat down in the living room, hoping the change of venue might clear her mind. The kids were asleep upstairs. It had been a grueling week. Run the kids to Tom's mother's, go to the hospital, pick the kids up, get home, sleep (in theory, at least), and repeat. The doctors told them to wait one full week to see if her mother would show any signs of life. It passed as of today, and now some decisions had to be made.

It was her father's call ultimately, but he had asked Sarah and Greg for their opinions. After all, who would want sole responsibility for ending their spouse's life? It was a decision for the three of them, but was there really a choice to make?

"Sarah, where are you?" Tom came downstairs after checking e-mails.

"In the living room." She sounded so little. He sat down next to her. She looked at him through swollen brown eyes. "How am I supposed to do this?"

"Unfortunately, you have no choice. Do you honestly think Patty Williams would want to spend the rest of her life attached to respirators and monitors existing as a shell?"

"Of course not. But, what if she comes around next week? People do that, you know, what if it happens, and I've made plans to kill her?"

"You are not killing her, honey. She is already dead."

Deep down, Sarah knew this was true. There was no trace of her mom's vitality in the body they visited day after day.

"Maybe you should get a second opinion. Would that help?"

"That's not a bad idea. I'll call Dad and Greg. We can try to get someone in tomorrow." She jumped off the sofa and sprinted toward the phone.

Annie threw a frozen meal in the microwave. It didn't matter which one; she could not taste it anyway. While it cooked, she ran upstairs, anxious to rid herself of the nylons that were digging lines in her stomach. She walked past the temperature chart and thermometer, omnipresent on the nightstand where she slept. The ovulation-predictor test on the vanity. The needles in her medicine cabinet. She glanced over at John's sink, void of Dr. Adams' (or was it Dr. Frankenstein's?) torture devices.

Washing off her makeup, Annie noticed a rash, no, a cluster

of pimples on the left side of her face. There were some on her chin also. Don't read anything into it, she told her reflection, they had to wait at least another week until the pregnancy test.

The microwave's timer had sounded awhile ago. Steam and condensation dripped out when Annie opened its door. The turkey tetrazzini's top was dark brown and crusty. The smell of it flipped her stomach. She threw it in the garbage and made some chamomile tea.

It was six-thirty. Annie knew she had at least an hour before John came home, thank God. His ridiculously positive attitude was the only thing she could identify in the multitude of things that bothered her about him over the past several months. Annie was grateful she did not have to pretend to care about what he discussed when he came home. A day or two ago, annoyance gave way to indifference. She didn't care if he worked eighteen-hour days or if he missed an appointment with Dr. Adams and she had to make up some stupid excuse. It would be just their luck. They would finally get pregnant, but would be estranged. The timer bell rang. Her chamomile tea was steeped. As she opened the trash to throw the tea bag away, the smell of burnt tetrazzini assaulted her nostrils. She ran into the powder room and threw up.

The second opinion confirmed the first prognosis. Patty Williams was brain dead. The family picked today, Tuesday, for disconnection, so the necessary people could say their goodbyes. Sarah laid out the makeup she used every day on the counter in front of her—concealer, eye shadow, eyeliner, foundation, blush and lipstick. If she did not wear mascara, it wouldn't run down her face when she cried. Her puffy eyelids would not hold the eye shadow she tried to apply. Buttercream, it was called. Shades of yellow, she read somewhere, made your eyes look brighter. But even Buttercream's alleged magic would not work on her today. Under her eyes were deep, black circles, which, no matter how hard she tried, would not be hidden.

She searched for something to wear. What does one wear to their mother's death? The thought was too surreal to fully comprehend. "Mom is going to die today" played like a tape on a continuous reel inside her head as she dressed. Sarah grabbed her purse, after forgetting it the first time she tried to leave, and got into the van.

"So what do you think, Dr. Adams?"

"You really should wait the full two weeks before you take the pregnancy test. The results will be more conclusive."

Annie lapped the center island in the kitchen. "But all the symptoms are there. Bloating. Acne. Vomiting. What else could it be?"

"Be careful not to jump the gun. You are receiving progesterone support, and your estrogen level is higher than normal right now. I'm not saying you are not pregnant, but I do think the hormones could be the cause of your symptoms."

"You think so?"

"Let's wait until next week to see."

"Okay. Thank you." Annie hung up the phone and patted her stomach. Just a little longer, sweetie, then they will all know.

At nine thirty, Friday morning, everyone processed to say their final good-byes to Patty Williams. Sarah bent over and touched her mom's hand. She jerked back, stunned by its coldness. "I love you, Mom" seemed so simple, so pat, but it was all she could filter out from the words and feelings inside her that made her dizzy. She watched Tom squeeze her mom's arm and, for the first time in their ten-year marriage, Sarah saw him cry. She put her arm around her father as he spoke to his love.

"Until we meet again, my dearest." He kissed her cheek.

"It's time to go, folks." The funeral director tried to usher them to the limousine, but Sarah just stood there.

"We'll be late for church." Her father put his arm around her.

"I can't go."

Greg took her hand, tears streaking down his face. "It's okay, sweetie, come on."

Mommy! Sarah held her heart, afraid of losing it.

Tom pulled her through the door as the casket lid came down.

In her bed, covers tight around her, Sarah sat shivering despite the unusually warm morning. She could hear Nicky watching cartoons downstairs. No loud banging had come from Alex's room yet signaling his desire to get out of his crib. Whoever thought of forcing a grieving family to host a public event when all they really wanted to do was stay in bed with the covers over their heads? To display that stiff upper lip stoicism that culture values so greatly? When is it okay to fall apart, Sarah wondered, to stare at a blank wall for god knows how long, afraid to close your eyes because every time you do, you see your her mother lying dead in a coffin?

Edwina Hipplewhite had paid her respects at the wake dressed in head-to-toe black lace, offering a kiss on each cheek and a book of bereavement poetry. Thaddeus shook her hand and mumbled "My deepest sympathies." Rosemary, Spring, and Larry all came as well. Catherine was at rehearsals, of all things, Edwina said. The poor girl had finally landed a bit part in a Shakespeare in the Park production for the summer.

Annie had seen the obituary in the newspaper and phoned as soon as she finished reading it. "Sarah, I am so sorry. I just read about your mom."

Grateful to hear Annie's voice, Sarah was unsure what to say. "Thanks for calling."

"Listen, I'm really sorry I didn't respond to your letter. It was just that our slot came up."

"It did? How did…are you…"

"We are waiting for the results. Should hear by Friday, actually." Annie's voice fell. It was the same day as the funeral. She had stayed close by her friend when Tom, Mark, and Greg were busy receiving condolences at the wake on Thursday. Did she need a tissue? A sweater? "Don't forget to eat something. You need to keep up your strength."

The night of the funeral, Annie brought over homemade chicken noodle soup, a loaf of bread, and a box of chocolate. "For you, madam. My cure for the bereaved."

"You didn't have to do this."

"Who wants to cook after the day you have had?"

"Come on in."

"No thanks. You need to be with your family now."

"You are wonderful." Sarah gave Annie a long hug. "How is everything going?"

"Still waiting for the results."

"I have my fingers crossed. Thanks again." Sarah was hesitant to say anything more.

"No problem. Talk to you soon." Annie squeezed Sarah's arm and ran off.

Tending to Sarah gave Annie a chance to do something other than obsess, at least for a little while. She could only imagine what it must feel like to lose your mother/best friend. Annie was almost touched by Marian's last call and olive branch extension, although that was a week ago and she had not heard anything else from her since. Annie didn't bother telling Marian about the procedure. She could not risk any negativity coming her way. No, Marian McDonnell would hear about the pregnancy when it was confirmed and not before.

CHAPTER EIGHTEEN

ANNIE CHECKED THE ANSWERING MACHINE as soon as she got home. "Hello, Mr. and Mrs. Jacobs. This is Debbie from Mitchell Adams and Associates. Your results are in. Please call us at your earliest convenience. Thank you."

"Was that the center?" John arrived home a few minutes later and put down his briefcase.

Annie jumped at the sound. "Yes. The message said the results are in. Damn it! I knew the minute I stepped out, they would call." She began twirling her hair, whipping it, actually. "I couldn't have been gone more than fifteen minutes. All I did was drop off the soup at Sarah's. I've been home all day, goddamn it. What time is it?"

"Just after seven. I'm sure the office is closed now. Doesn't it close at seven on Fridays? We'll have to call tomorrow morning."

"Maybe I can still get them." Annie dialed the familiar telephone number. "Hello. This is Annie Jacobs. I need to speak to Dr. Adams immediately. Well, no, it is not an emergency. Can you page him? Yes, okay, my number is…"

John was in the kitchen. Annie poured herself some water and guzzled it. "I got the service. The woman said she would forward the message."

"Yeah, I thought he wouldn't be there." John looked through the drawer by the phone. "Are you hungry? I was thinking of ordering a pizza."

"No thanks." Annie headed toward the library.

More waiting. Annie moved from sofa to chair to sofa again, incapable of comfort no matter where she sat. She flipped through the TV stations, but there was nothing worth watching. Annie picked up *The Great Gatsby*. She had seen Edwina at the wake who filled her in on next month's selection. After reading the first two sentences of Chapter One five times, Annie threw it across the room. Was she pregnant? Could this hell really be over? After two hours of pacing, crying, and suppressing the urge to drink two bottles of wine (just in case), she fell asleep. John walked into the study and saw Annie in fetal position on the sofa. He covered her with a chenille throw. He had thought about waking her and bringing her up to the bedroom, but somehow knew she would be happier by herself. He went to turn off the light. Annie's journal lay open on the coffee table.

"You can see it in their eyes. A brief moment of surprise, followed by a glance downward to divert attention. My supposed normalcy betrays me, ultimately revealing my fractional existence. I am a trained poodle attired in a ghastly pink tutu, jumping through hoops held by clowns. Denied membership into the world's largest sorority. Denied the very essence of womanhood."

John jolted awake on Saturday morning. What time was it? Six thirty. They had never received a call back from Dr. Adams. He went downstairs to make coffee. Annie had gotten to the kitchen first. She was sitting at the table, holding a cup of that damn fertility tea. He recognized that stench. "Good morning."

"What time does the office open?"

"Nine. Want some breakfast?"

"No. I don't feel like eating now."

"Me neither. I'll give the service another call."

Annie was in the shower when Dr. Adams called. Murphy's Law. John tried not to jump out of his skin when the phone rang. "I'm sorry I could not get back to you last night. I had an emergency. I called as soon as I got in."

"Okay, so…"

"I'm sorry. Neither one of the viable embryos attached."

"Oh."

"I am really sorry."

"I'll tell Annie."

"Please call the office and let us know if you will be attempting another cycle, so we can make the necessary preparations."

"Yes, of course." John hung up the phone. The IVF did not work. They were not pregnant.

Annie dried herself off after the shower and applied a coat of industrial-strength moisturizer. She could not use normal creams (not strong enough) or fru-fru moisturizers from a department store cosmetic counter (burned her sensitive skin). If Annie had to use this product at thirty-eight, what was next? Crisco?

John waited until Annie was dressed, but made sure to interrupt her before she put her makeup on. "Annie?"

She flung around. "What?"

"Dr. Adams called."

"I didn't hear the phone."

"You were in the shower."

"Oh." Annie sat down on the bed, her hands on her knees, bracing. "What did he say?" She could already tell what the outcome was by the tentative look in John's eyes, but she needed to hear the words.

"It didn't work," John said in a small voice.

At first, Annie said nothing.

She just sat there.

All of a sudden, she let out a huge primordial scream, exhaling every stabbing shot, every probing ultrasound device. She grabbed the Basal Body Temperature thermometer and threw it across the room. "Son of a bitch!"

She ran into the bathroom, cleared the counter of all fertility-related items, and hurled them toward the same wall. "Goddamit!"

Then she spied John. "How can you just stand there?"

John had imagined this day. He played out two possible scenarios in his head as he drove home from work yesterday. He even tried to anticipate how Annie would react. He thought for sure she would have crumbled onto the bed, sobbing. Maybe she did not have anymore tears left. Maybe humans only have a certain amount of tears allotted to them, and Annie had used up her ration during the last year. All he knew was that he felt nothing. He was dead inside.

"Well, this confirms it. We are complete biological oddities. The lab experiment failed." Annie glared at John.

"God, just stop it!"

"Most people can get pregnant after three years of trying, insemination, and IVF, John. Most people have two kids by our age. Haven't you paid attention to the statistics?"

"Lay off me, for Christ's sake. It's not my fault." As soon as the words left his mouth, John knew he shouldn't have said them.

Annie walked toward him, a hawk swooping down on her prey. "So that's it, isn't it? It's all me. It could not possibly be you, coming from such a large family, while I come from a line of only children, huh? How dare you spout out words placed in your head by your insane mother and sisters. You think I don't hear them every holiday? 'What's up with John and Annie? I'm sure *he's* always wanted kids, so it must be her.' 'She's too selfish to have children. Maybe it's better this way.' I can always count on Goneril and Regan to throw an Annie love-fest."

"Oh, please. It's so easy for you to make me out as a puppet, isn't it? Well forget it. I'm not playing along this time. You have held our childlessness against me every day for the past three years. You don't think I notice, do you?"

Annie stood still. "I don't know what you are talking about."

"Of course not. You are too mired in your own self-pity to pay attention to anyone around you. I see the disappointment in your eyes. I know our marriage has failed you. It hasn't produced the one thing you have wanted your entire life, a real family, not like the facsimile you grew up with. Try living with that every day."

"Do not insult my family. At least no one blubbers at every single holiday toast like your mother, whether it's Thanksgiving or goddamn St. Patrick's Day."

"I know this concept is foreign to you, people showing emotions other than depression, but my mother actually loves me and my sisters."

"Too bad there is no room in her heart for the daughter-in-law who could not produce the heir of her beloved son."

"Come off it. She asks how you are doing all the time."

"That surprises the shit out of me."

"Maybe if you rejoined the human race you would see."

"Shut up," Annie hissed.

"I am so sick of seeing your crying face every day. You are not the one to be talking about tears, Annie dear, you have shed enough to fill Lake Michigan. Most men get to come home and get some sort of welcome, even if it's just from the dog. I come home to nothing."

"If you even bothered to come home at a decent time.

Since when is midnight acceptable? Do you expect me to stay up, waiting to greet you wearing nothing but an apron? All hail the Neanderthal." Annie bowed.

"I do not think being greeted by someone who is genuinely happy to see me because she happened to get home from work earlier than I did unreasonable. Don't you dare pull that caveman crap on me. I'm the one who cleans and takes care of the house. You don't do a damn thing anymore. All you can do is brew that smells-like-shit tea and go on and on about how miserable your life is. Well, I'm sorry, Annie, but I am miserable too."

"Congratulations."

"God, you are such a bitch." John walked past her.

"How dare you!" Annie slapped him.

John held his fists clenched, but continued to walk across the bedroom.

"If you think I am going to the reunion with you tonight, you are delusional. You can go screw yourself for all I care," Annie yelled as he went down the hall.

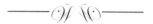

This time it was John who escaped to the library, though not on the chaise. That would be "too Annie," and John was, by no means, in the mood for anything Annie. He checked out the selections on the CD player. The ever-present *The Wall.* Wagner. The world's most depressing music collection. Here we go, some Peter Gabriel. John poured a scotch, not caring that it was only ten thirty in the morning, and sat back in the over-sized chair.

As if things were not bad enough, now he had to deal with the goddamn reunion. John thought he had five more years until such an ordeal, but St. Joe's restructured its reunion system last fall. Alumni relations decided to cluster graduating years in groups of five, so attendees could see more of the people they spent their college years with. This, however, conflicted with twenty years as an acceptable number at which to look into a mirror and say "look how I've matured... look what I've achieved" without choking. Besides, John was counting on those extra five years to make partner at Murdock and Stoddard, and, oh, yes, there was that nasty little thing about infertility.

He could only imagine how wonderful it would be seeing offspring photos of all the ex-friends who made him into a pariah after the Melanie break-up. Then there was the person herself to contend with. For no matter that he and Annie had been married right after college, everyone at St. Joe's still linked John and Melanie in the same sentence. Even Fred, one of the few who stood by John when he was shunned, was careful to note in his e-mail of two months ago that Melanie had not responded yet, so it probably would be safe to come.

John had responded positively to the reunion invitation six months ago so everyone could see how happy he and Annie were, how perfect they were together. What was he going to do now? He would have to show and make up some BS excuse why Annie was not there. She was sick. Yeah, sick in the head.

He would have to deal with seeing everyone alone, which was not very appetizing. He still remembered the looks he received the day after he broke up with Melanie. They all held him personally responsible for the disillusionment of at least fifty sorority girls and, consequently, their whipped boyfriends who had to endure the re-telling of the story as forewarning. When John and Annie got together in Rome, word around the Greeks was it had to be a rebound affair. He was sowing his oats with someone from another school before he came back to Melanie to beg forgiveness and ask her hand in marriage.

He chugged the scotch and slumped back into the chair.
"Is that a dagger or a crucifix I see?
You hold so tightly in your hands?
And all the while the distance grows between you and me.
I do not understand."

Was this guy married to Annie too? He tipped his glass to Peter Gabriel, a comrade in misery.

Annie washed her face, stripping away the artifice, until she was left with only the truth staring out from the mirror. Deep crevices digging in under swollen eyes. Pimples erupting violently from hormones dotted her otherwise unblemished skin. Meager strands of hair weakly covering naked patches of scalp from stress. So this was what she had become. This was all Annie had to show for it. The hours, months, years of false hope, of being subjected to medical procedures so intrusive Annie was left without her humanity. Of estrangement from the man who used to be her best friend, but now was another complication she could not face. She put on her pajamas and crawled into bed.

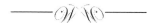

John had managed to avoid Annie all Saturday afternoon, which was not really all that difficult, considering she had burrowed herself in their bedroom the entire time. The only tricky part was getting dressed for the evening. As soon as his second foot crossed the master suite's threshold, Annie jumped off the bed and ran downstairs. "Good-bye to you, too," he shouted down the hall.

What was he getting himself into? Of course, at least he

could be somewhere else other than the morgue he lived in. Some radio station was into its second hour of flashing back to the eighties while he drove. John pushed the clicker to lock his Lexus.

"Hey, you old bastard!" It was Fred, along with a stunning redhead.

"Freddy." John greeted him with a hug.

"This is Fiona." Fred put his arm around her. She extended her hand to John. "Nice to meet you."

"A pleasure." This must be the wife number two Fred wrote about in the e-mail. The first, clearly a Midwesterner, must not have held enough intrigue for his old roommate, who changed girlfriends as often as sixteen-year-old girls change outfits on a Friday night.

"It's good to see you, sir." Fred smiled.

"Sir!" They heard a yell as they neared the dining hall. It was Bill, their other roommate. They high-fived, the three of them, two wives watching from the sidelines, the third at home wishing she were dead. They all entered the large wooden door under the gargoyle. It was 1986 again.

Faces from the past, altered by time enough to make some difficult to recognize off-hand, enveloped him. John was never very good at names, a trait he vowed he would change but never did. An exceedingly tall man was talking to a balding version of that guy who lived next-door to him freshman year…Jack… wait, he had it, Jack Taylor. Congratulating himself, he strode toward them. The tall one's name tag read Charlie O'Shea. Could it be? Charlie O'Shea was a thin, scrawny little scamp of a guy known as first floor's resident chess geek. Granted, they had lost contact after freshman year, when John moved to another dorm and Charlie settled into the computer science department, which some said he never left, but could it be? John guessed there were always those "geek turned Greek God" stories at reunions or, on the female side, the ugly ducking who blossomed into a swan cliché. No such luck for Stella Wichowski, whom everyone called "The Troll," still as portly and haggard as ever, talking with, hey, that's Kathy Cochran.

John joined Fred, Bill, and wives to claim a table for dinner. Stories of parties gone by, the prank of the century, and the mysterious stench that had emitted from the guy's dorm flew around.

"Where's your wife, John?" Bill was cutting his salad.

"Oh, unfortunately, she is sick tonight."

"Too bad. I don't think I ever met her." Bill was hiking through Germany and could not attend the wedding.

John gulped his wine and poured another. The obligatory child photos began circulating. He pretended to admire them, passing the pictures on with an "Oh, how cute!" and another drink of wine.

"Any kids, John?" This time it was Fred.

"No, not yet." Indicating hope would be better than nothing, right?

Fred and Bill exchanged looks. John could read their minds. Phantom wife. No kids. Maybe he would have been better off marrying Melanie. John drained another glass. "More wine anyone? Fiona, tell me about your boys." John heard random words. Baseball. Soccer. Trumpet. To each, he raised a silent toast. More missed experiences. Thankfully, dinner was over, and John was free to circulate. Sissy Bartholomew appeared at the microphone. John supposed she had a different last name now and a throng of kids. Goodie for her.

"Welcome everyone." She bent over the too-low microphone, unaware it could easily be raised. "Since I was president of the class of 1986, they asked if I'd say a few words. First, it is great to see you all again." Sissy flashed her still perfect smile. Caps. With age came the wisdom that the former cheerleader's toothy grin could never have been that perfect naturally. They used to debate the topic for hours, along with fantasizing about how flexible she really was. John could not help but wonder that now as he got closer to the small stage. Sissy still looked great. John felt flushed. Damn red wine. The room's decibel level had increased and not only because of the music. He was not the only one partaking this evening.

They used to have Winter Formal in these rooms, set up very much like this evening, but with an enormous Christmas tree sitting directly opposite the hearth. The seniors usually decorated it the Monday after Thanksgiving, and, somehow every year it was beautiful. Every year, that is, but his senior year, when some numbnuts bought the tree from the same lot where Charlie Brown shopped. Every time someone brushed past while running to class, at least ten needles came falling down. Needless to say, by Winter Formal many a branch lay bare. The tree was little more than a stick screwed into a stand, garland half-draped around two branches, a Norma Desmond Douglas Fir awaiting her close-up.

"Let's get this party started," a cheeky voice from behind the deejay table called out, then played "Like a Virgin," as if John's slightly spinning head was not enough to make him nauseous. He should have played "Burning Down the House," the official party-starting song of their generation. Or the Violent Femmes. Or The Cure.

"John Jacobs! Well, isn't that something! You sure are looking good." Sue whatever-the-hell-her-last-name-is-now was right in his face, her hands on both of his shoulders.

He backed away. "How are you, Sue?" Melanie's sorority sister, Sue Hyden-Smith, as her name tag read, had spearheaded the campaign against him and was Melanie's biggest advocate.

"Oh, just wonderful. Great marriage. Three kids. And you?" Sue looked around, noticing John was alone.

"Fine, thank you. My wife is home sick, though," adding "but she still wanted me to come. That's Annie. Very selfless." The words gagged him.

"Sounds like an angel."

Sarcastic or condescending? John was not sure which. "Well, good to see you, as always. I'm going to get a drink. Would you like something?"

Sue patted her stomach. "Oh, no, no. Can't."

John had not even noticed she was pregnant. Maybe if he made his way to the bar with his head down, he would not have to run into anyone else he was ill prepared to encounter.

"John!" Fred was there—an oasis. "What can I order for you?"

"Vodka tonic. I was just accosted by Sue."

"Who? Boo-hoo Sue? Oh, Christ. I think I'll join you. Two vodka tonics, please." Fred turned sideways to face John. "How's business?"

"I'm this close to making partner." He squeezed his thumb and pointer fingers close together.

"Great. Lawyer, right?"

John nodded. "How about you? I assume you finally made up your mind after grad school."

"Yup. Got my MBA, my first wife, and a dog. Quit Arthur Anderson. Divorced the wife. Dog died. My dad got sick, so I went to work at his company. Cancer, but he's in remission now. I'm still there. He's CEO. I'm CFO. It works." Fred's dad decided to become a builder after owning several quickie marts. Ground was broken for the first during their junior year. From what John had read in *Crain's Chicago Business*, they were now developing entire communities. "I met Fiona on a three-week Scotland excursion and brought her back with me."

"You're shitin' me."

Fred laughed. "No, really."

"Brigadoon, my friend." They lifted their glasses.

John patted Fred on the back. "I'll be back in a second." He had to piss like a racehorse. Weaving through the crowd, he tried to remember where the rest rooms were. Down the hall, to the right.

"I hope you're not leaving already."

John swirled around. It was Melanie.

"You look surprised." Her eyes twinkled, amused at his confusion. He was sweating just above the brow. "Don't worry, I left all projectiles at home. You're safe. Truce?" She held out her hand. As they shook, Melanie drew him into a hug, whispering in his ear, "I'm sorry I threw that book at you."

"Book? It was *The Complete Works of Shakespeare*. Damn near knocked me unconscious." He had seen Melanie only once after returning from Rome. She was coming out of the library and he was walking in. She had heard of his proposal to Annie. In a fit of rage, she had hurled the massive volume at him and ran out in tears.

Melanie laughed. "Not good enough aim, I guess. I was trying to kill you. Not a clean hit, though. Too many witnesses." She smiled. "It's good to see you, John."

"Could you excuse me for one second? I'll be right out."

John sprinted toward the men's washroom. He splashed some cold water on his face and ran his fingers through his hair. What the hell? Everyone said she wasn't coming. He pulled at his shirt collar, which now felt tighter than usual. His mind was whirling eighty miles per hour. He adjusted his suit coat and went out.

Melanie was looking at the recent class photos hanging in the hall, her hands crossed behind her back. "They all look so full of promise, don't they? Do you remember graduating thinking you could conquer the world?"

"No, actually I realized how much I didn't know as soon

as I donned the cap and gown and spent the rest of the day catatonic."

She punched his arm. "You did not."

"Yes, I did. I had this stupid business major, but no burning desire to really do anything. It took me awhile before I figured it out."

"Well something must have clicked. I think I read in the reunion booklet you're an attorney now?"

"Yes. Murdock and Stoddard downtown."

"Very impressive. Of course, you always did have a good tongue."

Their eyes met. John coughed. "So what have you been up to, Melanie?"

"Let's get a drink. Maybe we can find a little nook to talk in." She guided him back into the Social Hall. "This place reminds me of Winter Formal," she yelled, nearing the bar.

"I was thinking the same thing earlier."

Melanie smiled. "Still vodka tonics?"

John nodded. "You too?"

"Always."

They found seats in the far corner of the Social Hall. Melanie sat back in one of the big burgundy velvet chairs and crossed her legs. "I always loved these chairs. We spent many an evening here, didn't we?" John and Melanie were reigning Trivial Pursuit champions junior year, often challenged by naive newcomers. They won cases of beer, free lunches, and even a slave for a day once. Melanie shook her head. "You made poor Bob do all of your laundry."

"Hey, he just so happened to make the bet on the last day I had any clean underwear. What can I say?" They sat back, absorbing the scene. John finished his drink. "So you never told me what you've been up to."

"Well, I went to law school, too. I'm a patent attorney

in Milwaukee. I needed a little change after graduation, so I went to school up there. Anyhow, it's been good. I have a great place right on Lake Michigan, near the art museum. It's really beautiful."

"Hope you haven't become a Packer fan."

"No way. I still wear my Bears jersey faithfully every Sunday."

"That's what I always loved about you, Mel. You're one brazen chick."

"You bet. Remember going downtown for the parade after we won the Super Bowl? We must have partied for five days straight."

"Listened to 'We are the Champions' sixty-five times."

"Wore Bear attire every single day. Hoo. Hoo. Hoo." She howled like a junkyard dog, then suddenly changed expressions. "Where's your wife? Is she here? I hope I didn't steal you away or anything."

"Annie? Oh, no. She didn't come. Not feeling well."

"I'm sorry to hear that. Nothing serious, I hope."

"She'll be okay, thanks. What about you? Have you stranded your husband with Sue?"

Melanie shook her head. "I'm not married. Never quite found the right guy, I guess." She shifted in her seat. "Hey, did I tell you? I am staying in my old room at Gamma, can you believe it? They opened up the house for out-of-town alums."

The deejay returned after his break. "Let's start this second set with Modern English's 'I Melt with You.'" It was their song. Melanie put down her glass, stood up, and extended her hand. "Shall we?"

"Sure. What the heck?"

It didn't matter that Melanie gained a few pounds since college. We all have, John thought. What really mattered was that she was something Annie was not—happy.

CHAPTER NINETEEN

THE GRIEF WAS PHYSICALLY A part of Sarah now, like the open cut on her left-hand pointer finger that kept getting re-injured from thoughtlessly bumping it while changing Alex's diaper. She was attuned to tragedy around her, feeling other's losses as her own. Unable to control herself, she read the obituaries on Wednesdays, Fridays, and Sundays when the newspaper arrived at the Anderson house. Before Nicky was born, Sarah and Tom were daily newspaper recipients, but parenthood had stolen any extra time spent on current events. The papers went unread, stacking up a large pile of missed opportunities. She still had to go on living, everyone told her. Some had even uttered this nonsense while standing in front of Patty's coffin at the wake. How? How exactly does one go about doing that?

Sarah supposed the obituary people's families were told the same thing by awkward mourners on parade. Sometimes she tried to guess how each died by reading what organizations their families listed in lieu of flowers. American Cancer Society. Sad. Rainbow Hospice. Long, terminal illness. Horrible. There was no "freak of nature, lightening-induced car crash society," so her father thought it best to give the money to a home for orphans at which Patty volunteered.

———— ⁂ ————

For Mark Williams, every day life went on as usual. It was the extraordinary he would have issue with. He and his wife were full equals in their relationship. Patty was no martyr. She had no desire to control the house and welcomed sharing the chores with her husband. His daughter need not worry if Mark's laundry was done or if he had eaten a decent meal, like so many men of his generation who were incapable of any domesticity. Mark would merely have to incorporate cooking and paying bills into his schedule, along with a little grocery shopping. But what about holidays or birthdays? Creating special memories was Patty's talent and hers alone, whether it was knowing the right number of ornaments to hang on the tree or finding the perfect gift for the kids.

Mark sat down on the bed, their bed, the one he had shared with Patty for less than a year. The Williams both had back trouble, made worse by a lumpy old mattress they had slept on since Sarah was little. They finally purchased the new bed and their backs were improving. Chiropractor visits were down to once a month. Since that issue was settled, they had began discussing when Mark would retire from the bank and were planning on two years from last January, so they would receive the full Social Security benefits. Mark sighed. He might as well work until he was unable to now. What else would he have to do?

All the dreams of traveling to places they could never seem to afford while raising the kids were for naught. There would be no Caribbean cruise. No Vermont in autumn. No Turkey. Mark smiled for a second. Patty had always wanted to see Turkey; he was not sure why. She had talked to someone, a friend of a friend, who told her Turkey was a wonderful destination. "Most of the people speak English, so language wouldn't be an issue. And it's so exotic." Her eyes would get so large when she was excited, Mark couldn't help but smile, just for an instant, until reality invaded. But instead of spending retirement globe trotting, God saw it fit to pluck her out of this world and make Mark suffer the ramifications. He knew death was a part of life, yadda, yadda, yadda, but rhetoric is of little consequence when you lose the love of your life.

They were high school sweethearts, after all. Patty sang in the church choir during the nine thirty Mass at St. Cecelia's. Mark had watched her every Sunday, there in the front row. One morning, she sang a solo, "Ave Maria," and that was it. He had heard the voice of an angel. It took him several months to work up enough courage to ask her out. He passed her in the school hallways with his head down. One day, she gave him a small smile when he handed her change back at Jone's Five and Ten, where he worked part-time to save up money for his own car. Week after week, Mark stood in the back of church, feigning interest in the bulletin, hoping to make eye contact with her as the choir passed after Mass.

One such Sunday, Patty walked by him on her way to handing in her music folder. She stopped, turned around, and said "hi." He blushed and returned the greeting. Weeks of helloes turned into "The choir sounded great today" and "Don't you work at the dime store?"

When she said yes to his offer of a movie and a cheeseburger, all was right with the world. They dated for two years in high school and maintained a long-distance courtship through college, he at St. Francis, she at St. Mary's, although he had the more difficult time since St. Mary's was an all-girl institution, while St. Francis was co-ed. Patty told Mark during their sophomore year, and these were her exact words, he remembered them as clear as day, she would "rip his head off and pour maggots down his throat" if he ever cheated on her. The angel had an edge, which he was grateful for. It kept her off the pedestal and grounded in humanity.

Mark supposed he'd better take a shower. It was Saturday, and he had made an appointment with J.C. King and Sons Monuments to pick out Patty's headstone. His stomach flipped at the thought. He had been thinking of what it should look like and what it should say, but he was coming up empty. "Dear wife and mother" seemed so little, so mundane, to sum up a life. She was so much more, and Mark wanted to show the world that. Yet, realistically, Patty would never want him to spend a fortune on something so silly. He took a deep breath and started his day.

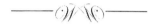

Annie emerged from the master suite at three o'clock on Tuesday afternoon. For many hours that morning, she had sat propped up in bed, a Raggedy Ann doll no one would play with. Alone. Unshowered. Unfed. John had moved his clothes and pillow into the guest room on Sunday. She remembered hearing something about him wondering if she intended to leave the bed, to which her response was to throw the remote control at him. Having no energy to retrieve it, the television had remained on a muted cable news station twenty-four hours a day for the past three days.

She slept for twelve hours straight from Sunday to Monday, which suited John just fine and afforded him time to grab his forgotten shaving cream and deodorant from the bathroom without Annie's knowledge. He had no desire for anything else to be flung at his throbbing head, having not felt this hung over since he had dry-heaved for an hour after the annual freshman quarters championships. Sprite and saltine crackers were all his body could handle, and he, too, spent most of Sunday asleep.

On Tuesday, she walked downstairs, Annie Van Winkle

descending the mountain, unaccustomed to the sunlight after hiding behind room-darkening roman shades. Obviously, life had gone on without her. There were no dirty dishes in the sink. No piles of mail to be searched through. John had taken care of everything per usual, bastard. *Wonder how the reunion went? After what he said to you? Who cares?*

Annie began filling the teapot with water, but stopped. There was no need for fertility tea. It obviously didn't work. Taking the unused boxes from the pantry, she pitched each one, cheering herself with every swish into the trash. She would make black tea, *caffeinated* black tea, which had not passed her lips for three years after reading that too much caffeine can somehow affect fertility. While the tea steeped, Annie whipped up some scrambled eggs and toast. Her stomach gurgled. It was used to only bathroom tap water for the last three days. Eating was a good thing. Annie made herself another piece of toast and sat down at the kitchen table.

What was she going to do today? For the first time since she could not remember when, Annie had nothing to do. No doctor appointments. No medications to take. Nothing to chart. No job to go to. Nothing. A shower? She lifted her arm and sniffed. Yes, she would definitely take a shower. She felt her legs. And shave, too.

Wednesday, Annie did a load of laundry. Thursday, she reorganized the junk drawer. By the end of the month, she had cleaned every room in the house, washing all walls, floors, draperies, linens, and cabinets. She had power-washed the outside and the deck, cleaned the gutters, and shined the windows.

She had even gone as far as to use her mother's tried and true mixture of dishwashing liquid and vinegar to clean each piece of crystal they owned, including vases, until they sparkled when the light shone through the window and rested upon the china cabinet. This was a feat, indeed, for it had never been done for the entire time they inhabited 208 W. Muirfield. Her mother, of course, performed the ritual each April along with countless homages to the season that beget spring cleaning, Marian McDonnell's Olympics.

She boxed up the torture devices and placed them in her closet, hesitant to throw them away, although she supposed some decision had to be made whether or not they would attempt another cycle. She had not gotten that far in her thought process, since that would require actually talking with John, something she had avoided for weeks now. It was the longest the Jacobs had ever gone without speaking. An occasional grunt could be heard between them when one stepped in the other's way, which seemed to happen more than usual. Annie was not about to let fate's hand to push her anywhere she was unwilling to go. The blow-out had spewed more than a year's worth of poison, which would not be easily rectified in one month's time. The other day, Annie could have sworn she caught him looking at her, but when she turned around, he'd left the room.

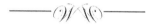

Every so often, the faint scent of cooking oats floated past Sarah's nose as she pushed Alex's stroller around the block for their almost-daily walk. A manufacturing plant was maybe two miles away, and on certain days when the wind was just right, their neighborhood became scented with the sweetness of baking cereal. It reminded her of coming home from school to a house filled with the aroma of baking Christmas cookies. Five different kinds, at least two batches each. There were red and green buttery spritz shaped like trees and wreaths, chocolate crinkles with powdery tops and chewy insides, thumbprints filled with raspberry jam and sprinkled with nuts, everyone's favorite chocolate chips, and Mom's private stash of oatmeal scotchies, which remained hidden until Christmas Eve when she semi-grudgingly shared them with the family. Sarah never did get Patty to reveal her hiding spot. Now she would never know.

"Mama?" Alex looked at her.

She leaned down. "I'll be okay, sweetie. I miss Grandma right now."

Alex reached up and gave his mom a huge hug. Sarah held him tight. What did her mom do all day in heaven? Did she have a job there? Probably something hospitality-related, like a greeter or tour guide. Oh, what the hell was she thinking? Heaven was not some Wal-Mart! Sarah wished she could talk to Patty one more time to make sure she was okay. To ensure heaven does not erase memories of people on earth. To ask her if she missed them as much as Sarah missed her.

For John, every day was a carbon copy of the preceding. Work. Eat dinner alone at miscellaneous fast-food restaurant on the way home. Sleep, still in the guest room. Leave early in the morning before Annie woke up. He did not dare to think, for that would bring his meaningless existence crashing down around him. Why didn't they accept their childlessness? What possessed such a grandiose attempt to cheat biology? Maybe Marian McDonnell wasn't speaking out of her ass. Maybe in her skewed view, she was onto something when she mentioned adoption. Of course, Annie could never resist the urge to do the exact opposite of what her mother wanted, so adoption was ruled out as soon as Marian mentioned it. John laced up his running shoes and headed out.

Soon after he began his run, shin splints jabbed his calves; he had begun too quickly and forgot to stretch out. He took it down a notch. His muscles loosened, and he settled into a good pace, a brief chill jolting his system. It had been a cold, rainy couple of weeks, which, even for the Chicago area, was odd in late spring. When he entered the zone, as John called around the second mile when he began to feel like he could run forever, images flooded his mind's gates. Dinner at the reunion. Talking at the bar with Fred. Sitting in Melanie's room. He shook his head, wishing the human brain's memory capacity was nothing more than an Etch-A-Sketch, and a few good shakes could dislodge the last two years.

When Sarah closed her eyes at night, her mind found its way back to the hospital room. There, the droll hum of the flat-lined heart monitor bored into her soul. She had tried reading before bed to combat this, and while doing so, irritated Tom through the large side table light that intruded upon his slumber. His wife offered to read downstairs and get in bed when she was tired, but that also woke him up. She had no choice but to deal with his snide comments of "Now I know why husbands and wives used to have separate bedrooms," as he pulled his covers over and constructed a bed linen cocoon around him.

"I can't help it, Tom."

"How am I supposed to be functional at work? I need more than six hours of sleep."

"What if I put the TV on low? That way the light would be off." Sarah reached over him for the remote and settled in.

Tom tossed about like a freshly caught fish, punctuating his movements with groans of exasperation.

Sarah sat up and turned on the light. "You are such a jerk."

"What now? Turn that light off." He turned to face her.

"No. I told you the reason I can't fall asleep, and you don't care."

"That's not fair. I loved your mom."

"I wish you'd act like you loved me."

"You are ridiculous."

"See? I can't even voice my opinion. You dismiss me like a child. I stood there and watched my mother die."

"I was there too."

"It wasn't your mother."

"Listen, can we talk about this some other time? I have an eight-thirty meeting tomorrow." He shut off the light.

She turned it back on. "No. There is no other time. You are always working."

"Here we go again. Tell me more about how negligent I am as I work my butt off to afford this house and all of our expenses."

"Oh yes, the great provider. There is more to parenting than bringing home a paycheck. There is more to marriage than a peck on the cheek and a long weekend in Boston once every ten years."

"I don't understand you." Tom sat up. "What more do you want from me?"

"I would like you to spend some time with me and the boys."

"Once I get through this project, I'll…"

Sarah put her hand up. "Save it. I've heard it all before." She turned off the light and rolled over, staring into the darkness. Once again, she found herself walking down the hospital corridor.

CHAPTER TWENTY

*A*NNIE BEGAN MAKING SMALL FORAYS into the real world. To the post office for stamps. For a walk around the neighborhood. To the video store to rent a movie. At last, she felt ready for the coffeehouse and prayed to God she would not run into anyone she knew.

Sipping her chai, Annie sat at the counter, watching the Napervillians going about their Saturdays. A white SUV came barreling down Main Street, its driver barely slowing down to make the turn onto Jefferson. Seemingly determined to kill herself one way or another, she zoomed down the street, cell phone in one hand, cigarette and steering wheel in the other, swerving from lane to lane on the narrow street, nearly side-swiping the Jaguar parked in front of the Mexican restaurant across the way. Grandpa Arthur's favorite pet phrase flashed into her mind. "Like a bat out of hell."

"Watch out, Annie. You came tearing around the corner like a bat out of hell. Where's the fire? Marian! Why are you running around like a bat out of hell? Ease up, dear. It's only Thanksgiving." Smirking, Arthur would retreat to the living room, martini in hand, and settle in to enjoy the company of others banished from his daughter-in-law's kitchen.

Marian had taken over the holidays pretty early on in her marriage, after Arthur's wife, Virginia, served canned jellied cranberry sauce and a refrigerated Cabernet one Thanksgiving. That simply would not do. Come to think of it, Annie could not remember one holiday on which her mother was not scurrying about. Maybe Valentine's Day? Pink hearts and roses were not a McDonnell favorite. Marian poo-pooed the day, lamenting over the made-up sentiments. What was the big deal, anyway?

She had dropped off a peace offering of Annie's favorite double-fudge brownies during the seclusion, but made up some excuse why she could not stay. George had kept uncharacteristically quiet, opting for e-mail as his preferred method of communication, which was fine because otherwise she would have had to deal with a melancholic, almost June Jacobs-like George McDonnell. He was a stiff-upper-lip guy about everything except when his daughter was hurt. First in the room after Annie had cut her hand on Aunt Harriet's crystal vase, he had just stood there, eyes wide and mouth open. Frustrated, Marian admonished him as she wrapped Annie's tiny hand in a towel and whisked her off to the hospital.

Fortunately, June had also stayed away. She did, however, send a bouquet of irises with a note saying she hoped Annie would not lose faith. Too late. Her mother-in-law had begun making an effort to talk with Annie a little more when she called, instead of asking for John right away, which turned out to not be as creepy as Annie would have thought. Joy had also phoned, and Julie sent a brief e-mail. That was big for them.

Two girls burst through the door, clad in hip-hugger jean shorts and black spaghetti-strapped tank shirts, hoop earrings, and flip-flops. Indistinguishable except for one's ringlet locks, they took seats facing each other at a bistro table and waited for their drinks to be called. They were having a conversation, it was true, only not with each other, but on their cell phones instead. Not the same conversation, mind you, not to meet up with a common third party, oh no, with completely different people. Annie hated to stare, but she couldn't help herself. It was so odd to see two people out together yet not.

"Tony? Oh, say hi to him," was the only spoken line of dialogue from straight brown hair to curly. When they finished their beverages, which happened to sync up with completing their last phone calls at least from that locale, they rose in unison and left, living symbols of society's communication breakdown. Annie rose and threw out her cup, dialing her own phone as she walked.

"John Jacobs."

"Hi."

"Annie? Is everything okay?"

"Will you be finished soon?"

"Um, eh, let me see." John had gone into the office today to make some headway on the new case he was given on Thursday, or at least that's what his note said.

"Will you be home for dinner tonight?"

"I'm not sure...um..."

"I thought maybe we could talk."

"Oooookay."

"What time?"

"How about..."

Annie could hear papers shuffling in the background.

"...seven? That will give me enough time to wrap things up here."

"Sure. Maybe I'll even cook." Her lame attempt at humor fell on deaf ears. They both knew she had not made a meal for God knows how long. "Okay. See you at seven."

John sat back in his chair. What was that about? She goes from not acknowledging my existence to "Let's have dinner?" He finished his work, not wanting to be late, then braced himself for the evening ahead.

Annie arranged the china, wedding gifts from George and Marian's friends which, prior to this evening, had been stored untouched in boxes. There. White roses and candles. Wine chilling in a silver champagne bucket. Perfect.

John emerged from the guest room toweling off his hair. "Wow! Nice. Should I change?"

"No, but you might want to lose the towel. Have a seat."

The Jacobs sat down for their first dinner together in three months. "I ordered some yellowfin sashimi." Annie passed the tray to her husband.

"Thanks." John was surprised she even remembered how much he liked it, considering it had been so long since they had eaten sushi. Annie had refused to even go near the stuff once she read it might be harmful to unborn children. He looked around the dining room, unsure where to rest his gaze. It was unusually clean. Even the glasses sparkled in the china cabinet. Marian would be proud, though he hardly thought that would be a welcome observation.

"I walked around downtown Naperville for a little while today."

"Really? That's great. It looked like a nice day, at least through my office window." Not wanting to sound like a martyr, he quickly added, "It was a bit warmer when I went for my run this morning."

Annie knew John was up to many miles a day, though how many she was not sure. She told him of the phone girls. "They reminded me of my parents. I always swore I would never be like them, yet here we are."

John was scared to say anything, so he merely nodded.

"I'm thinking of going back to work. If I take too much time off, they might realize they don't need me." Annie looked into her husband's eyes, trying to gauge his reaction.

"Are you sure?"

"It's time, John. I cannot live like this anymore. Insemination. In vitro. It's too much. My body can't take it. I am raising the white flag."

Dead silence.

She continued. "Um, I guess we need to talk about what this means."

John had been debating that very topic during his run every day for the last month. Adoption? Forget kids and work on our marriage?

"I want my life back. I mean, I want *our* life back. I let things get way out of control. I am so sorry. I am such an idiot. I know things can't be the same after all of this, but…"

The phone rang.

"Let the machine get it." Annie reached for her husband's hand.

"John, if you're there, please pick up. It's Melanie. I really need to talk to you."

He bolted for the phone and hurried into the study, leaving Annie and a barely eaten sushi platter alone in the dining room.

"Stupid Tom," Sarah muttered, pushing the lawn mower, trying not to roll over her foot. "I hope his system crashes."

Her husband had laughed so hard when she told him she was going to do this, he snorted soda through his nose. "What? Princess Sarah deigning to do peon work? I wish I could be there." But of course, he was not, hence the reason for Sarah's inaugural mowing. "Well, I can't wait for you any longer. I damn near lost Alex in it yesterday."

Tom attempted to sound defensive, muffling laughter. "I can't help it. I'm in San Diego."

"By the time you'd get around to it, I'd be wearing a long

calico skirt, and the boys would be calling you 'Pa.'" How dare Tom make her sound so pampered. Her brother cut the grass when they were teenagers. Sarah cleaned the bathrooms. That was how the chores were divided up. Tom would not scrub a toilet bowl to save his life.

"So, how are they?" Tom threw out the question.

Convenient diversion, Sarah thought, wondering if he even cared. She used to think the kids were their number one priority, but now it was clear only she prescribed to that. The great and powerful job had taken Nicky and Alex's place for her husband. Sarah wondered why Tom had bothered to marry and have a family. His life would be much simpler without them, she was certain. Maybe it was that masculine pride, continuing the family line thing. She was beginning to feel used.

Sarah's arms hurt from pushing the mower. This was taking longer than she thought. Didn't Tom usually finish in an hour? She had been out there for well over that and still had a bit more of the yard to go.

Alex pulled his bubble-blowing lawn mower out of the shed and walked alongside her. "Hi, Mama."

"Hey, sweetie. You cutting the grass too?"

He nodded, stopping every four feet to pop an iridescent sphere between his hands.

Nicky parked his bike against the house and walked toward Sarah. He had been riding around the block with Adam.

He eyed her strangely. "Your legs are covered with grass."

"Yes they are. Some day all of this pleasure will be yours." Sarah wiped her sweat-ridden face with the bottom of her tee shirt, leaving makeup stains. "Oh well. I have to take a shower anyhow. Finished at last. Why don't you guys go inside? I'll get you something to drink and you can relax for a bit while I clean up. Okay? Nicky, put your bike in the garage. Alex put away your bubble mower. Want to watch a movie? Nicky, could you pop one in please? Nothing too scary for Alex." Sarah trudged to the shower, each stair bringing a new level of pain.

Outdoor maintenance was now Sarah's permanent chore. "Crunch time, you know." Yes, Tom, she knew. More trips out of town. More dinner meetings. More shutting himself up in the office on weekends. So she developed her own lawn-care routine, even incorporating seasonal fertilizer and grub-be-gone or whatever it was called. The other day, Sarah went to the hardware store and inquired about an edger. She and the boys went on field trips to the plant nursery, wandered through landscape ideas, and purchased *Gardening Basics for Dummies*, along with a set of tools and gloves for each of them.

Sarah, Nicky, and Alex stood on the patio, surveying the yard. "All right, boys. Put on your gloves, and let's get to work." The three marched over to a mass of brown sticks on the left side of the house. From bed to bed, they assessed what had survived the winter, which was not much by the look of it. Tom was not one for flowers. Small evergreen hedges with a row of something or another in front was his extent. Any more would not be prudent.

There was not much to work with, at least nothing that would provide a decent beginning to her glorious gardening master plan. From her talks with Carolyn, her expert neighbor who had won the subdivision award for best garden three years running, Sarah now knew what she envisioned would take a complete restructuring of the existing beds, rototilling, edging, the list went on. It was nearing the end of prime planting season. Another month or so, and nothing would take properly. There was only one option. "Boys, I have an amendment to our plan. I'm going to make a few phone calls. You go play on the swings, and then we'll start gardening." Sarah went inside, looked up "landscapers" in the telephone book, and began dialing.

She returned, smiling. "Okay, guys. Get your gloves back on. Today's project is…" Sarah made a drum roll on the patio table. "…destruction. Yes, my gardening army, we are going to rip out everything and start fresh. Let's get to work!"

They removed the tiny evergreens, the brown sticks, and countless leaves still stuck in an unrecognizable ground cover from last fall, filling tall lawn bags as they went. The boys were especially good at it, attacking each plant with glee. After many hours, they sat on the patio, drank lemonade, and took a breather.

"First, let me congratulate you on a superb destruction. Next, let's discuss garden ideas. You had mentioned pumpkins before."

Nicky jumped in. "Yeah, that would be so cool. Could we make a scarecrow too?"

Alex's eyes lit up. "Yeah."

"Absolutely. I have decided to have a professional crew come in and create the new beds for us. After those are done, we will do the planting." Tom had received two bonus checks from his project. What better way to spend the money? "Besides pumpkins, what other vegetables would you like to grow?"

Her sons looked at her like she said it in Russian.

"Okay. How about corn? Tomatoes? Cucumbers?" Sarah saw the vegetable idea was not flying. "How about we go to the nursery and check out some plants?"

"Can we see the fishies?"

"Yes, Alex, we can check out the water features while we are there." She had learned the proper terminology from a show on HGTV. They put away their tools and gloves and ran to the van.

More research brought Sarah the knowledge of using perennials as a basis for the new beds and annuals for some highlighted areas or in the front. She knew she wanted certain plants for their scent and others so she could cut off their blooms and make arrangements for inside.

At last, Sarah was ready to place her plant order, and she was delirious with joy. A small traditional garden plot defined by boxwood in the back right would house pumpkins, tomatoes, chives, basil, mint, and a scarecrow come autumn, although Alex was doubtful. He did not believe those tiny seeds would grow into large orange pumpkins, even if they were taken care of well and watered properly. The entire project would take one full week. Sarah timed it for when Tom would be out of town for ten days total, seven at a conference in New Orleans and a three-day system check back in Boston. After the crews left, Sarah and the boys took over.

On the fifth day of planting, the three gardeners stood arm-in-arm admiring their work. Purple De Oreo day lilies lined the left fence wall. A shade garden was created in the back corner in which a black wrought iron bench sat nestled amid lady ferns and variegated hostas. Lilies of the Valley encircled a stone birdbath. Two black wrought iron planters hung on the fence, holding mixed-color impatiens and cascading English ivy. Three red hydrangeas along the back fence led the way to the vegetable and herb garden. Roses completed the outline to the right. The patio was surrounded with three dwarf lilacs and a crabapple on one side, a dwarf burning bush to the right. Dedicated annual beds bordered the rest, which today were filled with red and white geraniums. Come autumn, decorative cabbages would fill the spots. Then, Sarah and the boys would be planting once again, this time daffodil bulbs for spring.

The front was fairly simple. Snowball bushes and one burning bush flanked the stairs up to the front porch, while curved annual beds lined the walkway. This time, Sarah chose petunias for summer, which would be replaced with mums in the fall. The bulb of choice would be, of course, tulips. To the left, a large evergreen anchored the porch. It was their Christmas tree, as the boys called it, and the only thing left from the old landscaping. Behind it, Stella de Oreo day lilies lined the side of the house. An arbor completed the front yard welcoming visitors to the back.

Alex, still worried about the pumpkin seeds not growing, was the first to volunteer for watering duty. Bless his heart, he had watered a little too well. After the vegetable patch/mud pit dried out, Sarah purchased a thirty-six-inch watering wand for better aquatic control.

Tom was due to arrive the following night. Everything was set. Carolyn came over to congratulate them as they were cleaning up. The three gardeners showered and headed out for ice cream to celebrate.

CHAPTER TWENTY-ONE

JOHN EMERGED FROM THE STUDY, headed straight for the refrigerator, took out a beer, and chugged it.

"John? What are you doing?"

He ushered Annie mechanically into the family room. "Sit down."

"John! What the hell? What's going on?"

He took a deep breath. "Do you remember the night of my reunion?"

"Yes." Annie's mind raced through all of the things that could come out of a reunion. A DUI? A prank gone bad? But that was, what, three, four months ago?

"Well, it was a really hard night for me. The in vitro didn't take. You and I had just had that huge fight."

"I am well aware of what happened that night, John. Spit it out."

"A lot of my old buddies were there showing pictures of their kids, bragging about how their sons were good at soccer, great at baseball. I couldn't take it anymore." He stopped.

Annie knew this was not the end of the story.

"Everyone was drinking...it felt like we were back in school...hanging with the old group."

"Go on." This was not a request.

"I ran into someone."

"Who?"

"Melanie."

"I thought you said she wasn't going to be there."

"I didn't know…nobody knew…she just kind of showed up."

His wife glared at him.

"…and…oh, honey, this is so hard…" He looked at her with pleading eyes. "and somehow we ended up in her old room… and I found myself…"

"Found yourself doing what?"

In a very small voice, he answered her. "We slept together."

The full weight of his words did not register immediately.

"Okay. Well, we can work this out. I mean, after all, I did go a little psycho, and I guess it's understandable that…" her voice trailed off.

"There's more."

"More? How could there be more?" It was definitely sinking in now. "What else did you do? Have sex with all your friends' wives, too?"

"She's pregnant."

"What?"

"Melanie's pregnant."

She's pregnant? She sat there, silent and staring at the floor, until John could not take it anymore.

"Dammit, Annie, say something!"

"Well, I guess we know who's the defective one now, huh? What do you want me to say? Congratulations, you're not shooting blanks after all?"

"Oh come on. Don't say that."

"Now you're trying to tell me what I can say? You can't have it both ways, John. Oh, but wait, I guess you already have. You can't have a baby with me, so you screw somebody else? Here I am thinking we should try to work on our marriage, feeling guilty about not talking to you for so long." Annie stopped, turning her head to face him. "Have you been seeing her all this time? ARE YOU SEEING HER, JOHN?"

"No. No. It was only that night."

"Well, goodie for you. I guess one night was all it took, huh? Makes you kinda wish you had married her in the first place, doesn't it? Would have spared us all these wasted years." She rose and headed out of the room.

"Annie, wait."

"Do not come near me, do you understand? Get out of the house. I don't care where you go, just get the hell away from me."

"Annie, please don't do this."

"Go!"

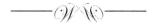

Tom Anderson did not mention the new landscaping until the morning after his limo dropped him off at ten o'clock at night. Per usual, her husband had recapped his trip in usual Tom form, during which Sarah mentally roughed in some accent lighting and decided on which tulip colors to purchase. She kept composed, knowing he was bound to notice after retrieving the morning paper, which lay at the end of the driveway. Fortunately the kids were not up yet or her surprise would be revealed. At last, even Tom tired of talking about himself and decided it was time to read about a world he was not the center of.

It took him awhile to come back in. Sarah snuck peeks out the window from behind the drapes. He circled the house, nodding as he walked. She heard the garage door close and ran into the kitchen, pretending to wash the counter.

"Sarah, what did you do?"

"Excuse me?" She put down the towel.

"How much did you spend?"

"What?"

"You had to have hired someone. Sarah, we don't have that kind of money."

"For your information, Tom, the boys and I put in every single plant and cleared all the beds before doing so."

"Really?" He was not convinced.

"Yes. We worked on it for days. We have the tools to prove it."

"But everything is edged perfectly."

"I bought one. It's in the shed."

"You're kidding."

"No, I am not."

"But the beds are curved."

"Okay, I had a landscaper create the new beds because that would have taken weeks for me to do alone, but the boys and I ripped out everything first, then they came in."

Silence.

"Looks great, doesn't it?"

"We still don't have that kind of money."

"Yes we do. I paid for it with your bonuses."

"You what? Oh, this is great, just great." Tom started pacing.

"The boys and I worked really hard to make our house look nice and all you do is ask about the money?" Sarah threw the scrubby in the sink.

He stopped right in front of her. "Usually we would discuss something as large as this."

Sarah stared right back at him and moved closer. "You're never home. I am here every day. This is my office, Tom. I decided it needed some beautification, and the boys and I needed a project."

"A project?" He whirled around and resumed pacing. "Make a birdhouse or something. Jesus Christ. Who re-landscapes their entire yard?"

"Once again, you were not available to do any outside

maintenance. I took that job over and re-landscaping was my decision."

"I was going to use some of that money to pay off the credit card bills."

"Should have said something then. If you want, I will take that over too. I might as well run the house inside and out."

"Are you going to proclaim yourself queen too?"

"It's better than dictator."

"Here we go again. I'm the big jerk. I'm never here for the kids. I'm not mowing the lawn anymore so you make a big dramatic gesture to drive the point home, right? Okay, I got it. Enough."

"It's not enough. You are either working nonstop or out of town. You do nothing with the boys or me. We lead completely separate lives. Doesn't that bother you?"

"How many hours are there in a day? What more do you want?"

A little voice broke in, barely loud enough to get his parent's attention. "Are you going to get a divorce?"

Sarah turned around and saw Nicky standing behind them. "Honey, I didn't know you were up. How long have you been standing there?"

He shrugged his shoulders, his brown eyes huge. "Adam's parents are getting a divorce."

"They are?" Sarah always thought the Christensens were a tightly knit family.

Nicky nodded. "Adam said his mom and dad fight all the time, and sometimes his dad never comes home."

Alex came down the stairs yawning. "Mama?"

"Over here, honey." Sarah outstretched her arms and pulled Alex into a hug.

"Adam said his mom, sister, and him are going to stay, but his dad's moving into another house. Is Daddy going to live at work?"

"Oh, honey. Come here." Nicky joined Alex in his mother's embrace. All three set their eyes on Tom, who ran up the stairs. Sarah tried to overcome the feeling of getting punched in the solar plexus by holding on tight to the boys until they began to squirm. "Everything's going to be okay. Don't worry. Mommy and Daddy love you very much. Okay? Come on. Who's up for pancakes?"

Nothing surprised Annie Jacobs anymore. Not that the insemination failed. Not that the IVF was unsuccessful. Not that John slept with Melanie. Not that Melanie was pregnant. Nothing. She was done, spent. Marian, George, even Grandpa Bill and Grandma Mary had tried talking to her, each leaving with Annie's empty reassurances. "I'm okay, really. Thank you for coming, but as you can see, I am fine."

June stopped by to retrieve some of John's clothes and toiletries. Annie had gathered the items matter-of-factly, telling herself they had not been in a real marriage for closer to a year now anyway. She even made small talk to help June feel less awkward, all the while thinking John was a coward for not facing her himself. "You know, I never thanked you for the flowers and prayers during the whole procedure fiasco."

"It was the least I could do." June's eyes went to the ground.

"None of this is your fault, June."

"I just…(sigh)…I can't imagine how you feel right now. I am so sorry."

Annie stopped her before the blubbering went out of control. That was the one thing she definitely could not handle right now. "Don't worry. Everything will be fine."

Her mother-in-law pulled a tissue from inside her sleeve and dabbed her eyes. "Well, good-bye for now, I guess, Annie, dear. Please take care of yourself."

"You, too."

After June had gone, Annie realized she would no longer be subjected to the Jacobs Family Christmas Spectacular, which temporarily lifted her spirits, until her thought process progressed to the reception John, Melanie, and the baby would receive in December. There would be gushing and cooing, and, above all, John would be absolved for his sins, contributing to the family in this way, while she sat stuck with Marian and George, drinking eggnog in silence.

John would be a great dad. Annie had known it since the first time she met the Jacobs en masse at Austin's baptism. John's interpretation of his godfatherly duties centered upon educating the baby on the finer points of baseball, not Jesus. He filled a Chicago Cubs mini-locker with jerseys, t-shirts, shorts, tiny gym shoes, baby-sized caps, a little mitt, a soft, chewable baseball, a bat, and, oh, yeah, a white cross with "You are a child of God" written on it, an afterthought Annie had thrown in, considering it was the kid's baptism.

John had carried Austin around all day, softly reciting the names of famous Cub players into the baby's ear. *Ernie Banks. Don Kessinger. Ryne Sandberg.* He even volunteered to put his nephew down at nap time and read him *Picture Me as a Baseball Player* before tucking the sweetie pie in. Austin's mother was furious.

"Take it easy, Julie. You get him every day. Besides, I'm the godfather." He flashed a Cheshire cat grin and off he went to grab a quick bite to eat while the baby was down.

Annie happily walked alongside him, thinking she was the luckiest person on earth to be dating a man who was so loving with children. What a great family they would have! How fortunate their kids would be, growing up surrounded by the large Jacobs family!

But come December, it would be Melanie receiving the

congratulations, bursting with pride at the inevitable oohs and aahs when she placed the baby on Santa's lap. June would have to find some other sap to don the red suit, since this year John would claim his rightful place among the father video camera corps.

Shit. Annie ran upstairs and threw open her dresser drawer. *Where is it?* She pulled out sweater after sweater, catapulting them across the room. There, tucked away under the red sweater she only wore on Christmas Eve, was a tiny Santa suit, size six months, which Annie had bought back when she and John decided they were ready to have children, a lifetime ago, back when they were still harboring under the unabashed, arrogant assumption of future parenthood. It was all for nothing. The want, the yearning, the pain that bored so deeply into her core Annie was scared she would never be free. All she had to do was go to the reunion with John. It seemed so simple now. Suck it up and put on a show like her parents often did. But no, she was possessed by maniacal tunnel vision. There were no other options.

Why hadn't they considered adoption? Did she really hate her mother that much to discard a valuable option merely because it was Marian's suggestion? How could she have been so foolish? They might have been parents right now. Right at this moment, she could be singing a nap time lullaby to Lizzie, small smile curling the baby's lips.

"Sleep tight, my little one," Annie would whisper, rubbing Lizzie's back as she brought the blanket around her daughter, all snug and cozy. "Mommy loves you."

Annie lay down on her bed, drew the mini-Santa suit to her chest, rubbed it's small footie between her fingers, closed her eyes, and fell asleep.

When she awoke, Annie tossed the tiny Santa suit in the garbage, along with her Christmas sweater, telling herself she never liked red much anyhow.

"How is Annie?" John lifted the clothes from the trunk of June's car.

"She is doing the best she can. Put on a brave face, but I knew she was hurting."

"What am I going to do, Mom?"

June patted her son on the back. "That's your decision, not mine."

"Gee, thanks." He laid his stuff in June's dining room. "I'm going to go for a run."

"Now? But the Weather Channel said…"

"I'll take my chances." The weather looked fine to him. Besides, John preferred running when it was overcast. Awhile later, he was in the zone and running at a pretty good pace.

"You should be castrated," Joy spat.

The wind picked up, blowing sharply against his face.

"Right after you found out the in vitro failed?" Julie chimed in. "Really, John. That's about as low as you can get."

He should have known better than to go to them for advice. A crime against one woman is an assault on all femininity. Don't mess with the sisterhood.

But it was one mistake. One night.

"There's not a snowball's chance in hell I'm going to stand by and watch you raise this child, muchless help you do so. Are you crazy? How could you even suggest joint custody with…with *her*?"

Wind gusts howled around him.

"Of course I am going through with it, John. This could be

my only chance to have a baby. Speaking of, the first ultrasound is Saturday. Wanna come? Do you think we should find out if Li'l Butkus is a boy or a girl? Let me know, okay? I'll call you tomorrow."

Torrents of rain bombarded him from all sides. There was no where to hide. No where to go for shelter. His head was spinning. He had never loved Melanie. They had plenty of good times, but that was it. Now, she was carrying his child. The words would not sink in. John had already made peace with the fact that he and Annie would be childless, and, in the back of his head, was planning a trip to Fiji for them to reconnect with no distractions. He loved Annie, no matter what had transpired between them, always had, right from that first meeting on the airplane.

"I want a divorce. I have already met with my lawyer, Claire Dupree. You will be hearing from her soon." Click.

GODDAMMIT! John punched a nearby tree, its bark shredding his knuckles. Stunned from the pain, John ambled his way back to his mother's house, where he stood on her front doorstep, dripping wet and bleeding.

"Good Lord, get in here." June ran for a towel. "I was worried sick. You could catch your death of cold. Good God, what happened?"

"Mom, what have I done?"

Annie walked amid a forest of large moving boxes. The last of John's suits hung in a cardboard armoire. The bubble-wrapped Victrola now rested among styrofoam peanuts. His law school books, childhood photos, sports equipment, all packed away, more traces of his existence being erased by the hour.

Annie supposed getting back to work was the sensible

thing to do, seeing as she would not be able to rely on John's salary anymore. She also supposed she should put the house up for sale. The furniture, too. One person did not need this much. Maybe she would move into a one-bedroom loft in downtown Chicago? She and John had talked about it when they were first married. Nevermind. Scratch the loft. A one-bedroom condo in Naperville would be just fine. Maybe along the Riverwalk.

Annie resisted the urge to burn their wedding album in the fireplace and instead removed her favorite photo, the one of them dancing and laughing together after the bride/father and groom/mother dance. June had held onto John for dear life several minutes after the song was over, large tears streaking her too powdered face. She kept fussing with his tuxedo muttering "My darling boy." When John tried to pull away, June only clung tighter. George McDonnell was well on his way back to the bar where his golfing buddies were sipping scotch by the time June eased her grip.

Annie slipped the photo into her desk drawer and packed the wedding album, along with their various framed travel pictures. As soon as that baby was born, he would be moving to Milwaukee, no matter what he said now. Annie had no doubt whatsoever.

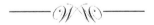

The garden was in full bloom. Every other day, Sarah and the boys perused it, pulling weeds, and dead-heading geraniums. Nicky became especially good at spotting intruders, be they plants or animals, and complained to his mom about the small bites in the hosta leaves.

"Rabbits, honey."

"Bunnies are cute." Alex often giggled while watching two of the furry woodland creatures frolicking in the afternoon sun.

"But you didn't plant those, Alex. I did. And the bunnies are eating them."

"The rabbits are sweet, but maybe we should get something to stop them from eating the new plants," Sarah said.

"Don't kill them though." Nicky became alarmed.

"Kill bunnies?"

"No. No. Sweetie, there are mixtures gardeners spray to make plants taste spicy so the rabbits won't want to nibble on them. That's all." The boys were relieved. Sarah put one arm on each of their shoulders. "It looks great, doesn't it?" Alex and Nicky nodded their approval. "Who's up for watering? Hey, while we're at it, let's put the pool out." The kids ran inside to get their swimsuits.

Sometimes Sarah came out here after she tucked the boys in, lit citronella candles, and let the night air's sweetness rush over her. The garden harbored no memories of the family that was, be it with her husband or with her mother. Sarah was tired of fighting with Tom. It made her less of a mother and turned her into a bloated devourer of all things chocolate. She decided to be grateful for her time with the boys, assuming normal conditions meant it would be the three of them. Anything with Tom would be a bonus. She would wait until he realized what he was missing, which would probably occur when someone younger, smarter, more innovative replaced Tom as the "go-to guy." Eventually, he would return to dinner at six, to Nicky's coach-pitch baseball games, to making sandcastles with Alex. To be her husband? Sarah was realistic; she would be content with father first.

Nicky ran out, towel in tow, followed by Alex hopping behind with both limbs jammed into one swimsuit leg.

"I did it myself." He smiled brightly.

"Good job, honey. Did you put on a swim diaper?" Alex shook his head yes. "Excellent. Come here and let me help you with your suit."

Nicky brought out the arsenal of aquatic torture devices (squirt guns of various sizes), and all three chose their weapons. Soon, not a dry soul could be found in the soaked pile of bodies that lay in a heap on the grass. Nicky watched his mom pull back the strand of hair responsible for a constant drip down her right cheek. "You were awesome. I can't believe the way you took both of us out."

"Thank you, sir." Sarah got up and bowed, making her way over to the patio, which had been declared a no-fire zone early on to keep the towels dry. She threw one to Nicky and picked up the other. "Come here, Alex. Let's get you dried off. Who's up for popsicles?"

Annie came down the stairs and flung a green and magenta beach towel at John. "Here. I'm sure you'll want this. It was on the floor in the linen closet."

"What is it?"

"Don't you remember? You picked it up in Cozumel after chewing that guy down to a buck. It was your triumphant prized possession of the trip."

"Oh, yeah. It was a great deal."

"You talked about it for hours. Told everyone we met," Annie said, shaking her head and rolling her eyes.

"Excuse me, ma'am."

Annie was jolted back to reality by a mover maneuvering a large box past her. They were not pleasantly bantering before leaving for work, like they had done so many times. John was leaving her to start a new life with his pregnant college sweetheart, as if their sixteen years of marriage never happened, erased away by a consequence they could not control.

Annie turned to him. "Anyway, you are free. Go to Melanie

and her baby." The last words caught in her throat, brutal in their finality.

"Honey." John tried to touch her arm, but Annie moved away and headed out the front door. He followed her, determined she hear him. "I have always loved you, not Melanie, you."

John pulled Annie close, snuggling his face into her neck.

"Please don't." She stepped back.

"Annie, I..."

"Good-bye, John." She ran inside.

Through the window, Annie watched her husband, ex-husband as of today, drive down the street and out of her life for good.

CHAPTER TWENTY-TWO

ONE YEAR LATER

"Guys, I'm going to make a phone call." No response came from Fort Anderson, constructed of family room furniture and strategically placed blankets. Nicky donned a coonskin cap and brandished a pistol, while Alex held a toddler-sized hockey stick that doubled as a rifle. It was the seventh viewing of *Davy Crockett* in as many days. Safely out of gunshot range, Sarah dialed Annie's number.

"Hello?"

"Hey, it's Sarah. Listen, Edwina scheduled a book club field trip to see *As You Like It* on the tenth at three o'clock. Catherine's playing Audrey. I looked up her character. She is listed as 'a country wench.'"

"At least it's not miscellaneous villager or court attendant. Her character actually has a name."

"True. And Catherine has a paycheck."

"All the better. Yes, I would love to go."

"Great. It's at Knoch Knolls Park. Don't forget a lawn chair. Edwina asked if we could meet there at two forty-five."

Annie's old lawn chair hung from her shoulder, clanking against her as she walked. She was pretty sure it had belonged to her parents at one time. Little bits of rust encircled the joints, but it was the only one she had. Scanning the crowd for book club members, Annie spied a large-brimmed straw hat with an equally large sunflower attached standing head and shoulders above the crowd. It had to be Edwina Hipplewhite. Who else would wear such a thing?

"Oh, Annie, dear. So good to see you. Come right over here. Make room, would you, Larry darling? That's right. Annie, do come sit here next to Sarah and me."

Annie's chair squeaked as she unfolded it. Everyone around her sat in dark green sling-back lawn chairs equipped with cup holders. Thaddeus' was more like a canvas Barcolounger, complete with a foot rest for reclining.

Edwina gave Annie's arm a little squeeze. A portly man dressed in tights and tunic sprung out from behind a tree. "Pray thee, noble gentlemen and fair ladies, your attention, if thou wouldst be so kind. We, the Elizabethan Players, are your most humble servants." He bowed deeply. "We hope you will enjoy this little trifle by Master Shakespeare, presented as it should be, in a forest. I give you, *As You Like It.*" His voice rose with every word. "Let the play begin!"

Long about Act III, Catherine/Audrey made her entrance alongside Touchstone and Jaques. "There she is!" Edwina beamed. Thaddeus and Larry were riveted. She made a comely wench, her ample bosom barely contained by her costume.

After the play, Catherine was greeted with applause and mutterings of "good job" from the book club members. "Bravo, my dear." Edwina made her way through the small crowd bearing a bouquet of roses. She handed it to the actress. "For you. An excellent performance, worthy of Lord Chamberlain's Men, if they were to hire a woman of course, which was not the case in those days, but, anyway, a triumph nonetheless."

Catherine curtsied, thanked everyone for coming, and ran backstage to remove her makeup.

"Would anyone care for a light supper?" Edwina surveyed the group. There were many nodding heads and a few rubs of the belly. "Lovely. Shall I call ahead to, oh, I don't know, oh, how about that Argentinean steak house? What's it called? It's the one with that lovely roof top patio."

"What did you think of the play?" Sarah asked Annie.

"Pretty good. Catherine made the most of the wench role."

"Okay, darlings. I have made a reservation. Shall we meet up there in about fifteen-twenty minutes?"

The bibliophiles packed up and headed to dinner. Sarah dialed her cell phone while she walked to her car. The boys were at Greg's for the afternoon. After several rings, he answered. "Hello?"

"Hey, it's me."

"It's your mother," he whispered. "Hey, you. What's up?"

"The book club is going out for dinner. Can you keep the boys for a little bit longer?"

"Sure. No problem."

"Where are you? The signal is breaking up."

"We're at Lincoln Park Zoo. Heading toward the farm area now."

"Is everything okay?"

"Absolutely. Little angels."

"Okay, well how about I pick them up around eight o'clock?"

"That would work. I was thinking of taking them out for pizza. Is that okay, mom?"

"Sure. Thanks. Tell them I love them."

"Hey, boys. Your mommy says she's having a great time without you, so she is leaving you here with me forever."

Sarah heard cheering through the phone. "You suck, Greg."

"I know. See you later."

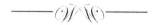

A rooftop garden supper would be lovely on such an evening, Edwina thought. They could discuss *As You Like It* and celebrate dear Catherine's temporary employment. She also hoped today's adventure would shake things up a bit. The bibliophiles were so used to the community center, perhaps thinking, or in this case, being out of the box might do the trick. Miss Hipplewhite was interested in what would come about, particularly with the re-emersion of Annie Jacobs, who had been MIA for quite some time.

Small white lights intertwined with grape vines enclosed the roof's perimeter. Purple clematis climbed wrought-iron trellises. It was a small space, only six tables, three of which were pushed together to accommodate Edwina and company. Despite not remembering its name, Miss Hipplewhite seemed very familiar with the restaurant, referring to the host and waiter by their first names. She took her place in the middle of the table facing the clematis and waited for her guests.

Annie and Sarah took their seats across from Edwina and Rosemary respectively, as Thaddeus, Spring, and Larry were heard ascending the stairs. Spring entered, giggling, while Thaddeus smiled, not quite knowing where to rest his gaze.

The evening called for Sangria, Edwina announced. The idea was met with approval all around, and the waiter, whose name was Joe, Edwina informed them, prepared three pitchers of the fruity wine at their table. He left an empty glass for the guest-of-honor, who seemed to be running late, and got an iced tea for Rosemary.

"My darlings, some think the forest in *As You Like It* represents a world compensating for injustices. Others say it harkens back to an age of innocence and abundance. What do you think?"

"The Forest of Arden reminded me of Robin Hood," Larry said, punctuating his utterance with a hearty slam of his Sangria glass.

"I didn't see that at all." Spring looked around the table, hoping for once someone would come to the same conclusions she had.

"What did you see, dear?" Edwina asked.

"I'm not sure. Shakespeare never was my thing."

"An honest response. I can respect that."

That made the thin girl smile as she sat with a small sweater around her shoulders, despite the warm evening.

"I enjoyed that the god of marriage's name was Hymen," said Annie.

"Hear. Hear." Larry rapped on the table, amid their laughter.

Catherine made her entrance sweeping through the door. Edwina knew the thespian would be better off if only she were more genuine, personally and professionally. Before *As You Like It*, the audition with her friend Lacy had not gone well. Edwina was trying to figure out how to suggest an improvisation workshop her other friend ran, but had yet to master the delicacy of delivery required.

"Bravo!" Miss Hipplewhite clapped for her pupil, knowing one can never go wrong with positive reinforcement.

Catherine waved and blew air kisses. "Sorry to be late. I had to help take down the stage. You know small theater companies." Her voice rose for the last few words, ensuring the other three tables knew she was an actress. "Ah, Sangria!" She sat down and poured herself a glass. "Fabulous. I'm famished. Have you ordered yet?"

"No, dear, we were waiting for you, of course." Edwina was perusing the menu, deciding between the steak and paella.

"Would anyone like to split some tapas?" Sarah threw out.

"Not me. I'm going for the biggest piece of beef I can find."

"Well, Larry. Enough about your sexual preferences." Rosemary eyed him across the table. He rose his glass to her, a simple smirk on his lips.

"You know what? I'll take you up on some tapas, Sarah. How about some empanadas?" Annie's stomach was rumbling.

"FYI, darlings. They have the most wonderful portobello mushroom sandwich, in case you are interested. Let me know when you are ready to order, and I'll call Joe over. Don't take too long, though." Miss Hipplewhite used her gentle, yet firm, school teacher voice.

"I'll have a salad." Spring closed her menu and folded her hands on the table.

Annie glanced sideways at her. "Really? You look like you could use some meat."

"Oh, no thanks. I don't eat it much. I prefer fruits and vegetables. Oh, and an occasional piece of turkey." She shrugged her shoulders. "It's the way I've always been. I'm not trying to make a political statement or anything."

"I didn't mean…" Annie began.

Spring waved her hand in dismissal. "It's okay. I know you didn't."

"Wish I could be that way." Unfortunately for Sarah, a passion for bakery items haunted her, a sugared-up specter bearing brownies and donuts.

"Enough talk of it, dear ones. Let us construct our repast. Joe, darling, I believe we are ready."

They placed their orders and refilled their glasses. Edwina ordered another three pitchers of Sangria.

"So, where have you been, Annie? We were worried you abandoned us." Larry patted his heart.

Annie exchanged looks with Sarah, unsure how to proceed. "Well, I, um…"

"That's Annie's business, Larry darling. Glad to have you

back amongst our ranks." Edwina raised her glass. "Cheers, everyone."

THE END

ACKNOWLEDGMENTS

I had never planned on writing a series. I was busy trying to find the time to finish this idea for a novel that would explore two sides of womanhood, comparing and contrasting wanting a child with the realities of having one, while raising two boys of my own.

In my mind, *A Whisper to a Scream* was a stand-alone novel throughout most of the writing process, until I needed a way for Sarah and Annie to meet. Being a former English major, the choice was clear—a book club. What better way to illustrate an immediate bond between two strangers than over great literature?

As soon as Edwina Hipplewhite walked through the door of Room 204 for their first meeting on March 20, I fell in love with the bibliophiles. Their voices so strong in character, their interactions so much fun. I knew I had to write their stories.

Most series follow one character through various adventures, but I wanted mine to be a little different. I'm fascinated by people's backstories. How did they get to where they are today? What ramifications does the past have on the present? So, I decided to have each novel "star" one or two of the book club members. Sarah and Annie kick the series off, followed by Catherine's story. The third novel will focus on Thaddeus and Spring. Rosemary will be up next, followed by Larry. Edwina's adventures will wrap up the series. I hope you will grow to love them as much as I do.

I would like to thank two wonderful professors who shared their wisdom and amazing knowledge of the English language with me, even long after I graduated from their hallowed halls. Thank you, Sister Mary Clemente Davlin and Sister Jeanne Crapo, from all of us who have been lucky enough to have been inspired by you.

Thank you to everyone at Streetlight Graphics for their amazing cover and interior design.

Thank you to Geraldine A. Young for her excellent book discussion questions.

And a huge bouquet of thanks goes to David, Tim, and Danny for all of your support, encouragement, and constant love. I am forever grateful for the insight, wisdom, and wit you share with me every day.

Karen Wojcik Berner
March 20, 2013
The first day of spring

READER'S GUIDE

for

A *Whisper*
—TO A—
SCREAM

THE BIBLIOPHILES: BOOK ONE

QUESTIONS AND TOPICS FOR DISCUSSION

By Geraldine A. Young

1. As a stay-at-home mother of two young children, Sarah has definite concerns about her life. What does her self image say about her frame of mind?

2. Annie feels uncomfortable with John's extended family because of her failed attempts at having children. Do you think Anne overreacts when she hears her sister-in-law is pregnant with a third child? How is Sarah's reaction some of her in-laws different or similar to Annie's reaction to her own in-laws?

3. What do you think of frequent Tom's late nights at work? Would you say Tom or John, in the first chapters of the book, appears the most supportive husband and family man?

4. Annie and Sarah both have very busy lives: Annie as vice president of a public relations firm and Sarah as a homemaker. Do you think they are unreasonable to be dissatisfied with the lives they have chosen? Are their situations typical or atypical for many women? Who do you sympathize with the most?

5. Was a book club a good choice for Sarah to spend some time away from her housework and chores? What other activities could she have chosen? How important are Edwina

Hipplewhite and the Classics Book Club to Annie and Sarah at this time?

6. Sarah's mother is supportive of her in every way. How is Annie's mother different in responding to her daughter's need to have a child?

7. Annie and John waited to have successful careers before starting a family. Now John is not sure he even wants a child. Do you think Annie, by considering artificial insemination and in vitro fertilization, is going too far in trying to have children?

8. Even after learning about their diagnosis of "unexplained infertility," why is Annie not open to adoption?

9. Sarah's visit to Tom during his business trip to Boston seems to change things between them. How is this significant?

10. Were you surprised when Annie was asked to take a leave of absence from work? Why or why not?

11. Annie and Sarah both have ethical and religious decisions to consider, Annie regarding fertility treatments that her church frowns on, and Sarah about prolonging or cutting short the life of her mother who is in a vegetative state. What do you think of the decisions that were made?

12. What is the importance of the garden that Sarah and her family planted after the death of Sarah's mother?

13. Anne tells John to leave after she found out about his affair with Melanie. Did Annie's decision to cut John out of her life for good seem inevitable? If you were to write a sequel to this novel, what would you plan for Annie? Do you find her a sympathetic or unsympathetic character?

14. In the last chapter, the book club discusses Shakespeare's play, *As You Like It*. Does this add another level of meaning to the ending of the book?

15. How apt is the title of the book, *A Whisper to a Scream*? How many people or situations in the book could this apply to?

16. What do you think the author's message was in this novel?

Geraldine A. Young is a freelance writer (and retired English teacher) in Ohio.

READ ALONG WITH
THE BIBLIOPHILES

Would you like to start a Classics Book Club of your very own? Wouldn't Edwina Hipplewhite be proud? Here are some ideas for menus and discussion questions for the classic literature pieces found in *A Whisper to a Scream*.

A Portrait Of The Artist As A Young Man
by James Joyce

Food and Beverages
James Joyce was Irish, so naturally, Guinness must be served. Pair that with bite-sized ruben sandwiches or bangers (sausages) and mash (mashed potatoes). A Bailey's Irish Cream cheesecake would be lovely for dessert.

Discussion Questions
1. *A Portrait of the Artist as a Young Man* is known for its innovative use of stream of consciousness. As Stephen ages, the writing becomes more sophisticated. How does that enhance or detract from the overall novel?

2. What role does Emma play?

3. Religion focuses prominently here. How does it motivate Stephen's actions?

As You Like It
by William Shakespeare

Food and Beverages
In lieu of someone hosting the book club for this one, wouldn't it be fun if your group attended a Shakespeare in the Park performance like the bibliophiles instead? One of you could even wear a huge hat like Edwina Hipplewhite, if you choose. Afterward, head to the restaurant of your choice that has outdoor dining.

Discussion Questions
1. One of the main themes of *As You Like It* is country life versus city life. Can a person's sense of balance really be restored by a few days in the country?

2. Analyze Jaques' famous "All the world's a stage" speech. What does it mean to you?

3. Love, obviously plays a large role in the play. How are the themes of true love versus romantic love and appearance versus reality illustrated here by Shakespeare?

Read on for the first chapter of

UNTIL MY SOUL GETS IT RIGHT

The Bibliophiles: Book Two
Karen Wojcik Berner

CHAPTER ONE

BURKESVILLE, WISCONSIN

1985

*I*T TAKES A LOT OF effort to be ordinary-looking. Catherine performed the same morning routine the pretty girls did. The same shampoo, conditioner, blow dry, style, spray. The same moisturizer, concealer, foundation, blush, eye shadow, eyeliner, mascara, lipstick. She checked herself out in the mirror. *Ugh, still me.*

Still a senior in high school who hesitated to use the term "farm girl" for fear of it being too clichéd after her English teacher defined the term as "the lack of thought." Clearly, nobody aspires to be a stereotype, but, really, is everyone that original?

Who hasn't grown up knowing the bitchy cheerleader, a dumb jock, the computer nerd, an overbearing mother, a distant father, a misunderstood old person, or an alienated artist, writer, musician, or dancer? If everybody knows these people, are they really clichés or merely categories? Maybe the various cities, towns, neighborhoods, and blocks are really replicating microcosms? The same strands woven together to create one large tapestry of life?

Anyhow.

Still living in boring-as-shit Burkesville, Wisconsin. The entire town consisted of a bank, post office, drug store, gas station, church, two schools, and four taverns, all within a four-block area. Anyone could walk through it in about two seconds unless old Ben got a hold of you. Ben practically lived on the third-from-the-left bar stool at Pat's Bar and Grill, Burkesville's only real restaurant.

One day, Catherine and her friends were there for pizza and old Ben started blabbing to anyone who'd listen about how Bart Starr was the greatest quarterback who ever lived. Then this guy, Ernie, who usually goes to Padowski's, but it was closed because the furnace broke, piped up with "Well, what about Dan Marino?"

Ben turned to Ernie like he was going to beat the shit out of him for even thinking of someone besides Starr, (a) because he's a Miami Dolphin and (b) he's not a Packer. Heaven forbid! Like there aren't any other teams in the NFL. Catherine could not have cared less about the Packers. Who would wear green and yellow together anyway? Vomitosis.

"Ma! I hate sunny-side up." There was something about the way the yolks jiggled, like teasing, googly eyes. *Eat me, Catherine. Eat me.*

"Everyone else likes them well enough." Vintage Clara Elbert. Don't deviate from what the men in the family want for breakfast. Eggs. Bacon. Homemade bread, toasted. Would it kill her to buy some fruit?

By nine o'clock on Saturday morning, her father had already put down fresh hay for the pigs and milked the cows. "Here ya go, Clara," he said, placing a filled pitcher in front of her.

"Thanks, Hank. Boys, wash your hands."

No matter how old the brothers were, Clara always referred to them as "the boys." Of course, since they acted like little kids, maybe she was right. Catherine fiddled with her eggs, eventually covering the oozing yolks with bread. "So, Mr. Leary is nagging me about 'my future plans.' How am I supposed to know what I want to do with my life? I'm only seventeen."

Clara scoffed.

Russell smirked. "Yeah, like you're so good at makin' decisions."

"Remember Dairy Queen?" Laughing, Peter pulled his sleeve over his left wrist and ran it across his face. Ma shot him a pulverizing look. He grabbed his napkin and wiped his mouth properly.

"I mean, really, even if I do go to college, what am I supposed to major in?"

Hank glanced at his wife, then at the boys. "You could work with us here."

How could she tell her family that staying on Elbert Farm was the only thing Catherine was certain she could never do?

With February looming, its contemptible blend of pink hearts and dateless nights, the only bright spot in Catherine Elbert's endless gray winter days was the spring musical. Three years of paying dues were about to end. Seniors were guaranteed to get the leads. She was a dancer in *Li'l Abner*, a chorus member in *Hello, Dolly!*, and had two lines in *Bye Bye Birdie*. This year, she would be the one coming on stage last for curtain call, receiving a huge bouquet of roses, bowing her head in appropriate humility, and then rising to continuous applause.

The choir had begun rehearsing the *Oklahoma!* score two

weeks ago in anticipation of tryouts. Anyone interested in solo work was welcome to book a time before school with Mr. Gusselman. So, every morning at seven thirty, Catherine began her day singing "Out of My Dreams" and ended it running lines with Beth, who would rather skydive than get up on stage. She was happy running the crew, safely tucked backstage.

At three o'clock on Tuesday, the usually dark auditorium had become a flurry of activity. Every few rows, seemingly schizophrenic teenagers mumbled lines to themselves. On stage, dancer hopefuls practiced a combination step. Mrs. White, the elderly organist from St. Agatha's Church, was brought in as an accompanist, so Mr. Gusselman could focus on his directorial duties. He sat with student director Ted Swanson ten rows up, dead center.

"Denise Nelson. Please come to the stage. Denise Nelson. You're up," Ted yelled through a megaphone.

Catherine slipped into the seat next to Beth. "How's it going so far?"

"Pretty good. Nobody as good as you yet, but Denise is up next."

"Hey, Smellbert." Bill Davies biffed her on the back of the head as he worked his way through the row behind.

"Cut it out, juvenile."

Bill faked a "What did I do?" smirk that made Catherine flush.

"So, are you ready?"

"Ready as I'll ever be. Besides, my competition is pretty lame." He sat back, kicking her seat as he crossed his legs.

Bill was right. Arrogant, but correct. The only other boy with a decent voice looked like he would be more likely to play "Curly" from *The Three Stooges*.

"So, Bethie. Do you think our little smellbag has a chance?"

"Absolutely. She's gonna nail it."

"Bill Davies to the stage. Bill Davies."

Bill rose. "Break a leg, Smellbert."

"Yeah, you too." Her stomach churned with about fifty thousand butterflies.

"Catherine Elbert. Catherine Elbert to the stage."

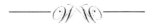

Now the waiting began. Clara told her daughter there was nothing she could do about it, so she might as well get on with things, but Catherine couldn't help but wonder if it went well. Mr. Gusselman was smiling, but then he had started talking to Ted halfway through the song. What was that about?

Before she leaned her head against the window of Bus 79, Catherine checked for splattered bug remnants. Halfway between Burkesville High School and Elbert Farm was the only true Victorian house in or near the town, quite possibly in all of Muskegee County. It was built in 1892 by a gentleman from Milwaukee who supposedly made his money in beer. Probably one of the Pabst relatives. Sophomore year, her class toured the Milwaukee mansion on a field trip. Dumbass Mike Wurhauser kept asking the tour guide where all of the beer was, like the Pabst family had the brewery in their basement or something.

The Pabst mansion had a gorgeous, ornately carved staircase in the foyer, perfect for grand entrances. Catherine imagined herself, long skirt flowing as she descended, extending a gloved hand to greet guests. "Hello, Mr. Taylor. How wonderful to see you." "My dear Mrs. Banks, you look beautiful this evening."

The Gazette reported that the people who bought it were going to turn the Burkesville Victorian into a bed and breakfast. One time when the bus drove by, there was a little girl in a floral pinafore dress jumping rope on the front lawn.

263

Her mother, clad in a denim jumper and straw hat, watched nearby, trimming away the overgrowth. Today, ladders and furniture were strewn about the lawn. A sofa, almost identical to the one Great-Grandma Gribbons had given Clara, sat on the front porch.

No one knew much about the family. One of the ladies who sat behind the Elberts in church had told Clara that the missus was wife number two and was way younger than the man. Hank had heard the guy had taken early retirement from a bank in Milwaukee to settle into a more peaceful life in the country. If "peaceful" was a synonym for "boring," then maybe he got it right. Otherwise, he was delusional.

The newspaper also stated the bed and breakfast would be opening on Memorial Day, and that the owners "were hoping to draw boaters from Lake Sikapu in the summer and to capitalize on some of the Sleepy Hollow Fall Festival traffic," which was a mile or so down Route 36. Catherine wished she lived in Sleepy Hollow, even if it was not the real one. At least the name suggested a link to literary greatness, not like Burkesville, with absolutely no associations whatsoever.

Visitors flocked to Sleepy Hollow every weekend in October to view the fall colors, purchase corn stalks, hay bales, and Halloween costumes at Johansen's Pumpkin Farm. If they were lucky, they might even catch a glimpse of Ichabod Crane out for a stroll or run into Katrina Von Tassel, both played by the Johansens themselves.

When the Elbert children were little, Hank made them pose for pictures next to the "How Tall This Fall?" wood cut-out of a scarecrow holding a measuring stick. The photo collection of little Catherine only went from barely standing at two to age seven, the year Peter hurled a pumpkin at Russell's head for calling him a baby. Hank sped to the emergency room, where the doctor informed a distraught Clara that her eldest son had a concussion. Peter was banished to his room for one week, and that was the end of the Fall Festival excursions.

From then on, Halloween costume choices consisted of whatever was leftover from last year at the Quickie Mart, which turned itself into a lame "Halloween Spook-Quarters" every October. Clara Elbert was not about to drive all over Muskegee County for some outfit Catherine would wear only once.

Consequently, when she was eight, Catherine was a ballerina. Year nine, Sleeping Beauty, who really had the best gig of any fairy tale princess, slumbering away while the prince had to go fight that awful Maleficent and her dragon-and-thorn extravaganza. Best gig, worst costume. Cheap fabric and a plastic mask that damn near suffocated Catherine when she was trick-or-treating. Year ten, a godforsaken butterfly. By the time she was eleven, Catherine had had enough with the cheap crap and bought her own costume with leftover birthday money from Aunt Ida. She was Lizzie Borden.

The bus left her off at Blather's Hill. Elbert Farm was about a mile up the road. Most days, Catherine enjoyed this solitary walk before the onslaught of parental questioning. It gave her time to process the day's events, figure out what to tell Beth on the phone after dinner, and what to keep from her mother. She threw Clara a bone every once in a while to delay the incessant nagging about future plans. Like they ever had to make such a decision. Hank inherited the farm from Grandpa Elbert, and he and Clara got married a month after high school graduation.

Catherine stopped to breathe in the fresh, non-farm-animal air courtesy of the World's Largest Christmas Trees, huge pines that divided their house from the soy bean field. When she was little, Catherine had asked her parents if they could decorate them for the holidays.

Russell laughed. "Yeah, right."

"How stupid are you?" Peter added.

Hank cut in. "Cat, honey, it would be impossible to run electricity all the way over there."

"Those trees were planted ages ago to block the farmhouse from the wind, not for your own personal decorating pleasure, missy." Clara gave an exasperated sigh and left the room.

A faint clucking came from the chicken coop. Winter was a good time on the farm. The frigid air canceled out a lot of the animal smells. Next door, the pigs lay asleep, as they were apt to do in the late afternoon. Pigs are actually some of the cleanest animals on the farm. They change the straw for their beds every day and never poop where they sleep. Poor misunderstood creatures.

"It's you and me, Penny." Catherine petted the over-sized swine slumbering near the sty's fence. Each Elbert, from as far back as anyone could remember, was either a farmer or a farmer's wife. Even on the Gribbons' side, Ma's relatives. Didn't any of them want to be a teacher? A banker? A truck driver? An artist? Butcher? Baker? Candlestick maker?

Clara left the large farming to Dad and the boys, but was totally in control when it came to cooking ingredients, which were grown in a small garden plot to the side of the house. There were vegetables and a few herbs, even an occasional flower or two—nothing fancy. One of Catherine's chores was to weed the thing, cringing every time she donned those dumb denim overalls and gardening gloves so thick with mud that even industrial-strength detergent could not remove. Somehow, dirt always got through the gloves anyway and jammed under her fingernails. Gross.

"Cat, is that you?"

"Yeah. It's booger-freezing cold out. Can we have some hot chocolate?"

"Watch your tongue. Don't have time for hot chocolate. I've got these clothes to fix, and then I need to get dinner started."

Why mending holes would take precedence over a nice, hot afternoon beverage she did not know, but then again there was little about her mother Catherine understood anyway. The sewing could have waited, but Clara Elbert operated on an internal time clock from which there would be no deviation.

The telephone rang.

"Hey, Miss Catherine."

"Hey, can you hang on just a second? Ma, I'm going to take this in my room. Would you hang it up when I yell down?"

"Who is it?"

"Beth."

"Didn't you just see her less than an hour ago? I'll tell you, frivolous time-waster, the telephone."

"I got it." Click. "Okay, my mom's off. So how are things with our dear Fred?"

"Nonexistent."

"But I thought you said the situation was heating up."

"Only because we are chemistry lab partners."

"Give it time. Pretty soon, he'll be igniting your burner."

"Stop it." Beth giggled. "Oh, crap. My mother's yelling for me. Call me after dinner." Hank had mercifully bought Catherine her own phone for her sixteenth birthday. Well, not really her own line, just a phone for her room, but she was the first one of her friends to have one. You would think it was 1946 instead of 1985. Beth was still stuck talking right in the middle of the kitchen where her entire family could hear every word.

She was pretty quiet about anything related to guys, but last week Beth let it slip she thought Fred Schmidt was cute. She would never ask him out or anything, so Catherine got him to build sets for the musical after overhearing Mr. Jones talking to Pop about Fred building bookcases for him. Beth was always the stage manager, so that would give them a chance to work together after school, romantic strains of Rodgers and Hammerstein music floating sweetly in the air—albeit blended with the buzz of circular saws—but maybe Fred liked that sort of thing. They would be dating by prom!

ABOUT THE AUTHOR

Karen Wojcik Berner grew up on the outskirts of Chicago. After graduating from Dominican University with degrees in English with a writing concentration and communications, she worked as a magazine editor, public relations coordinator, and freelance writer. A two-time *Folio Magazine* Ozzie Award for Excellence in Magazine Editorial and Design winner, her work has appeared in countless newspapers and magazines. She lives in the Chicago suburbs with her family.

To learn more about Karen, please visit her website at www.karenberner.com.